The Owl and the Wolf

Book 2 of the Elektros Saga

Marcellus Durrell

The Owl & the Wolf: Book 2 of the Elektros Saga

Marcellus Durrell

Cover art: *The Sword of Oiorpata* by

Leeanne D'Alesio

Cover design by Marcellivision

A NOTE ON PRONUNCIATION & SPELLING

No one knows how ancient Greek words and names were pronounced. Languages evolve constantly. Pronunciation changes over time, so modern Greek gives us few clues, just as modern English cannot tell you with any certainty how to pronounce Old or Middle English words.

So go ahead pronounce the names in this book any way you damned well please, because no matter what you do, no one can prove you wrong.

If you want some sort of a guideline, here's what I do. When I orally or mentally pronounce ancient Greek names that have three or more syllables, I usually put the emphasis on the third-last syllable:

Themistocles	- The-MIS-to-klees
Neocles	- NEE-o-klees
Miltiades	- Mil-TIE-a-dees

I make exceptions for names that sound awkward if you use the third-last-syllable rule. Aristides, for example, just trips the tongue if you say it this way, so I put the emphasis on the second last syllable: Air-ris-TEE-dees. For two-syllable names, like Kimon or Hermes, I just put the emphasis on the first syllable. For all names and places, I assume there are no silent letters.

Most ancient historical names and places have acceptable alternate spellings, and in some cases several, so do not be alarmed if you see an unfamiliar one in these pages. I've seen Halicarnassus, for example, as Halicarnassos, Hellikarnassos, and Halikarnassos. There seems little point in trying to determine which one is the 'right' spelling, so I just pick one, usually the first that comes to mind, and stick with it.

I also do not use the words *Greek* or *Greece* anywhere in this book, apart from this intro, because these terms did not exist in the 5th century B.C.E. The southern coastal regions of Italy were colonized by the ancient Greeks as early as the 9th century B.C.E. The Romans called these regions Magna Graecia–hard *c*–and its inhabitants the Graeciae. This eventually became their term for all Hellenes. It was anglicized, many centuries later, as *Greek*.

The ancient Greeks called themselves *Hellenes,* descendants of a mythical hero named Hellen (not to be mistaken for Helen of Troy). They called their language *Hellenic* and the lands they occupied *Hellas,* which they loosely applied to any place where the dominant language and culture was Hellenic. I have followed this practice.

–Marcellus Durrell

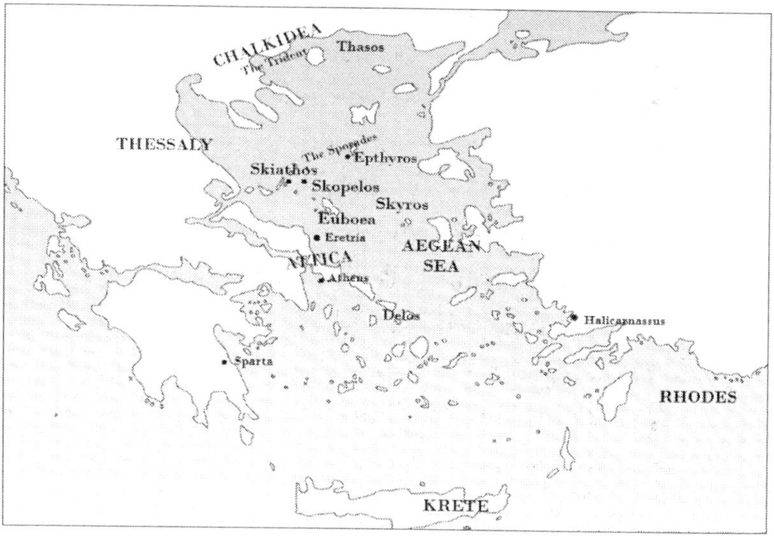

CHALKIDEA
The Trident
Thasos
THESSALY
The Sporades
Epthyros
Skiathos
Skopelos
Skyros
Euboea
Eretria
AEGEAN SEA
ATTICA
Athens
Delos
Halicarnassus
Sparta
RHODES
KRETE

ATHENS

1–ARRIVAL

"Blubber-arse!" the merchant yelled at the fat wheezy harbourmaster. "Lard-bucket! If my cargo is lost, I'll cut you up and spit-roast you like the pig you are!" Several other merchants muttered their approval of this idea.

I lugged my heavy trunk off the ship and onto the dock at the Phaleron, the port of Athens, on a smothering hot spring afternoon. The Phaleron was four times the size of the main port on Skiathos, but the Athenians complained that it was too small. Impressed as I was at its size, they were right. The port was over-packed with merchant ships. Some ships had to hover around the entrance to the port for hours, or even overnight, until there was room for them, and more ships were coming. The new port under construction at the Piraeus was sorely needed.

At first, I pitied the harbourmaster as the Athenian merchants yelled at him. The harassment must have been ongoing: he had two armed bodyguards who glared at anyone who came too close. The merchants were angry because their cargos were in the holds of ships that couldn't get into the harbour. One merchant punched the harbourmaster in the side of the head, bloodying his ear. One of the bodyguards quickly rammed the pommel of his sword into the merchant's face and knocked him over backwards. As blood dripped down his chin, the merchant, flat on his back on the ground, continued to curse the harbourmaster. With everyone shouting, it was initially hard to understand what was going on, but the upshot was that merchants had to bribe the harbourmaster to gain entry to the harbour. The owners of the cargos on every ship in that cramped harbour had paid up. But so had the owners of the cargos in the ships stuck outside the harbour. The water there was too deep to drop anchor, so the ships' oarsmen worked nonstop to prevent the vessels from drifting out to sea. They couldn't keep this up forever. A storm could be disastrous. When I learned this, I pitied the harbourmaster less. The merchants now wanted three things: their bribe money back, their cargos safely unloaded in the port, and the harbourmaster's head on a stake.

The angry merchants were joined by others. The harbourmaster had made himself many enemies. The merchants were joined by labourers, whores, drunkards, and anyone else who either had a grudge or just liked being part of a mob. The bodyguards growled at people to stand back, and whacked a few men over the head with the flat sides of their swords, to intimidate rather than kill, but this only made the burgeoning mob angrier. More than twenty men and a few women now cursed and jeered the harbourmaster.

As the situation got uglier, the bodyguards showed their true mettle: they ran. One dropped his sword and shield, which some skinny little boys fought over.

The harbourmaster's jowls jiggled as he screamed. "You'll all end up as mine slaves if you don't leave me alone," he shrieked, eyes wide with terror. "I'm an important man in Athens. Mark my words, anyone who lays a hand on me will regret it."

"Then we'll use our feet," replied one of the merchants, who then kicked the harbourmaster in the balls. Everyone laughed, and soon the entire mob was trying to kick the harbourmaster, who'd collapsed to the ground and tried to protect his face with one hand and his testicles with the other.

I thought the harbourmaster was a dead man, or at the very least he'd be stomped to a bloody pulp. Then a loud whistle suddenly shrilled the air, and everyone instantly stopped kicking. The mob backed away from the bloodied man on the ground. Two brightly dressed men, who towered over everyone else, broke through the mob and stood over the harbourmaster. Both of the men were well over six feet tall, and their long dark hair and big black beards made them look feral. The mob had seen through the bodyguards' bluster but stayed clear of these two. The tall men were dressed for war. They carried spears and had swords in scabbards. Belted to each man's waist was an extra-large quiver, called a *gorytos,* which held not only a bow but seventy-five arrows. They wore orange tunics with ornate designs up and down the sleeves, and orange trousers. They didn't glare or growl, they didn't point their weapons menacingly at anyone, and so far, they hadn't said a word. Yet the mob backed off immediately. I was struck by the calmness of these bizarre foreigners. They *expected* the mob to back down, and that's exactly what happened. The mob thinned out as people lost interest in the harbourmaster and went back to whatever they were doing before.

The harbourmaster jumped to his feet. His bloodied jowls jiggled. "Arrest that man!" he said, pointing at one of the departing merchants. "He's the one who hit me first."

"Arrest is no our job," said one of the tall men. "We keep it peace. Break up fightings. No more we do."

"Sue him," said the other tall man. "That's what the courts are for. You've got plenty of witnesses." His flawless Hellenic had a Euxine twang.

As the crowd dispersed, I lugged my trunk, which contained the new armour Uncle Damon had made for me and some clothing, toward the road that led to Athens. A skinny little boy offered to help me carry it. He was maybe nine years old, filthy, the type of dockside orphan the locals called *wharf rats,* who would do anything up to and including prostitution to survive. He was one of the boys who'd fought over the bodyguard's dropped sword and shield.

He put his hand on my trunk. I drew my sword from its scabbard. "Take your hand away," I said, "unless you want to lose it."

The kid backed away, but I felt sorry for him. He looked hungry. I tossed him an obol. Big mistake: suddenly a dozen other wharf rats swarmed around me. I swung my sword over the head of the tallest one, just close enough for him to feel it pass over his shaved head. "Back off! All of you!"

They still crowded around me, so I punched one of them in the face, knocking him down. Then something hit me in the back of the head, probably a stone. My scalp bled, and I was a little dazed. The next thing I heard was a loud whistle.

The wharf rats ran away. One of the tall men had made the whistling sound, the same one I'd heard earlier, by putting two fingers into his mouth and blowing hard. It was startlingly loud, and it definitely got everyone's attention. The tall men came up to me, and the older of them spoke in his own language, apparently thinking I'd understand it. When I didn't answer, he said, in his battered Hellenic, "You no Saka? You look like."

Now I remembered who these guys were. They were Scythians. They called themselves *Sakai.* Grandfather had told me that the Athenians used them to keep order during assemblies and trials and in the streets. I had just witnessed their effectiveness–these two Scythians scared an angry mob away just by showing up.

"My father is Hellene," I said. "But my mother was Saka. She died when I was four years old, so I only learned a little of her language."

"Don't giving it money to boy whores," said the older man. "Big mistake. Ceramicus girl whore cost more but no cut you."

"I wasn't paying the boy for anything," I said. "I felt sorry for him. I gave him a coin so he could eat."

The Scythians just looked at me like I was insane. "You give money for nothing to do?" said the older one. "You crazy. I Scylurus. He Madyes," he added, pointing to his companion.

"Elektros, son of Belkos," I said.

Scylurus' eyes lit up, and he pumped his arms back and forth in a running motion. "Belkos you father? Running man famous?"

I nodded. Father was so famous that even a Scythian who barely spoke Hellenic knew who he was.

Then Scylurus' eyes lit up even more. "Father fastest man in world and mother Sakai? You born warrior, Lectoros!" He laughed loudly and clapped me on the back so hard he almost knocked me over. He would never get my name right. "You buy me wine. We talk."

He was an easy man to like. I told him that I'd buy him wine, but not today, as I had to report to the ephebe barracks in the city. After I'd hired a wagon and driver to transport my trunk to the city, two other Scythians arrived at the port, which signaled the end of Scylurus' and Madyes' shift here. They were headed back to their own barracks in the city, so they came with me. But they refused to ride in the wagon. "For womens and babies, or man with arrow in leg, or old man," said Scylurus. "Young mens ride horses. If no horses have, walk." So I got off the wagon and walked with them.

Grandfather told me that many years earlier the Athenian tyrant Hippias brought in Scythians to police the streets of Athens after the assassination of his brother Hipparchus. Hippias chose Scythians because they were fierce, loyal, and willing to work cheap. In theory, they were state-owned slaves, but in practice they had more autonomy than slaves normally did. They served terms of five years in Athens, after which they returned to their homeland north of the Euxine Sea. They were politically neutral because they had no ties to any of the city's contentious leading families, and their sense of personal honour was so acute that they were nearly impossible to bribe. When Hippias first brought them here, his enemies claimed they were just his hired thugs. Yet when Hippias and his faction were ousted, the Scythians stayed, and more were brought in. Now no one doubted their effectiveness. They feared no man and would never run from a fight. I'd already heard stories about what happened to young hotheads who lacked the sense to back down from the Scythians, who were skilled with all weapons and could break arms and legs without working up a sweat.

They had free time some evenings and could pretty much do what they liked. They were bored and away from their families, so it's not surprising that they hung out in a tavern. They liked whores too, of course, but were not paid well enough to visit them often. Madyes had his own solution to this problem: when he wasn't on duty in the city, he worked as a doorman at a brothel, where he was paid not in coin but in services. The Scythians had limited authority to arrest citizens, but could do whatever was necessary, including busting heads, to keep order. The litigation-loving Athenians would not hesitate to sue any private citizen who looked at them the wrong way, but the Scythians' state slave status exempted them from lawsuits.

"Athens big honk fuck *monkey* town," said Scylurus as we walked. He spat, and I'm not sure if it was intended to punctuate what he'd just said or if he just needed to spit.

I looked to Madyes for help, and he just laughed and said, "Hey, don't look at me, I don't know what the fuck he's talking about either." Madyes spoke little, but his Hellenic was perfect. Scylurus spoke constantly, but never quite got the hang of our language.

Their biggest adjustment from their previous life was more philosophical than linguistic. "In Saka land, man free," said Scylurus. "Go place you want go, *when* you want go. In Athens, no man free, not even free man. Is crazy."

"What he means," added Madyes, "is that Athenian men always seem to have to be somewhere at a specific time. Then when they've finished there, they usually have to be somewhere else at a specific time. The more important the man, the more he has to do this. On the Sea of Grass, only slaves have to do that."

"Curfew fuck-it crazy dog bugger-time look you," Scylurus added, spitting again.

"What he means," said Madyes, "is that we initially had a lot of trouble understanding that we had to be in our barracks at a certain time and had to wake up in the morning at a certain time. We're used to it now, but no one does that in Scythia, unless they're at war and have to rise with the sun."

"How did you guys end up in Athens?" I asked.

"Cannot say, story fuck too long," said Scylurus. "Walk to city only five miles."

"I heard the Sakai are born cavalrymen," I said.

"Is true," said Scylurus. His face hardened into a slight grimace. Madyes looked away. I realized, too late, that I'd unintentionally hit a sore spot. The Sakai measured a man's wealth by the number of horses he owned. Here, Scylurus and Madyes didn't have the money to own even one. It wasn't their fault, but they were still ashamed, and their shame would deepen if they returned to their homeland on foot.

Scylurus quickly changed the subject. "Son of Belkos is runner too?"

"Is true," I said, teasing him about his Hellenic, and he looked at me like he wanted to kill me. Then he guffawed loudly and again slapped me on the back so hard that I swear I stopped breathing for a few seconds.

"I like you, Lectoros!" he bellowed. "Like make fun! Father best Hellene, mother Sakai! You want fight me?"

"Are you serious?" I said. "Now?"

"Yes, we fight. Not today, later. Wood

swords, no killings. Or wrestle. But no rubbings with olives oil. Uck! Wrestle like men."

"Sure, I'll fight you," I said. "You'll probably kick my ass halfway back to Skiathos, but I'd learn a lot from the Saka. You wouldn't get into trouble for fighting a free Hellene, would you?"

"No," said Madyes quietly. "We'll just make sure no one finds the body."

The three of us just looked at each other intensely for a few seconds. Then we all burst out laughing. Madyes had a deadpan delivery that, pardon the pun, killed.

I learned later that I'd answered correctly. If I'd said I didn't want to fight, they would have accepted it but also lost respect for me. They might not consider me enough of a Saka to share any kinship with them—I'd be just another effeminate Hellene who quaked in his sandals at the sight of a Scythian. I'd agreed to fight, and acknowledged that I'd probably lose, which showed that I did not fear pain. That was the way of Saka warriors. They feared nothing. To lose a fight was not shameful, but to back down from one was.

On a clear day you could see the Acropolis of Athens after you'd barely left the Phaleron. The countryside around us was rocky. There were a few thin vineyards and olive groves on both sides of the road, but no steep hills or tall trees to block the view. I just gawked at the Acropolis like a bumpkin. Along the road, there were merchants' stalls, food-vendors, and shrines, all taking advantage of the traffic going in both directions, although this late in the day most of it headed back to the city. Several stalls sold roast goat, salted fish, bread and cheap wine. There were also a few ramshackle huts on the road and the occasional beggar.

"Marta will ease your burdens, young sir," said a rich, full-throated female voice.

The lady wore a blond wig and wildly painted eyes. She stood by the side of the road with the top of her tunic pulled down to reveal ample breasts. She was past forty and missing a couple of teeth, but still attractive enough to make a living. I gawked at her rosy-nippled splendour with the same reverence I'd had for the Acropolis. Remember, Ephander, I was seventeen and randy as a drunk lapith. I had money. I was tempted.

Madyes stepped between Marta and me. "Not today, Marta," said Madyes. "Our young friend has business in town."

Madyes was diplomatic. Scylurus was not. "Fah!" he spat. "Diseases! Make cock shrivel up and fall off. Ceramicus whores cleaner."

Madyes laughed. "Scylurus, since when have you worried about diseases?" he said. To me he added, "He'll fuck anything that's warm. Women, men, dogs, goats, chickens. If I were you,

I wouldn't even leave my dinner unattended when he's around."

"No chicken!" protested Scylurus. "Duck maybe, but chicken? That sick!"

Madyes told me that Athens had a bylaw that prohibited prostitutes from operating within a stade of a shrine, unless it was a shrine to Aphrodite. There had been an ocean of sanctimonious rhetoric about it: prostitutes, because of their disreputable profession, would pollute the precincts of a shrine. Everyone knew this was only about money. A location next to a shrine would be good for a prostitute's business but bad for the shrine's. A man on his way to donate money to a shrine might change his mind if he saw bare-breasted Marta on the way. The Ceramicus brothel-keepers were trying to enact a bylaw that prohibited shrines from being built within a stade of a brothel, although they were probably doing this just to irritate the priests.

About halfway to Athens, we passed a man who would draw your portrait in charcoal on a small piece of papyrus for five obols. He had just finished drawing a rich matron, who'd gotten out of her six-slave litter to pose on a stool in front of the artist. She was moved to tears over the drawing. The artist had taken twenty years off of her face, and the portrait was of a lovely woman who only slightly resembled the matron. She was so pleased that she gave the artist double his fee.

The foolish woman couldn't take her eyes off the drawing as she climbed back into her litter.

Madyes went over to the artist and quietly asked, "Are you going to be here tomorrow when her husband comes to demand his money back?"

The artist chuckled. "I'll be here," he said, "but he won't be. She won't even tell him about it. Before she gets home she'll realize how much I've gilded the lily, and she'll be too embarrassed to even show it to him." Madyes laughed, and clapped the man on the shoulder.

As the three of us walked beside the wagon, I observed how people reacted to the Scythians. Athenians considered Scythians savages, half-feral, little more than animals. No respectable Athenian would ever let his daughter marry or even speak to one. The Athenians were, however, clearly comforted by the Scythians' presence, which meant safety for all. The Athenians looked down their noses at the same men they looked up to for protection on the streets.

Most people were outwardly polite and greeted the Scythians as they passed. One older man, a paunchy fellow who sold sandals from a little stall, saw the three of us and said, "What's this? Are you horse-milkers invading? Should I hide the women?"

"Absolutely, Koros," said Madyes. "By the time we're through, you'll all be wearing orange trousers and your women won't want you anymore. Once they go Sak, they don't go back." Koros howled with laughter and went back to his sandals.

Madyes and Scylurus were both physically powerful, and their colourful Scythian clothing made it impossible for them to go unnoticed, but Madyes was tactful and reserved, while Scylurus said whatever came to his mind. As we walked, many women furtively admired the Scythians, especially Madyes. The sandal vendor's wife had a flirty smile for Madyes when her husband wasn't looking. Madyes was very fit. He worked out every day. He drank his wine neat, like most Scythians, but he paced himself and I never once saw him sloppy drunk. He was one of the few Scythians who could read. He loved Homer and other Hellenic poets. Men pulled their wives and daughters close when Madyes approached, not because they feared what he might do, but because they feared what the women might do. Madyes was also discrete. If an Athenian lady favoured him, he did not boast of it afterwards. He knew that it was a bad idea to embarrass fathers and husbands.

Scylurus, on the other hand, had no discretion whatsoever. On the rare occasions that he romped with a Hellene woman who wasn't a whore, he boasted loudly and often. He was an Athenian father's worst nightmare, a drunken unrefined barbarian, loud and crude, but still charming enough to get female attention, though not as much as Madyes. Scylurus did not work out every day, and it showed. He complained that the Athenians never fed him enough, but you rarely see a paunch like his on a starving man. He ate and drank anything that came his way, and sometimes drank until he passed out. Sober or drunk, he told very crude but very funny stories. More than once I helped carry him back to the barracks when he was too drunk to walk.

When we got close to the Acropolis, it was even more magnificent than it had been from a distance. Back then, Ephander, there were only a few buildings on it. The Bluebeard temple amazed me. Its pediment had detailed carvings of three men with the bodies of snakes. The men's beards were all painted dark blue. And I marveled at the temple of Athene Polias. It was the largest temple I'd ever seen. I was thrilled to be in the city that had the cleverness and skill to build it.

"Look like big dumb farm-boy," said Scylurus, laughing at my state of paralyzed wonder.

"Go to your barracks," said Madyes, 'before someone hits you over the head and steals your trunk."

Before we departed, both men gave me bear hugs that constricted the breath out of me. If the Scythians liked you, they showed it without reservation. They were equally unreserved if they hated you. I agreed to visit Scylurus and Madyes soon. I'd buy them wine, and they'd tell me about my mother's homeland, and how they ended up so far from home in a land so strange to them. But now I had to find the barracks where I'd spend the next two years.

2–EPHEBE

The first year ephebes stood at attention, naked, in the cool morning on the open square outside our barracks. There were about fifty of us.

"Listen up, goat-fuckers," our instructor Proxenos bellowed, or attempted to. His voice was nasal, and when he tried to project, he sounded like an irritated mallard. His nickname was Ducky. It fit. Several boys laughed at his voice.

"You don't fucking laugh when I talk!" Proxenos quacked at us. "Everybody do fifty pushups. *Now*!"

Some boys groaned. "No fucking groaning, either," Proxenos added, "or I'll make it a hundred."

Ephebes were divided into barracks by tribe. Themistocles had sponsored Phylo and me as honorary members of Leontis, his own tribe. Athenians had to be eighteen years old to begin the training. I was only seventeen, but because I was a *metic*, a resident foreigner, I wasn't as closely bound to Athenian customs. At the end of the training, the other ephebes would be full Athenian citizens. I wouldn't be, so my age didn't matter so much.

Proxenos, despite his voice, thought himself an orator. After the pushups, which most of us handled easily enough, he made a windy speech about the duties of citizenship and our responsibilities as citizen-soldiers of Athens. "Yes, even you fucking foreigners," he added, looking directly at me.

Proxenos, Themistocles' cousin, did not share his kinsman's respect for the talents of non-Athenians. He told us, on this day and many others, that he'd fought for years in the phalanx. "I risked my life all those times for the defense of Athens alone," he would say, "and not some fucking backwater where the goats are prettier than the girls." A few boys chuckled at this.

After the speech, Proxenos had us compete in athletic contests. The first one was the discus. I'd never thrown a discus—in fact, I'd never even seen one before. Proxenos made me throw first, so I did not even have the benefit of seeing how it was done. Proxenos wanted to embarrass me, but I thought the discus was ridiculous. It had no military application, and it wasn't particularly fun to throw. I was pretty sure the Persians wouldn't quake in their silk trousers at the thought of Hellenes throwing dinner plates at them.

In later years, I came to know some excellent discus throwers, and I gained more respect for their efforts, but on the training ground that morning with the other ephebes, the discus was a joke to me. The other boys laughed at my pathetic throw. I did too.

This enraged Proxenos. "Listen, you feathered foreign fuck," he said. "You'll take your training seriously or you're out of here today."

"No disrespect intended, sir," I said, quickly realizing it had been a mistake to laugh. "I've never thrown the discus before. I don't know how."

The boys thought this was hilarious too. Proxenos then jumped on my speech inflections. Hellenes from the Sporades, the island group that includes Skiathos, speak Hellenic with more of a drawl than Athenians do. The Athenians thought their own manner of speaking Hellenic was the right way and everyone else's was wrong. When I said the word *thrown*, for example, it almost had two syllables. *Discus* almost had three.

Proxenos walked up and stood only inches away from me. I was taller than him, so I kept my eyes forward, looking over his head. I could see the grins of the other Athenian boys, but I knew that every one of them was thankful he wasn't the one being yelled at.

"What the fuck language you speaking, boy?" Proxenos said, attempting to growl. He was spraying spittle on my neck. Duck spit. "During the rare occasions that I want you to open your fucking mouth, you'll speak proper Hellenic or you won't fucking speak at all. Understood?"

"Understood, sir," I said.

Our next athletic contest was a hundred-yard sprint across the training square. Many of the Athenians were good athletes, and a few were talented sprinters, but I won this race with an explosive finish. We were only a few feet from the finish line when I passed the boy who'd led from the start. I recovered my wind quickly, while he was doubled over and gasping for breath. He would not shake my hand afterwards, even though others did. "Nicely run," said the boy who'd finished third. "At the end, you were just a big blur. You're not even breathing hard!"

"Neither are you," I said.

"My name's Simeon," he said as we shook hands.

"Elektros," I said. "I'd be willing to bet you're a distance runner." Simeon nodded and smiled, proud that I'd noticed. He had the lean physique and ropey leg muscles of a distance runner.

"Well, maybe the goatfucker from Bird Turd Island isn't completely useless," huffed Proxenos. So far, Proxenos had not spoken to—or about—any of the boys but me. This did not bode well. I did not want to be his whipping boy for my entire two years here.

The next event was the javelin. "This thing, farm-boy," he said to me, "is called a javelin. Ever seen one before?" Proxenos laughed, and so did a few of the boys.

Again, he made me throw first. I considered myself no more than adequate with the javelin. I'd always focused on running and sword work. Even so, my throw was the third longest of the day. This seemed to anger Proxenos, who clearly wanted me to fail. You can't belittle the skills of someone who's among the best at something.

The next event was a distance run. We were to run, still naked, to the Phaleron and back, a total distance of about ten miles. Proxenos would pace us, on horseback.

"Hurry up, girls," Proxenos said. "Your mascara runs faster than you do." He loved this joke, and repeated it several times during the run, and many times afterwards.

I won this race easily. I was so far ahead of the others that I was alone with Proxenos, who seemed irked that his horse would have to trot a little faster than he'd planned. "So the island farm ape can run a little," he sneered. "I will fucking break you, boy."

He was wrong. He would not break me. Compared to Xenocrates, Proxenos was an infant. He was a few years past thirty. He wore his hair and beard close-cropped, in the military fashion, and he was fit, so he at least looked like a soldier. Maybe he always had to have one boy to pick on, so he chose the one whose father was too far away to cause trouble over it. So I tried to reason with him. I had nothing to lose.

"Permission to speak, sir," I said. I trotted beside his horse. The pace was not particularly strenuous to me, so I spoke easily as I ran.

"Go ahead," he said.

"Sir, have I offended you in some way?" I asked.

"No, *you* haven't offended me," he said. "Your presence in my barracks offends me. Ephebe training is for Athenians, not for foreigners."

"Sir, sooner or later we'll fight the Persians. Skiathos will ally with Athens against them. We're Hellenes, so how can you consider us foreigners?"

He snorted and laughed. "Boy, you're foreign in a hundred different ways. For starters, I can barely understand a word you say. You gawk at the architecture here like you've never seen a fucking building before. Do you live in mud huts over there on Bird Turd Island?"

"No sir," I said. "My father's house is large and made of stone and Anatolian oak."

"Well, it has to be large. How else would you fit the goats in?"

"Sir, is it the practice here to house goats and people in the same building? On Skiathos, the goats stay outside. We shelter them in a barn in severe weather."

"When you're not fucking them. Now shut

up and run." This last command was not necessary. I had picked up my pace while we were talking. Proxenos' determined ignorance frustrated me. When I'm frustrated, I run faster.

We continued in silence for a while. "Sir, may I say one more thing?" I asked.

"Yes, but keep it short. Your caterwauling is ruining my pleasant ride in the countryside." I almost laughed at this. He was hardly a paragon of oratory. His voice grated. At the best of times, he sounded like a duck that had just been stepped on.

"I just want to say, sir, that I take my training very seriously. If you hadn't ordered us to run ten miles today, I would have done it anyway, on my own, after you dismissed us. I realize that as a metic, I am fortunate for this opportunity to train in Athens. I will work hard, sir, and follow all commands without question."

"Fucking right you will," he snorted. There was no point in saying anything more, so I finished the run in silence. He did too.

As we returned to the training field, I was half a mile ahead of Simeon, who finished second. There were about forty other ephebes there, clustered around one of their fellows, and a sudden burst of laughter exploded from them. They were the second-year ephebes of Leontis, and the boy they'd gathered around—the one who'd just made them all laugh—was Phylo. When I approached the square, he smiled at me and winked, but said nothing. Several of the others handed him coins. I laughed. They'd wagered on the outcome of our ten-mile race, and Phylo was the only one who'd bet on me.

"I had to do it while I could," Phylo explained later, "because after today, everyone here will know that you never bet against Elektros of Skiathos in a footrace."

"If they have any sense," I said, "they'll also learn that you never bet against Phyloctetes of Skiathos *on* a footrace."

Proxenos rode towards Phylo and tossed him a coin. "How did you know the farm boy would win?" he asked, smiling. His loathing for foreigners did not include Phylo.

"I've seen him run before, sir," said Phylo.

"Really?" said Proxenos. "Where?"

"On Skiathos, sir."

Proxenos did not ask Phylo why he was on that gods-forsaken backwater, and he apparently did not know Phylo was my brother. It wasn't obvious. I was tall, athletic, dark, bearded. Phylo was average height, pudgy, pale, and his beard was a few scraggly white wisps on his chin and upper lip. And Phylo now spoke differently. He didn't sound completely like an Athenian, but he now concealed most of his Skiathan drawl. He'd been here over a year and had obviously worked at it.

After the last of the first-year ephebes ran back to the barracks, Proxenos gave us a half hour to rest and put on our armour. When we reassembled on the training ground, he divided us into pairs with practice swords and shields. He paired me with a boy nicknamed Krios, 'the ram.' He was broad-shouldered, had a neck like a tree trunk, and considered himself a swordsman. The second-year ephebes were watching us, and I heard one of them say to Phylo, "Krios is the best swordsman here. Do you think your farm boy can take him?"

"No," said Phylo, "but the farm boy has already made me some money today, so I'll bet on him out of loyalty." Five or six of the others also bet on Krios. Again, I laughed to myself. Phylo had just gotten them to bet against me again, even though they'd all just lost money doing so.

"I will crush your skull, bumpkin," Krios said to me in a low growl, trying to be menacing. "You'll be shipped back to Bird Turd Island in a Ceramicus yellow." A Ceramicus yellow, Ephander, was a cheap pot that poor people used to store the cremated remains of their dead. The yellowish colouring was a result of the high sand content in the clay. These pots were so flimsy that you could almost break one by just giving it a dirty look.

I said nothing. I sized up my opponent quickly, as Xenocrates had taught me. Krios was very strong in the arms and shoulders, but he looked muscle-bound. His bulging biceps impressed the girls but slowed his movements, especially in armour. I was taller and had a reach advantage. His brute strength was greater than mine, so I would not try to overpower him. His legs were not nearly as developed as his upper body, a sign that he didn't run any more than he had to. The ten-mile run had taken a lot out of him, so I had a stamina advantage. My strategy would be to get him moving, to tire him further. His strategy would probably be to try and end the bout as quickly as possible.

As it turned out, I didn't need strategy against Krios. When Proxenos gave us the order to begin, Krios thrust his wooden sword at me so clumsily that I thought it was trickery, like he wanted me to think his awkward lunge was his best shot. I easily sidestepped it. After a few more of these artless thrusts, I realized that these *were* his best shots. The lack of fluidity in his movements was no ruse.

His thrusts were powerful but inaccurate, and he had no defensive skills. His nickname suited him: his entire strategy consisted of the mindless charge, like a ram, powerful but predictable. I lowered my shield a little so he'd think he found my weakness, one of the oldest tricks in the book. He fell for it. As he lunged at my left shoulder, I brought my shield up against the bottom of the wrist of his sword-arm, then quickly slammed my wooden sword down on the top of his wrist. If we'd been using real swords, I would have cut off his hand. He dropped his sword and shield, then sunk to his knees and yowled like a burnt piglet.

"What the fuck just happened here?" squawked Proxenos.

"I was limbering up, sir," said Krios, as he tried to rub the feeling back into his wrist. "The farm boy suckered me."

The second-year ephebes all protested, even as they handed coins to Phylo. "Not true, sir," shouted one of them. "Krios made the first move."

"Silence!" Proxenos yelled at the second-years. "When I want the bitch brigade's opinion, I'll ask for it."

"He was ready, sir," I said to Proxenos. "He'd already lunged at me a few times."

"Who told you to talk, asshole?" he yelled at me.

"Sir, you asked us a question," I said. "I answered it. As you allowed my opponent to do."

He ran up to me and again yelled and sprayed spittle on my neck. "What the fuck is wrong with you?" he said. "Do you think you can get away with taking sucker-shots at Athenians?"

"No, sir," I began to say. "It wasn't a—"

"That was a *rhetorical* question, moron," he shrieked at me. "Have you ever heard of those?" His face was red with rage. A vein in his neck looked like it would burst any second. I wouldn't have been too surprised if his head exploded.

The next thing that happened I've replayed in my mind a hundred times. How I wish I'd acted differently. Proxenos tried to punch me in the jaw. I'd trained for years with Xenocrates, who constantly lashed out at me unexpectedly to develop my reflexes. Before Proxenos knew what was happening—Apollo's balls, before *I* even knew—I'd redirected his fist with my left hand, then countered with a hard right to the chin that flattened him. I did not think. I reacted. I immediately regretted it. If I'd known it was coming, I would have let him hit me.

All of the ephebes fell so silent you'd almost think they'd stopped breathing. "My apologies, sir," I said, taking Proxenos' arm to help him up. "That was a reflex."

"Don't fucking touch me!" Proxenos yelled. "Striking a superior officer! I'll have you fucking executed."

"Proxenos," called a calm, clear voice from the vicinity of the barracks twenty yards away. A man, an officer by his bearing, leaned against the barracks wall, his horse beside him. He walked over to Proxenos who, angry as he was, deferred to the older man and calmed down a little.

"Captain," said Proxenos. "This fucking metic struck me. Everyone saw it. He's an uncontrollable maniac. I want him out of here, sir."

"He reacted defensively," said the man. "If you strike a man without warning, you can't blame him if he defends himself. What an army we'd have if all our ephebes had such reflexes. You know as well as I do that he disarmed his opponent in a fair fight. Krios, how's your wrist?"

"Sore, sir," Krios said.

"Broken?"

"No, sir, just sore."

The officer nodded to me. "Come with me, boy. You too, Proxenos." He led us into the barracks and closed the door behind us. His next words were for our ears alone. "This metic is hardly out of control. He could have broken Krios' wrist but did not. Is that right, lad?"

"Yes sir," I said. "I disarmed him. I did not want to cripple him."

"Proxenos, more metics will be coming to train as ephebes. You're going to have to accept it. The fucking Persians will have us outnumbered. We'll need to train as many hoplites as we can, and Athens cannot supply all of them. That's the reality we face. I don't want you to treat metics favourably, just fairly. Understood?"

"Understood, sir," Proxenos mumbled, even though his eyes still flashed hatred at me.

"Go back to your men, Proxenos," said the officer. "Boy, you stay. I want another word with you."

When Proxenos left, he said "I'm Phocas. I was the Leontis strategos last year." A *strategos* was the general who represented his tribe in the Athenian military command. Each of the ten Athenian tribes elected one every year. The current strategos of Leontis was Themistocles.

"Elektros of Skiathos, sir," I said.

Phocas smiled. "Yes, I know who you are. My cousin Themistocles asked me to look in on you. I must tell you, if you ever strike a superior officer again, you'll not only be expelled from the ephebes but prosecuted. Execution is a punishment option. Clear?"

"Understood, sir. I reacted without thinking."

"I know that, but it won't be overlooked a second time. I know you're a first-rate runner and you're good with weapons, but you'll need to learn how to fight in the phalanx. I'm guessing you have no experience."

"True, sir. This is only the second time I've had the armour on. It feels strange. I don't know how to use the spear."

"In the phalanx, you fight as a member of a team, not as an individual. It's a completely different mindset from what Xenocrates teaches, but you'll get it soon enough."

"Yes, sir."

"I also hear you're not very good with the

discus," he said with a smile.

"True, sir. I don't even know how to grip it."

"The discus is for show, not for war, so don't lose sleep over it. Know also that Proxenos is testing your mental toughness. That's part of his job. Today he's singled you out, but eventually he'll get to everyone else."

"Yes sir."

"What I want you to do now is apologize to Proxenos in front of the other ephebes. It will let him save face. Then after the day's training is finished, you will repeat the run to Phaleron and back, except this time you'll do it in full armour. Proxenos does not have to oversee it, so I want your word that you'll do it."

"You have it, sir."

When I returned to the ephebes, they were still sparring with the wooden swords.

"Permission to speak, sir," I said to Proxenos.

"Fucking keep it short," he said.

"I apologize for what happened earlier, sir," I said. "I was in the wrong. I reacted inappropriately, and I swear by sacred Athene it won't happen again."

"If it does, you're fucking dead, boy," he said. "Now pick up your training sword."

I could see that most of the boys were straining with the weight of the wooden swords, which were heavier than real swords but about half the weight of the training swords Xenocrates made me use. A ten-mile run followed by weighted-sword-training was a new experience for them. With Xenocrates, it was only a portion of a day's training.

Proxenos paired me up with Simeon, who was nervous after what had happened to Krios. "Go easy on me, big guy," he said. "If you kill me, every whore in Attica will mourn for a year."

I laughed. I liked this guy. He joked when he was nervous. I sensed courage in him. "Krios tried to bash my head in," I said. "As long as you don't do that, we'll be okay."

Proxenos didn't really tell us what to do, he just wanted us to get used to the feel of sword and shield. Instead of sparring, I showed Simeon a drill that Xenocrates made me do hundreds of times. I put my shield forward and told Simeon to strike the top of it with his sword. Then I pulled my shield back and had him put his forward, and I struck the top of it. We did this back and forth, again and again, slowly at first but gradually increasing to a rapid-fire pace that had us sweating.

"I must stop," Simeon said, out of breath. "I really feel that in the arms."

"Then it's working," I said. "It builds shoulder strength and stamina. We probably shouldn't overdo it today."

"Why not?" said Simeon. "Can't handle

it?" Then he suddenly pounded his sword against my shield. He laughed. I did too, and we began the drill again. The pounding of sword into shield became a percussive rhythm. Then the rhythm started to get louder. The other sparring pairs had picked up on it and were doing the same drill, in rhythm with Simeon and me, and the sound became progressively faster. When Simeon and I stopped this time, the sound continued as many of the others kept going.

I expected Proxenos to yell at me again, but he just shook his head. "I wondered if I had a bunch of Theban ribbon dancers on my hands," he said. "I wonder no longer."

We continued with this drill and others for a couple of hours, then Proxenos told us to call it a day. "Tomorrow," he said, "we start phalanx training. All day. Rest up."

The next morning, I was a little tired but otherwise okay. I'd run twenty miles that first day, ten of them in full armour. While twenty miles wasn't a typical day's training on Skiathos, I'd done it many times. The only ill effect I had was some chafing from the armour. Before the second run, my armour was stiff. The metal below the breastplate arm-holes chafed my underarms, and the greaves, which went from above the knees to below the ankles, hindered my leg movements. I initially wondered if I could run one mile, let alone ten. But I soon got used to it. It wasn't a race, so I ran a slow, relaxed pace. By the time I returned to the barracks, the straps on the greaves, breastplate, arm guards, and helmet had softened. Everything was broken in. Phocas did me a favour when he gave me the second run as punishment.

What Phocas had told me about Proxenos was true. He needled me regularly. “How’s our pathetic metic today?” was something he said almost every day. After that first day, though, he didn’t focus on me exclusively. I kept my mouth shut and trained. I was always the first ephebe on the training ground every morning. Some days, Proxenos didn’t work us particularly hard. On those days, I’d run another ten miles after he dismissed us. The other ephebes thought I was nuts. But I was accustomed to that physical workload.

When the day’s training was over, the ephebes who didn’t have sentry duty would hang out in the barracks, playing dice or singing. Sometimes they’d go to a nearby wine-shop, and even though Proxenos had expressly forbidden us to go there, it was not a rule he enforced. Sometimes he joined us there. I never understood this. By declaring repeatedly that we were forbidden to go there, and then not doing anything when we ignored this rule, he undermined his own authority. I’ve never been commanded by anyone who was so little respected by his men. I wondered how he even got this job. He was a complete fuckup. Themistocles must have made him the ephebe trainer as a favour to his family.

I went to the wine-shop a few times. It was like the Athenians and I were from different planets. They were all more educated than me. Once, when the wine-shop talk turned to poetry, I mentioned how much I loved Homer.

"Oh, Homer is terrific," said Metion with his flawless aristocratic diction, "*if you're eight years old!*" Metion was blonde-haired, blue-eyed, and extremely handsome. He was one of Proxenos' favourites. This alone made me dislike him. My face flushed with anger, which I tried not to show. Homer was sacred to me, and this mollycoddled tit had just dismissed him.

"So if Homer is for children," I asked Metion, "who writes poetry for men?"

"Archilochos is hot these days," he said. "Pindar too. Anacreon, if you like words that can be sung easily. But my favourite right now is Simonides of Keos."

Simonides? Kandra once told me that her father was from Keos. It couldn't be the same man.

"I know a man from Keos named Simonides," I said. "Any idea what he looks like?"

"Yes, I met him once," said Hyperion, Proxenos' other aristocratic pet. "He's old, past sixty. Brilliant poet, but a complete swine. Always drunk and always smells like rancid garum. I couldn't talk to him for very long because his smell made me ill."

"Where do you know him from?" Metion asked me.

"I was mistaken," I lied. "That doesn't sound like the guy I know." I'd caught myself in time: if I said how I knew Simonides, it might compromise the work he did for Themistocles. We were not supposed to acknowledge our fellow operatives to third parties. If it wasn't already common knowledge that Simonides lived on Skiathos, it would have been a mistake for me to reveal it.

I had little in common with these guys. I could read both Hellenic and Persian, and my knowledge of Homer was pretty good, but by Athenian standards I was uneducated. They understood mathematics, rhetoric, philosophy and literature at a far more advanced level than me. When they spoke on these topics, I rarely knew what they were talking about.

To them, I was a big dumb hick. For some reason, they thought superior education made them better soldiers. When they talked of going into battle, which none of them had done before, *they* were the big dumb hicks. They mused about what it would be like to kill a man. Like little boys, they glorified it. Even though they knew they were training to fight in a phalanx, which depersonalized combat and turned it into killing by committee, they still thought battle would be as glorious and noble as it was in *The Iliad.* In their minds, they'd be heroes.

I had never fought an actual battle either, but between taking down Persian sentries and fighting my way out of the mines at Thasos, I'd already killed fifty or sixty men. It was never glorious. The men I killed would have killed me if they had the chance. As they writhed at my feet, as their bowels emptied in terror and their blood soaked the ground, my only thought was how easily that could've been me. Next time, maybe it would be. They spoke no immortal last words. The only sounds they made were confused groans. I saw no glory there, no heroism, only ugliness and horror. I did not imagine I was Achilles.

Of course I couldn't tell them this. The work I'd done for Themistocles was not for their ears. Also, if I told them about what happened on Thasos, they wouldn't have believed me.

So I stopped going to the wine shop. Wine itself was no incentive: my lifelong dislike for it was a social disadvantage sometimes. When men drink together, they bond, became closer. When *I* drink wine, I get a headache. Instead of getting happy, I get wretched. I will drink it well watered on important occasions—for example, when a friend or family member is celebrating a birthday—but even then I hate the taste and will rarely take a second cup. Grandfather once told me that my mother never drank wine. He always figured it was because she was used to powerful Scythian *koumiss*—fermented mare's milk—but it may also have been simply because wine disagreed with her as much as it did with me. At the wine-shop, I was tolerated but not particularly welcome. Once the boys started getting tipsy, I no longer wanted to be with them. A drunk man gets on well with other drunk men, especially if they started drinking together and have matched levels of intoxication, but to a sober man he's a dribbling idiot. A wine-shop full of drunks is no place for a sober man. In my spare time, even on feast days, I worked out and practiced with sword and shield.

After I'd been in Athens a couple of months, I had no friends in the barracks. Not one.

I was not like Phylo, who could make friends in the Persian section of Hades. I was not talkative by nature and had no knack for chitchat. In our mess hall, if I sat down at a table with other boys, they got up and left. If I was the only one sitting at a table and there were no other spaces available, boys would cram themselves onto the occupied benches and almost sit on each other's laps, just so they wouldn't have to sit with me. Phylo couldn't join me because the second-year ephebes took their meals at different times than the first-years did. The boys were civil towards me, never blatantly hostile, but no one was friendly. They were relieved when I stopped coming to the wine shop.

In the barracks, Simeon's bunk was next to mine. "Why am I being treated like a leper here?" I asked him one night just before lights out. "Everyone seems to hate me."

"Not true," he said. "It's nothing personal." His face flushed a little and he couldn't look me in the eye.

"What is it?" I demanded.

"Sorry, I can't say." Simeon wanted to be my friend, but something prevented him. The deep fear in his eyes was real, so I dropped the subject.

The next day I asked Phylo why everyone avoided me.

"Several reasons," he said. "The first is that you look like a Scythian. For all their education, these boys have led sheltered lives. Some think Scythians are savages and it will diminish their reputations if they befriend one. As they get to know you, this will change."

"If they never talk to me," I asked, "how will they get to know me?"

"When you go out on overnight maneuvers, which you'll do in a month or so, they'll see your quality. They'll see you as the best man to stand beside in battle. Right now they're actually scared of you. When you slugged Proxenos, everyone saw your hands move like lightning. They thought it was superhuman, and while they were impressed, they were also unnerved. You spooked them.

"The biggest reason, though, is Proxenos. He told them to shun you. He's promised some inventive revenge on anyone who befriends you. That's why they don't want you in the wine shop. Simeon's a good man and wants to train with you, but Proxenos threatened to have his sister raped if he did."

Proxenos, in his bullish hatred, wanted to either drive me out or make my two years with him as hellish as possible. He would not succeed. As I said before, Ephander, he was nothing to me. Xenocrates was a hurricane. Proxenos was a light drizzle. I wondered if I could somehow turn this around, make *his* life as hellish as possible.

I finally visited the Scythians, as I'd promised Scylurus and Madyes. They hung out in a shit-hole tavern just outside Athens on the road to the Phaleron. I'd put it off because I did not want to hang out with drunkards, and Scythian drinking was legendary, but I felt obliged to visit them at least once.

Turned out to be one of the smartest things I ever did.

The tavern was barely a building. It was called Dio's, named not for the god of wine but for the barman who claimed his name was Dionysos. The unpainted wooden walls had so many holes and cracks that you felt the wind outside. When it rained, the roof leaked in a dozen places. The tables were coarse wood, chipped and cracked and unfinished, and the benches left splinters in your arse. The floor was covered in gravel and sawdust, to absorb spit and blood and spilled wine. Only hard men drank here. Almost every non-Scythian customer was missing front teeth or an eye, as were most of the half-dozen whores. There were knife scars on a lot of faces here, but the rugged clientele suited the fearless Scythians. The wine here, which I'd heard people compare unfavourably to horse piss, was cheap, which also suited the Scythians, who had very little money.

I saw seven or eight Scythians sitting at a table in the corner. In their bright orange trousers and tunics, they stood out, especially since most of the other customers were thieves and thugs who avoided drawing attention to themselves.

Madyes and Scylurus both spotted me at the same time. "Lectoros!" Scylurus roared. He jumped to his feet and crushed me in a bear-hug. "We think you coming never!"

One of the Scythians had a barmaid on his lap and was trying to get her to leave with him, but she insisted she'd only do it for money, and he didn't have enough. Another barmaid came up behind him and dumped a pitcher of water over the Scythian's head. The woman on the man's lap scrambled free, wet but laughing and relieved.

"Aki tries this every night," Madyes told me, "and every night he gets his face slapped, his balls kicked, or water dumped on his head. Aki, why do you do this?"

"Free water," said Aki, "and sometimes free kick in balls."

"My friends, this Lectoros," said Scylurus. The other Scythians nodded polite greetings. Then Scylurus said, "His father Hellene, his mother *Saka*." This got their attention. Most of them got up, came over to me and shook my hand.

"Saka mother!" said Aki, still dripping wet, smiling so broadly that his mouth seemed wider than his head. "You lucky!" Several of the Scythians clapped me on the back so hard I thought I'd have bruises the next day.

All except one of them, who hadn't left his seat on the bench. He just stared at me, unblinking, transfixed, like I was some kind of fearsome miracle. "Thoas, you fucking slug," Madyes scolded. "Show our guest some manners."

Thoas stood up quickly, embarrassed. Fierce as they are, Scythians pride themselves on their hospitality. Thoas shook my hand, but there was still something on his mind. There was a long awkward pause before he spoke.

"Forgive it me, Lectoros," he said. "Thoas not want rude to guest. You remind me of aunt. Tall, strong Saka lady, many year ago pirates take."

Ephander, do you ever get a tingling behind your eyes when somebody's about to say something that you know will change your life? It doesn't always happen like that. More often than not, life-changing words catch you completely by surprise, but I almost knew what Thoas was going to say next before he actually said it. His Hellenic wasn't good, and in his excitement he forgot most of the little he knew. He said something in his own language to Madyes, and spoke so rapidly that I didn't understand much of it, but I clearly heard him say *Roxella.* He pronounced it Rocks-AY-la.

"That was my mother's name," I said.

"What?" said Thoas.

"I didn't understand most of what you just said, Thoas, but you said 'Roxella,'" I said. "That was my mother's name."

"Roxella my mother sister!" cried Thoas. "You my—uh, Madyes, what word in Hellene talk?"

"Cousin," said Madyes.

"My coo-zen!" said Thoas. He was overjoyed, and he hugged me, but there was also sadness in his eyes, like he already knew that Roxella's story did not end well.

"Are you sure?" I said. "Is Roxella a common name among the Sakai?"

"No, not common," said Thoas. "Not matter anyway. I *know* family. Uncle Borysthenes you look like."

One of the other Scythians said, "You right, Thoas. Borysthenes look like!" Thoas and I also resembled each other. Not exactly twins, but we looked related.

"Lectoros and me talk alone," said Thoas.

I put two tetradrachm coins on the Scythians' table. "Fill your cups again, friends. On me."

Their eyes widened. They looked at me like I'd done something wondrous. Athens gave them room and board—a dilapidated barracks and two bowls of stew every day, and sometimes they were given extra wine during festivals—but no money. They could earn extra money in their spare time, acting as bodyguards—a citizen might pay a few obols to a Scythian to walk him home after dark—but these little jobs were infrequent. The two coins were enough to pay for two nights' worth of the cleaning fluid that passed for wine at Dio's. I was just being friendly—I didn't drink, and I slept and ate in the ephebe barracks for free, so I didn't spend much money in Athens. Two tetradrachms were nothing to me. But generosity was sacred to the Scythians, especially when it was unexpected and unasked for. Madyes later told me that this seemingly minor gesture made every Scythian in Athens my friend, and all of them would help me if I was ever in trouble.

Thoas and I went to a small table in a different corner of the tavern. I bought another pitcher of sour wine. Thoas drank his neat. Mine was well watered, but I could still barely get it down. I told Thoas what I knew about Roxella. I told him how she died, how she killed three of the men who attacked her and wounded the fourth, how my Father never forgave himself for allowing it to happen, and how he never loved another woman after her. I knew so few details that this part of the conversation did not take long. We were both in tears by the end of it.

Thoas had much to tell me. "Roxella have sister Gia, my mother, and brother Borysthenes. Him and you mother great warriors."

"Really?" I said. "The Sakai allow women to fight in battle?"

"No, not *allow*," Thoas laughed. "We not can stop. They kill us if we try. Better they kill enemy!"

When Hellenes go to war, they don't want their women anywhere near the battlefield, but Thoas told me that some Scythian women fought beside the men and were just as dangerous. They rode horses and trained with bow, sword, and spear from childhood, just like the men did. According to Thoas, our mythical tales of Amazons had a basis in fact. The Scythians lived north of the Euxine Sea, which was where the Amazon nation was supposed to have existed.

"Roxella famous," Thoas continued. "Great shoot, fight with sword, kill hundreds mens in battles. *Oiorpata*, we name her. Man-slayer. King Skunxes want marry her, but Oiorpata not want husband who take more than one wife."

To live in Hellas, even as a respected citizen's wife, must have been torturously dull for Roxella. Hellene women are barely allowed to leave the house without their husbands' permission.

"Do you have any idea," I asked, "how she got captured?

"Know not much. Bandits take. One night, Roxella patrol, no come back. Next day, we find her horse, broke leg. Signs of fightings. Three dead bandits near horse. We think horse step in gopher hole, break it leg. Oiorpata fast runner, faster than most mens, but not outrun bandits on horses. Bandits probably sell Oiorpata to pirates." Thoas' face was pained as he said this. His family's grief at losing Roxella was great enough, but she was unavenged, which only increased their torment. The bandits, whoever they were, disappeared.

Thoas was about to sink into grief, so I changed the subject. "Tell me about Gia," I said.

Thoas smiled again. "My mother. Gia tall, beautiful, good with bow and spear. Good fighter, but not like Oiorpata. Less serious, more like to laugh. Healer-woman. Know potions, clean wounds. I learn from her."

"And what about Borysthenes?" I asked.

"Very important man. Very tall. Even taller than king. Blood brother to King Koraltes. Great, great warrior. Once ten men attack and Borysthenes kill all. No fuck with Borysthenes and live. But he heartbreak for lose sister."

"I'd like to meet Gia and Borysthenes," I said hopefully. "Would they want to meet me?"

Thoas jumped to his feet. "Yes, yes!" he bubbled, then he gave me another bear hug. "Borysthenes and Gia want meet Lectoros! More you cousin there too. But Thoas not go back for four years—finish duty in Athens first. But Lectoros come with?"

I said I would if I could. We took what was left of the wine pitcher back to the table with the other Scythians. They all seemed to know that Thoas had something solemn to say. All of their conversations suddenly stopped.

"Oiorpata kill by pirates many years ago," said Thoas, "but die with enemies' blood on sword. Die like true Saka warrior. We drink to Oiorpata, and Lectoros' father who love her before she die." All of the Scythians filled their cups and drained them quickly. They all knew of her, some had met her, and several brushed away tears. I was touched by this. I thought they might resent my father for having taken a Scythian noblewoman as a slave, but instead they admired him because he treated her with the honours of a wife. It didn't matter that Father never actually married Roxella. He'd treated her well. To the Scythians, nothing else mattered.

They all looked at me in near shock when I told them that I didn't like wine—for the toast, I'd sipped some wine but did not drain the cup—but they got over it quickly enough.

I spent the next couple of hours listening to their stories, and I promised to wrestle with Scylurus and one or two of the others soon. Thoas pulled out of his pocket a little device made of animal bones tied together with flax thread.

"I have one of those at home!" I said. "What is it?"

Thoas smiled, said nothing. He put the device to his mouth and blew into it. The sound that came out of it was soft but haunting. It was a small set of panpipes.

"Little flute," said Scylurus. "Make from vulture feets bone."

The one I had at home was brittle and falling apart. I kept it because it was my mother's. I thought it was an amulet or a hair-clip. It never occurred to me that it was a musical instrument. When I saw Thoas play it now, I wondered how I could've missed it. Hellenic panpipes were larger, and made from reeds instead of bird bones, but very similar in design.

I didn't want to leave the tavern. These so-called barbarians made me feel far more welcome than the Athenians did. They were rough and didn't particularly like Hellenes, but they were far more easygoing by nature and less judgmental. They held their drink better than my fellow ephebes did, too, so it was easier to be sober in their presence.

And I was one of them now.

3–REVENGE

I sprinted across the open field all the way to Dio's tavern. I touched its shaky wall and hoped the damned building didn't collapse as a result. Madyes, Scylurus, Thoas, and several other Scythians ran behind me. I was way ahead of them. They were all out of breath. I wasn't.

They laughed about it afterwards. "No one catch son of Oiorpata and Belkos running man famous," said Scylurus. "Not like human run!"

They could laugh. I outran them, but they'd bested me in everything else. I thought I was passably good with the javelin, but their worst throws were five yards longer than my best. When I wrestled with Scylurus, he twisted me into a knot and had me flat on my back in less than two minutes. When Madyes and I sparred with wooden swords, I held my own until he used a trick I'd never seen before. He feinted high with his sword, blocked my counter-thrust with his shield, then dropped into a one-legged crouch while his other leg swept low and kicked my feet out from under me. I was so impressed with this move that I insisted he teach it to me right there and then.

"It works best," he said, "if you first give your opponent something high to block with his shield. When he raises it, you drop under his line of vision and sweep-kick at that precise moment. Do it wrong, you end up low and vulnerable, but do it right and you take your man down." I tried it at least twenty times before Madyes was happy with the way I did it. He also taught me how to defend against the move by jumping over your opponent's sweeping leg.

I was banged up and bruised. The Scythians were pleased that I took my lumps and came back for more. To them, a true warrior learns whatever he can from better fighters. Pain was part of the learning process. They also surprised me with their athleticism, even paunchy Scylurus. They went to Dio's often. I'd assumed they'd all be out of shape, but they rarely drank as much as they were reputed to. Back in Scythia, they lived like Spartans—plain food, water instead of wine or koumiss, weapons practice and physical training every day—and only drank to excess during feasts and celebrations. They liked wine but were not slaves to it. They spent time at Dio's because they were far from home and bored. When they needed to focus on training, they stopped drinking wine altogether, for months if necessary. How many Hellenes could do that?

Meanwhile, my ephebe training continued. We worked out with spears and shields, we sparred, we wrestled, we boxed. Sometimes we had athletic competitions—I always won the long and short running races, always came close but never actually won the javelin throw, and always finished last with the discus—but mostly we drilled and drilled and drilled in phalanx techniques. Proxenos excelled at this. Repetitive drilling was simple and not beyond his limited capabilities. We practiced holding formation, fighting as a single entity, and rotating in and out of the phalanx so that the enemy always faced fresh men. We sometimes spent entire days drilling. We marched in step, turned in step, and hoisted our nine-footers in unison. Mindless as it was, I actually liked it. For the first time in my life I was part of a team, even though the Athenians did not socialize with me.

We also had sentry duty. Every night, four of us patrolled a section of Athens' walls for the first half of the night, and four others patrolled for the second half. Even with reduced sleep, sentries were expected to participate in all training exercises the next day. "It's dull," said Proxenos. "Even in the field, sentry duty is uneventful most of the time. It is essential, however, and you must learn to deal with the boredom. Know now that no god will help the ephebe I catch asleep on duty."

It made perfect sense, but Proxenos still played favourites—Heracles' balls, it was impossible for him *not* to. Metion rarely drew sentry duty, and never during feasts or holidays, which was when I was always scheduled. Proxenos did Metion no favour here. When Metion went to war as a hoplite, Proxenos would not be his commander, so he'd have to do sentry duty without having learned how. Unless he planned to be the bum chum of every officer he served under, he'd be better off learning to stand watch like the rest of us. Hyperion, Proxenos' other favourite, was also given very few sentry shifts, but once he realized this he insisted that Proxenos schedule him in, including feast days and holidays. Hyperion, tall and aristocratic and probably the most handsome of us, was also the most principled. I admired him for it.

There was a woodworking shop close to the barracks. I had the woodworker make me an extra-heavy practice spear of Anatolian oak—very precious wood in Attica, where there were no oak trees and few forests of any kind. Oak was denser and much heavier than ash, which most spears were made from, and I had this spear weighted with extra iron on the tip and on the butt. When I went to the shop to pick it up, I could barely lift it. "Good luck with that, Achilles," the woodworker teased me.

"I can't heft it now," I said, "but give me a month."

Proxenos permitted me to train with my extra-heavy spear and let me store it in the barracks. At first, I struggled to keep it hoisted at shoulder height, and Proxenos would not let me rest it on my shield. "You may use your big spear, fuck-face," he snarled at me, "but only if you use it properly." But within a few days I was able to hoist it without pain. When I switched back to the lighter regulation nine-footer, it felt like a toothpick in my hand. When Proxenos wasn't looking, Simeon asked me where I'd gotten it. I told him about the woodworker's shop. Within the next half-month, other ephebes started showing up with custom-made heavy practice spears. Being Athenians, most of them wanted the heavy spears to not only strengthen their spear-arms but also display their fathers' wealth. My spear was varnished, and the iron had been coated with beeswax to help prevent rust, but the spear wasn't decorated. Some of the others' spears were absurdly ornate. They'd tried to outdo each other. Battle scenes, usually involving Heracles or Achilles, were carved into some of the shafts, and some of their spear-tips had gold plate over the iron. I laughed to myself. Some of them had completely missed the point. Metion's heavy spear had gems embedded in the butt-spike, and there was gold leaf on the entire shaft, including near the centre, which should have been left clear for easy gripping. The point and the butt spike were both solid gold, which was much too soft for combat training. This spear was worth the price of a small farm. Metion was proud of it, but the first time he drilled with it, a few gems fell off, and the gold leaf got scratched every time the spear came in contact with a shield or another spear. He left a trail of gems and gold behind him. Proxenos was amused. If I'd ever done something like that, he would have flown into one of his quacking rages, but he and Metion were lovers. Proxenos quietly told him to go back to the barracks and fetch his old unadorned spear. Proxenos had to stifle a laugh.

Proxenos still needled me every day, but as Phocas said would happen, he rarely focused on me as he did that first day. Proxenos continued to greet me every day with attempted wit.

"How's the Bird Turd King today?" he'd ask me, or he'd say "Greetings to the Prince of Goatfuck Island."

Once, when Hyperion and I sparred with wooden swords, Hyperion tripped and fell over backwards. As I helped him up, we were both laughing.

Proxenos flew into a flurry of fury. He didn't see what had happened, so he assumed that I'd knocked Hyperion down. Within seconds he was in front of me, screaming in rage, his crimson face knotted and throbbing, as the veins in his neck and forehead looked like they'd burst. We'd all seen this many times by now and weren't particularly intimidated by it. Proxenos was an embittered, deeply unhappy man. There's no other explanation for the way he became engulfed in fury over trivial things.

"It's okay, sir," Hyperion said. "I tripped on my own."

"Don't cover for this lunatic!" he screamed at Hyperion.

"I'm not, sir. My greave came loose and I tripped over it. I'm not hurt." Hyperion pointed down to his greave, which had come unbuckled.

Proxenos ignored him completely. "Asshole!" he screamed at me. "What did I tell you about damaging your Athenian betters?"

I did not answer. There was nothing I could say that wouldn't make him angrier.

"Answer me, you island turd-ball!"

"Sir, you will disbelieve anything I tell you," I finally said. "I await my punishment."

He punched me in the jaw. I flinched, but more for show than because I needed to. One of the first things Xenocrates ever taught me about fighting was that you cannot do it well if your body is tense. Never fight angry, he often said, because anger tightens your muscles and muddles your thoughts, and you must think clearly to fight well. Proxenos, enraged, didn't get much on his punch. He punched me in the stomach, but I saw it coming, flexed my abdominal muscles and barely felt it. My biggest problem was not the little bit of pain: I had to focus every last iota of my concentration on not retaliating, because that's what my reflexes had been conditioned to do. Proxenos hit me ineffectually a few more times, then made us all run to the Phaleron and back in full armour.

"When one of you fucks up," he said, "all of you will be punished. Blame this one on the Island Goat King here."

The boys were unhappy about this punitive run, but none of them blamed it on me. Hyperion had insisted from the start that he and I were sparring amiably, and everyone had seen that his greave was loose.

The loose greave gave me an idea.

A couple of days later, we stood in formation on the training ground. The sun was at its mid-afternoon hottest, which was when Proxenos usually made us sprint in full armour.

One ephebe, Alexandros, had been kicked in the knee by a horse when he was a child. It had never healed completely. He could handle a full-armour jog to the Phaleron and back, but he could not sprint well. A quick trot was the best he could manage. This shouldn't normally exclude a man from the phalanx. Sprinting in armour strengthens your legs and improves your overall fitness, and we did it in training almost every day, but you almost never do it in battle. Your phalanx would fall out of formation and you'd tire quickly. It would also make you sweat too much. A hoplite's armour already weighs forty pounds. When the armour's inner padding absorbs perspiration, it gets even heavier, and if sweat gets into your eyes, you can't see the enemy clearly. You wear the hoplite panoply to stand and fight, not to run. Good commanders know this and will even order you *not* to sprint as you approach the enemy.

Alexandros, despite his wonky leg, was an excellent soldier. Even though he worked hard on conditioning and mastered all training exercises, Proxenos was merciless to him. When he made us sprint the hundred yards across our training square, Alexandros was slow and Proxenos always rode him about it. What rankled us most was that Alexandros was never the slowest. There were two others who usually finished behind him. One was Proxenos' catamite Metion, who could get away with laziness, and the other was Ableros, who suffered from asthma. Ableros had trouble with any kind of running, but we admired him because he worked so hard at it. Exertion left him wheezing, which would make him vulnerable in battle. Proxenos' never picked on Ableros because Ableros' father was a former archon. Alexandros' father was dead, and mine was far away, so Alexandros and I were fair game for Proxenos. He wouldn't dare pick on any ephebe whose father was near enough to give him grief over it.

One day Proxenos was particularly harsh on Alexandros. "You're no soldier, you sack of goat shit with feet," he shrieked at him. "I wouldn't have you in my phalanx. Who wants to form up beside a gimp?"

That was unfair. Alexandros was strong and brave. I would stand in battle beside him anytime. The rest of us felt the same.

It was Hyperion who spoke up. Proxenos' favoured him because he wanted to marry Hyperion's sister, rumoured to be jaw-droppingly beautiful. Proxenos never knew how much Hyperion despised him and would never suffer him as a brother-in-law. Hyperion idolized Aristides the Just, and like his hero, he abhorred any form of unfairness.

"Sir!" Hyperion called out. "Show us how it's done."

"What you talking about?" Proxenos snapped.

"Pardon me for speaking out, sir," replied Hyperion, "but I think the slower ephebes might benefit if you demonstrated a proper sprint in armour for them."

Proxenos didn't want to do it, but he'd been called out. If he refused, Hyperion might report this unmanly reluctance to his lovely sister.

"Okay, girlies," said Proxenos. "Watch and learn."

Proxenos was actually a good athlete, a fine runner and superb with the javelin—with the discus, too, although that didn't count much with me. He crossed to the far side of the training ground, limbered up his legs a little, then began sprinting in his armour towards us. His form was excellent—in fact, he ran like the armour wasn't there. He strode smoothly, faster than a spring hare. Then when he was about twenty strides away from us, he fell flat on his face.

We all howled with laughter. One of his greave straps had broken, and he tripped over the loose greave. There was nothing he hated more than being laughed at, even though he seemed to go out of his way to make himself ridiculous. He stood up, murderously furious. He shrieked at us like a harpy's mother, and ordered us to run to the Phaleron and back in full armour. Some of us still laughed as we ran.

Proxenos thought Hyperion had tampered with his greave, but he had no proof and didn't want to alienate the boy whose sister he desired. So Hyperion was never punished. A good thing, too, because Hyperion knew nothing about it. A few nights earlier, I'd snuck into Proxenos' quarters and cut one of his greave straps just enough to make it come loose if he ran while wearing it.

In Dio's tavern that night, I told Scylurus and Madyes about Proxenos and the aggravation he caused me.

"We kill," said Scylurus. "Make look like accident."

He was joking. I think.

"He is kinsman to my sponsor Themistocles," I said. "We can't kill him. I just want him to suffer."

"I can help you," said Madyes with a wink.

Ten days after the incident with the greave, Proxenos showed up on the training ground without his armour. He wore only a loose tunic and sandals.

He was an unholy mess. He looked like some pestilence had had its way with him. His face was swollen and red, but the redness was uneven, mildly pinkish on one side and a huge purple splotch on the other. He had open sores that had scabbed over on his cheeks, forehead, arms, legs, and neck. He had black circles under his eyes. Whatever ailed him kept him up at night. We were all horrified at the sight, though not necessarily displeased about his suffering.

"Sir," said Hyperion, "that's not leprosy, is it?"

Horror flashed in Proxenos' eyes. That his ailment might be leprosy hadn't occurred to him. He told Hyperion to supervise our training today and limped away to suffer in private.

He limped because his testicles were swollen. It was a symptom of this particular rash. Madyes had given me a small vial of oil that had been extracted from deadly nightshade, giant hogweed, and stinging nettles. This Scythian concoction, fatal if ingested, prevented infection in wounds if diluted and used sparingly. I'd rubbed the stuff inside the front of Proxenos' breastplate, on his greave straps, on the inside padding of his helmet, and any other spot that would come in contact with his skin.

I initially thought the stuff didn't work. I'd expected Proxenos to start scratching as soon as he wore the treated armour. After three days, I thought maybe the oil had dried out in the summer heat, or maybe I'd applied it incorrectly, or perhaps he'd had his armour cleaned. On the fourth day, however, Proxenos scratched at his neck, where the flesh looked raw. The next day, as he stood in front of us on the training square, he scratched his armpits and his buttocks.

When I saw Madyes the next day, he asked me if the concoction worked. "Superbly," I said. "I've never seen a more wretched man,"

When I showed him the empty vial, his eyes widened. "You used *all* of it?" he said. "I thought you said you didn't want to kill him."

"You told me to use all of it," I said.

"No. I told you to rub a bit of it into his armour. The whole vial might kill him."

Proxenos' would suffer severely, Madyes told me, but if he survived, there would be no permanent effects except for some skin discoloration. Phocas had arranged for a shoemaker named Linos to supervise our training until Proxenos recovered. We all liked Linos. Past sixty, he was no longer required to serve in the phalanx, but he did so anyway. He'd fought in dozens of battles and remained fighting fit. He tolerated no nonsense and made us work harder and longer than Proxenos did, but he didn't play favourites and didn't gratuitously harass any of us. We would be sorry to see him go, not least because it meant Proxenos was coming back.

Proxenos was away for seventeen days. We'd heard that he had a high fever at one point and teetered between this world and the next, but he returned to us almost completely recovered. His skin had peeled in places, but he was no longer scratching or limping. He had new armour. He'd figured out that his old armour had caused the rash—or perhaps the acidity of the concoction had eaten holes in the bronze. I was a little disappointed. I wanted him to wear the old armour and get the rash over and over and over again.

The Scythians wanted to meet my brother, so one evening I brought Phylo to Dio's. I was worried. Would they like him? The Scythians admired warriors and had little respect for soft Hellenes. Phylo was an adequate soldier at best and no athlete. He did all of the weapons and athletic training required of ephebes, but he never did more. He struggled with athletic activities. In the phalanx and with the sword, he was mediocre. His fellow ephebes liked him as a friend but did not respect him as a soldier.

I needn't have worried. The Scythians liked

Phylo right away. If he was unnerved in any way by the lowlife clientele at Dio's, or by the Scythians themselves, he didn't show it. I was as tall as the Scythians, but Phylo barely reached their shoulders.

When I introduced him, his first words to Scylurus were, "Elektros is a big ugly fuck. Now I see where he gets it from. *All* you Scythians are big ugly fucks."

The Scythians were initially stunned by these bold words. For a second I thought Phylo was going to get beaten up. Then the Scythians all erupted with laughter.

"Lectoros brother, brother mine," said Scylurus, as he and the other Scythians greeted Phylo with handshakes and hard slaps on the back.

No other Hellene, not even Themistocles, could have spoken to the Scythians like that and gotten away with it. Phylo had a knack for it. He understood how the Scythians respected boldness.

"I learned that from you," he told me later.

"What are you talking about?" I said. "I'd never call Scythians a bunch of big ugly fucks."

"No, but you agreed to wrestle Scylurus the first time you met him," Phylo explained. "That was bold. No one else in Athens would do that. They respected you for it, so I applied the same principle when I met them, except I used only words. And I don't have to wrestle any of them."

Phylo, always a better talker than me, got along famously with the Scythians. He would visit them at Dio's regularly. They spent a lot of time singing together. Phylo never shared my aversion to wine, and drank Dio's horse-piss like it was Chian supreme. He was thrilled to learn Scythian songs, particularly because he hadn't heard any of them before and always wanted to expand his repertoire of lewd ballads, which was becoming legendary in Athens. He also picked up words and phrases of their language very quickly, and occasionally made jokes in Scythian.

Unlike me, Phylo talked to the non-Scythian customers at Dio's. Once I showed up there and Phylo was rolling dice on a corner table with a sailor. Known as Cutter, the man had many knife scars on his face and arms. I left Phylo to his game, and sat down with the Scythians.

Cutter was losing and getting surly about it.

He finally exploded. "You cheating prick!" he yelled at Phylo. He then knocked the table over—wine cups and dice went flying—and pulled out a knife. I thought Phylo was a dead man. He was up against an experienced knife fighter, and I wouldn't get to him in time. Then Phylo stomped on Cutter's foot, punched him in the throat, then followed with another hard shot to the ribs. Cutter held on to his knife, but fell backwards against the wall. Phylo grabbed Cutter's wrist with both hands and wrenched the knife away. He then kicked

Cutter's feet out from under him and left him sitting on the floor.

"Here, shit-pail, take your fucking money," Phylo said, dropping coins on the floor beside Cutter. "I didn't cheat. You were just losing. But I don't want there to be bad blood between us."

The Scythians told Cutter to leave Dio's and never return. Cutter eagerly obliged. We never saw him in there again.

"I thought you were dead," I said to Phylo. "Where'd you learn to fight like that?"

"You cannot be brother to Elektros of Skiathos," he said, "without learning *something* about fighting."

Impressed as I was, the Scythians were even more so.

4—KRITES

One evening I walked into Dio's tavern and saw a little guy at a table with four or five Scythians. The little guy had his back to me. Scylurus, animated at the best of times, seethed.

"Sakai best archers in world!" he shouted, jumping to his feet. "Best warriors in world!" He slammed the top of the table with his open hand, spilling the drink of anyone who didn't see it coming and failed to rescue his wine cup in time.

If the little guy was intimidated by the size and apparent anger of the big Scythian, he didn't show it.

"I'm not saying otherwise, Scylurus," he said calmly, with traces of a Lydian accent. "I'm just saying that in certain terrains, Kretan archery would have an advantage over Scythian archery. I've heard how well you guys shoot, but it's mostly from horseback. That's perfect for the Sea of Grass, or on an open battlefield, but in rough terrain, like rocky hills, forests, or mountain-sides, you'd need to focus too much on your horse. An unmounted Kretan archer would have the advantage."

"Bah!" bellowed Scylurus. "Sakai never need focus on horse! Little bastard have big mouth!"

I knew Scylurus. He wasn't nearly as angry as he pretended to be. The little guy, who'd just met him, was perceptive enough to see this.

"Lectoros!" Scylurus shouted when he saw me. "Little bastard with big mouth say you him friends."

The little guy stood up and turned to face me. It was Agapios, Xenocrates' slave. He was fifteen years old now, barely five feet tall—he would grow no taller—and his attempt at a beard had resulted in a few weak blonde wisps on his cheeks and chin. But he was impressively muscular in the arms and shoulders.

I'd always liked him, and sometimes Xenocrates let him run with me. It's no simple thing to befriend a slave. His fate is never his own. If his master sold him, there would be nothing I could do about it. Amongst Hellenes, it wasn't proper for a free citizen to befriend another man's slave. Owners did not want their slaves' loyalty diverted. I've never been particularly observant of social norms, but I was respectful of other men's property.

All these things went through my head as Agapios stood in front of me surrounded by Scythians. He held out of his hand for me to shake it, and for a moment I just looked at it. Then I said, "Give me a hug, little bastard with big mouth."

He laughed. We embraced. I was glad to see him. He made me think of home. "What are you doing in Athens?" I asked him.

"Looking for you, sir," he said. "Master told me to serve as your squire for the rest of your time as an ephebe."

"He should've contacted me first," I said. "I don't need a squire."

"But sir," he said, "who polishes and maintains your armour?"

"Ephebes maintain their own armour," I said. "When they become full citizens and go to war, they might take a slave along, but now we're expected to do it all ourselves so we'll learn how."

Agapios looked devastated.

"You don't have to go back right away," I said. "Stay for a few days. I'll find you a room somewhere, and one evening when I don't have sentry duty, I'll take you to one of the city's finer, uh, *entertainment* establishments."

Agapios looked at me blankly. "What I mean, buddy," I said, "is that I'll get you laid." When I said this, the Scythians all hooted and howled.

"Take me too, Lectoros!" said Scylurus. "I show little bastard how to do!"

Agapios was not cheered by the idea. "Sir, I cannot go back," Agapios said. "The despotis told me that if I serve you for the remainder of your ephebe training, he'll free me, which he probably won't do it if I return. If you do not need a battle squire, I will serve you some other way."

I didn't need a slave. I took my meals in the ephebe mess, and there were slaves there who cleaned and maintained our barracks. The tribe Leontis might give him some barracks duties, but I was reluctant to allow this. If he became a barracks slave, I could not protect him. They sometimes had to submit to the sexual advances of the lustier ephebes. Proxenos was also cruel to our slaves. One time in the mess, a slave spilled a cauldron of soup. He claimed that the handle had broken off. Proxenos whipped the boy until his back was almost completely skinless, then pissed on his wounds to complete the humiliation. He made us all watch. The slave's wounds festered and he died from fever a few days later. I also knew that Proxenos would not need a pretense as flimsy as spilled soup to torment a slave from Skiathos.

So what was I to do with Agapios? Our troubles were forgotten for the moment, though, because the Scythians wanted to have a little archery contest with him.

We all went behind Dio's for the contest. Scythians are always in high spirits when they have weapons in their hands. Krites could not take his eyes off Scylurus' gorytos. He'd heard of goryti, but he'd never seen one before. He was fascinated with the Scythian compound bows. His own bow was a simple one made of pinewood, effective enough for hunting small game but of limited use in battle because of its short range. Scythian compound bows are made of wood, bone, and animal sinew, melded together flawlessly. The materials had to be heated, cooled and polished to perfection. The process took two years. The bows were strong but pleasantly smooth to the touch. They were works of art, truly beautiful, with ornate designs and inscriptions on the handles. Agapios peppered Scylurus with questions about how the bows were made. I thought this might annoy Scylurus, but he loved talking about his bow, and answered Agapios' questions gladly.

For the archery contest, I leaned a broomstick up against Dio's back wall, handle down, bristles up. From thirty yards, Scylurus, Madyes and Aki hit the bristles of the broomstick easily.

It was Agapios' turn. "Remove one of the Scythian arrows, please," he said to me. "I'll put my arrow into the hole it made."

"You not do," laughed Scylurus. "Not is possible. How you see hole from here?"

"Can't be done," agreed Madyes, "especially with that kiddie bow of yours."

Agapios said nothing. After I removed one of the Scythian arrows, he drew back the bowstring, took a few seconds to get a bead on the target, and let it fly. The arrow went exactly where Agapios said it would, right into the hole left by the removed arrow.

The Scythians loved it. They hooted and hollered. "Excellent shoot!" said Scylurus. "With shit bow, too!"

The Scythians wanted him to do it again from fifty yards instead of thirty. They repeated the shots and again Agapios put his arrow into an arrow-hole on the broom-head.

Then they wanted him to do it from one hundred yards. The three Scythians again hit the target easily. I removed one of the arrows. Instead of aiming at the target, Agapios turned around and shot in the opposite direction. The arrow hit something and we heard a yelp.

I ran back to where Agapios had shot his arrow. An old man, dressed in the coarse tunic of a slave, sat dazed on the ground. His straw hat was on the ground beside him, an arrow through the top of it. The old slave had pissed himself but was unhurt. I gave him a few obols for his trouble.

The Scythians laughed so hard they almost pissed themselves too.

"Why didn't you shoot at the target?" Madyes asked him.

"It's out of this bow's range," Agapios said.

"Why didn't you just say so?" I asked, shocked at his recklessness.

"Because knocking a slave's hat off," he

said, "was a lot funnier. My Saka friends would agree."

"Never do that again, you crazy little fuck," I said to him. "If you'd killed that old slave, we couldn't protect you. You could be forced to take the man's place as a slave in his master's household. "

"I didn't kill anyone," he protested. "I just knocked his hat off."

"What if you missed?" I said.

"I don't miss."

He said it with such confidence that I truly believed him, but I still made him vow to never again shoot at Athenian citizens, slaves or animals.

"Try my bow," said Scylurus. "Shoot target, not slave." He held his bow out to Agapios.

Ephander, I cannot overemphasize the significance of this gesture. A Scythian warrior may have several bows, each for a different purpose, but he treats each one as an extension of his own body. You *never* touch a Scythian's bow without permission, which is almost never given. Yet Scylurus offered his bow to a Hellene boy he'd just met.

It was a sign of deepest respect. It was also a test. The Scythian longbow is famously difficult to use. It requires great upper body strength just to draw back the bowstring, and even greater strength to hold it steady. The Scythians wanted to see if Agapios could handle it.

Agapios tingled with excitement. He held the bow a little unsteadily at first and drew the bowstring back several times to get the feel of it. When he finally shot, he missed the broom, hitting the wall a foot above it.

"Wow!" said Agapios, eyes wide. "This bow is amazing. I missed because I underestimated its power. May I try again?"

Scylurus smiled and nodded. Agapios missed the broom-head target with his second shot by only a couple of inches, but he hit it with his third shot. With his fourth shot, he put an arrow into an arrow-hole left by an earlier shot.

The Scythians cheered. They spent another couple of hours shooting. On foot, Agapios was more accurate than the Scythians. They loved him for it.

I shot too. None of the Scythians offered to let me use his bow. I used Agapios' little bow. From short range, I hit the broom-head more often than I missed it, but I was not remotely close to the skill levels of Agapios or the Scythians.

The sun sank into the red sky. "I must go," I said. "I have to return to barracks, and I also have to find Agapios a room."

There was a passable inn just inside the city. We'd go there first. As Agapios and I left, the Scythians argued, sudden as thunder and almost as angry. I didn't catch all of what they said, but their meaning was clear: the other Scythians *scolded*

Scylurus.

Whatever was happening, I didn't have time to get involved. Agapios and I left the tavern, but we'd barely gotten outside when Scylurus came running after us.

"Lectoros," Scylurus said. "What name for Krete man?"

"Krites," I said. It meant simply *the Kretan.*

Scylurus pointed to Agapios. "Krites come with us," he said. He'd just given Agapios a new name. "Give work in Sakai barracks. Give bed and to eat. If okay with you, if okay with Krites. What is word for boy train for working?"

"Apprentice," I said.

"We make Krites a-pren-tos," said Scylurus. "He sweep barracks, cook food, we teach how to use it sword."

"So what do you think, Krites?" I said. "Want to work for these big ugly fucks?"

Krites' grin was the only answer I needed.

5—PERSOS

I often sparred with the Scythians—with wooden swords, with fists and feet—and I learned something every time, but they always made a competition out of it. Sometimes I just wanted the peaceful repose of repetitive practice drills. When I trained with Xenocrates, I did hundreds of repetitions with weighted practice swords every day. In Athens, I missed it. I needed a place to train alone, without distraction or interruption.

I found a secluded spot on an abandoned goat trail a few miles beyond the Itonian Gate on the south side of Athens. There was a forested area near the Ilissos River that no one had cut down yet—timber was scarce in Attica, so it was only a matter of time before someone did. There was a grove of ash trees in the middle of the wood, beside a patch of flat ground. It was high ground, and I could see the river from there, but the trees gave me enough cover that no one on the river could see me. It was perfect. I hid an old shield and a practice sword under a rock there, so I wouldn't have to always carry them with me. There were many rolling hills with dirt paths in the area. I liked running them because they reminded me of Skiathos. So I'd run for an hour, do some sword-and-shield repetitions to build my arms and shoulders, then I'd go for a swim in the Ilissos before I headed back to the barracks.

One evening as I did shield drills, four figures approached my little grove. I cursed myself for not hearing them coming. They all wore hooded cloaks and had daggers in sheaths belted to their waists.

There were two ways out of here. One was over the cliff behind me. Suicide.

The other was down the trail, but only if I went through the four of them. Slightly less suicidal.

Xenocrates always taught me to size up situations quickly. As I looked these four over, I wondered why they hadn't drawn their daggers yet. Amateurs. They didn't even know that their long cloaks would hamper their mobility. Were they cocky because they had me outnumbered?

I chose to fight. "I'm going to kill at least one of you," I said, "and probably two. Right now you should ask yourselves how badly you want me dead."

"We're not here to fight you," said the one closest to me. Even with the hood over part of his face, I could see it was Krios, 'the ram,' the boy I'd beaten in sword practice my first day as an ephebe. He'd avoided me ever since. The others were probably ephebes too.

"I agree, Krios," I said. "It won't be much of a fight. And what's with the hoods? Think they make you look scary?"

I was up on the balls of my feet, ready to charge. If their daggers had been drawn, I already would have. Xenocrates had taught me that hesitation was fatal, and when you're outnumbered, your best chance is to quickly incapacitate one or more of your opponents to improve your odds. Their daggers were still in their sheaths. So I waited.

"We're armed," said Krios, "because these woods are dangerous at night."

"Horseshit," I said. "There haven't been bears or wolves here for a hundred years. No bandits, either, because there's no one up here to rob."

One of the other boys stepped in front of Krios and pulled his hood back. It was Damoxenos, a small quiet ephebe. He and I had never spoken, so I couldn't imagine what grudge he had against me. He smiled nervously and drew his dagger. I was about to cave his head in with my wooden sword, but then he dropped his dagger on the ground in front of him.

"My older brother knows you," said Damoxenos, "and he told us we shouldn't bring weapons. He said it's a mistake to provoke you, even if there are four of us."

"There won't be four of you for long," I said, "if you don't cut the shit and tell me why you're here." The other three hooded figures drew their daggers, dropped them on the ground, and pulled back their hoods. Besides Krios and Damoxenos, the other two were Capros and Philostratos, ephebes I didn't know at all, apart from their names.

"We want to learn how to fight," said Damoxenos. "We want you to teach us. We'll pay you. My brother saw you defeat a Persian giant named Firuz."

"Who is this brother of yours?" I asked.

"Persos," said Damoxenos. "He met you in Chalkidea, when you both spied on the Persians."

I saw the resemblance now, but I was not comfortable with this conversation. Damoxenos shouldn't have known that I'd spied on the Persians. Themistocles always told us that we weren't to talk about our spy work, even with family members. If Damoxenos and his friends knew, then who else did?

"Persos exaggerates," I said. I changed the subject. "Why do you want me to teach you to fight? Proxenos trains us every day."

"Proxenos only teaches phalanx techniques," said Krios. "They're important, but we want you to teach us to handle a sword the way you do."

"Why would I trust you, Krios?" I said.

"You hate me."

"No, I don't," he said. "I swear, I don't. I was angry after you bested me on that first day, but after I had a chance to think about it, I realized that I wasn't even close to you as a swordsman, and that you'd already given me my first lesson. I would have made amends sooner, but Proxenos ordered us not to talk to you. So I say right now, I'm sorry about the bad blood between us. I hope we can start over."

He held out his hand. I grasped it and said, "It's forgotten."

"You're easily the best fighter in the barracks," said Philostratos. "We wanted to ask you to train us months ago, but because of Proxenos, we were afraid to. So we followed you up here. We feel like cowards." The others nodded.

"That's why we've got the hoods," said Damoxenos. "We don't want Proxenos to know we came to see you."

"Is it true you trained with Marg Tufan?" asked Capros. *Marg Tufan*, Persian for 'Death Storm,' was one of Xenocrates' nicknames. He absolutely hated it. *Hades* was another, because if you fought him, that's where you went. He hated that too.

"Holy shit," I said. "What *didn't* Persos tell you about me?" The guys all laughed, but they were still a little nervous. They may have thought that I still planned to kill one or two of them.

"It was Pudger who told us that," he said. Pudger: Phylo's boyhood nickname had followed him here, but it was now less accurate than it had ever been before. Ephebe training had slimmed him down, although he would always have baby fat around his face and wouldn't maintain his fitness once he completed his ephebe training.

"It's true," I said. "Because of Xenocrates, I do not fear Proxenos. Xenocrates is a charging bull. Proxenos is a spring calf. When Proxenos punches me, I barely feel it. When Xenocrates punched me, I ended up on my ass. Luckily, he also trained me to duck."

They laughed again and started to relax. This wasn't necessarily a good thing, because then they bombarded me with questions faster than I could answer them. Is it true you killed a guy with one punch? Had you really never thrown a discus before, or were you just fucking with Proxenos? Is it true that you didn't scream when the Persians burned you with a hot poker? It was like they'd hoarded their questions for months. In a way, they probably had.

They were astonished that I trained with the Scythians. Wasn't I afraid of them?

"Yes, at first," I said, "but they were impressed that despite my fear, I sparred with them anyway. They value courage and honour above all else, and do not fear pain or death or any man. They train with all weapons from infancy, and are far more disciplined than you'd ever expect. They are the best fighters in the world, but they also like to laugh. Hospitality and generosity are as sacred to them as they are to us. They consider me and Phylo their guest-friends. My mother was Scythian, and one of the Scythians here in Athens is my cousin."

Eventually, I had to stop talking so I could finish my exercises. They wanted to join me. "So will you train us?" said Damoxenos.

"No," I said.

"No?" Damoxenos was stunned. We'd all been getting along so well. He misunderstood.

"No, I will not train you," I said. "I will show you some exercises and drills, I will spar with you, I will advise you, and I will even make up training schedules for you. Ultimately, I will not train you. You will train yourselves." Xenocrates said it often. It was futile to train someone who wouldn't work at it. The success of training depends entirely on the effort of the trainee.

Damoxenos was relieved. "So let's talk about your fee," he said. "How much do you want?"

"I don't want your money," I said.

"Hey, we don't expect you to do this for nothing," Krios said. The others agreed.

"I don't need money," I said. "I need the four of you to train *me*."

Damoxenos chuckled. "We don't know anything you don't, Elektros," he said. "What could we possibly teach you?"

"Ever seen me dance?" I said.

They laughed. At the end of each year of training, Ephander, ephebes had to perform the Pyrrhic Dance in armour in front of the elders of the tribe Leontis. Proxenos had begun to teach us. I was horrible at it. My awkwardness was a running joke in the barracks. Proxenos taunted me about it ruthlessly. I had rhythm, and my co-ordination was exceptional, but I had a mental block about the Dance. Xenocrates always taught me to limit my movements to preserve energy during combat, and I worked at this so much over the years that it became natural to me. The Dance required you to do the opposite: we were supposed to spin and twirl and do other completely unnecessary movements. The Dance was even more idiotic than the discus, because it took up more time and energy. The discus I could ignore, but the Dance was mandatory. If I couldn't do it passably, I would not be permitted to continue with my ephebe training.

So the five of us set up a training schedule. They would meet me here at the grove every other day, after Proxenos had dismissed us. If any of us, including me, had sentry duty, the others would still come here and train. We would still keep what we were doing secret. I advised them not to wear the hooded cloaks because they only drew attention to themselves. I told them to wear tunics and sandals, and tell anyone who asked that they were just doing hill training in the countryside. They would also hide practice swords and shields here in the grove.

I wanted to improve their conditioning, so I told them to always jog to our training sessions, and jog back to the barracks afterwards. I will admit, Ephander, that I didn't expect these pampered sons of affluent Athenians to stick with it. They did no farm labour, which built strength and stamina. Their ephebe training was the most strenuous thing they'd ever done in their lives. I deliberately made our first sessions long and tiring to test them, to gauge their dedication. I figured that if I worked them to exhaustion a few times, they'd give it up.

I couldn't have been more wrong. They liked the challenge of this extra work. There were a couple of times, during those first sessions, when they were so tired they could barely stand. Not once did any of them complain. I was surprised, impressed, and delighted. Xenocrates would have considered all four of them worthy.

I started by strengthening their arms and shoulders, as Xenocrates had done with me. We used a low branch on one of the ash trees for chin-ups. I had them do repetitive drills with shields, including just holding the shields over their heads for half an hour. Ever tried that, Ephander? Harder than it sounds. We also sparred and sparred and sparred. Within days, I saw improvement. Instead of going to the wine shop in their spare time, they trained with me. They had also sworn off wine.

They helped me with the Dance. Capros would bring a flute and Philostratos would tap his practice sword against his shield to keep time, while Krios and Damoxenos showed me the dance moves and critiqued my form. I'm embarrassed to admit that the four of them improved their swordwork more quickly than I improved my dancing.

"You're still swinging your shield like you're trying to kill somebody with it," Damoxenos said to me. "Pretend you're just trying to knock an apple from a tree branch that you can't reach with your hands. You just want it to fall, not go flying across the orchard."

The only reason I'd ever swung a shield before was as a combat move. It had never occurred to me that there was any other reason. My footwork was also wrong. I'd always sought to maintain balance and minimize foot movements, but the Dance required moves that would get you killed in combat. Twirls were particularly problematic for me. Even in sparring sessions, only an idiot presents his back to his opponent. I just couldn't get my head around it. It went against every instinct I had and everything I'd ever practiced.

During our daytime ephebe training, we still did not speak. I insisted on this. They wanted to defy Proxenos and openly socialize with me, but I convinced them that it would serve no purpose and would probably result in extra punishments for both them and me. So in the barracks and the training square, we did not acknowledge each other. Within a month, however, the four of them had improved noticeably.

Proxenos didn't catch on. "Haven't seen you in the wine shop lately," he said to Krios one day.

"The fucking Persians are coming, sir," said Krios. "I plan to be ready for 'em. I'm trying to drink less wine, get more sleep, and do extra training."

Proxenos just nodded. "Good idea," he said. He suspected nothing.

None of the ephebes openly socialized with me, but I no longer felt the unspoken disdain I'd felt earlier. Even the ones who had initially disliked me now respected my abilities as a soldier. I was the fastest runner, long distance or short, with or without armour. I was the best swordsman, and had mastered all the hoplite drills. I was among the best with the javelin throw. My dancing improved slightly, even though I still moved like a bear with a spear in its guts.

Persos, through his brother Damoxenos, had invited me to dine with him at his father's house. It was my first time as a house-guest in Athens.

Persos had changed since I'd last seen him. In Chalkidea, he'd been deer-slender, an athlete. Now he was thirty pounds heavier, bloated, red-faced, and he even wheezed when he breathed. He'd destroyed his conditioning in only a few months. He was half drunk by the time I got there.

"Whenever I saw a bridge out," said Persos, "I knew that Elektros of Skiathos had been busy. Did you notice how often the Persian wagons broke axles? That was my specialty. I'd sneak into their camp at night and cut the axles just enough so they'd collapse after a few miles."

I never knew this. I'd thought the Persian axles broke so often because they just couldn't make axles worth a damn.

This is a conversation I dearly would have loved to have had with Persos in private—but we were not alone. He had nine or ten dinner guests here, his drinking sluggards, and he spoke so loudly that they all heard every word.

It was a bad start to the evening. I was proclaimed guest of honour and seated next to Persos. One of the first things he asked me, very loudly, was if I was 'getting much.' He didn't care, of course. He only asked me so he could boast about his own prowess with the ladies. I hate guys who do this, not least because their boasts are usually untrue.

"A gentleman doesn't tell," I said, hoping he'd talk about something else.

"Exactly the words of a man who isn't getting *any*," he said, to laughter all round. "I tell you, Elektros, the ladies love the spy stories. Tell them a few of those and they'll be moist for you in no time at all. Try it if you don't believe me."

He was right about one thing: I didn't believe him. Persos looked like he didn't leave the house much. His conquests, if he actually had any, were probably slave girls who did not have the option of refusal. He would not need to impress them with spy stories or anything else.

He talked too much. It could get him killed. Whenever he brought up our spy work, I tried to change the subject. I asked him about the fine house he lived in, asked him to introduce me to the other guests. These subjects diverted his attention, but never for long.

He talked about my encounter with Firuz.

"You should've seen it," he said loudly. "I thought Elektros was a dead man. The guy they put him up against was *huge.* I'm not kidding. He was nine feet tall. I didn't know it was possible for humans to grow that big. But Elektros took him down in two seconds by kicking him in the balls. Then the Persians burnt him with a hot poker and he didn't even scream. Never seen anything like it.

Everyone raise your cups to Elektros the Brave!"

The other guests cheered, raised their cups and drank heartily. Most of them drank their wine neat and were already shit-faced. I drank only water, which of course offended Persos. He insisted, repeatedly, that I drink wine, and I insisted, repeatedly, that I did not like wine. I drank it only on important occasions. Dining with this fool didn't qualify.

Whenever Persos or anyone pressed me for details about the Persian spy mission, I told them I did not wish to talk about it. Several of them thought me antisocial, or at least rude. Yet Persos spoke of almost nothing else.

As we dined, the talk died down. Persos, who'd had a boar roasted for the occasion, busily shoveled pig meat down his gaw. He'd stopped talking for the first time that evening. I tried to caution him about his loose tongue.

"Persos," I said in a low voice only he could hear. "When you talk about your spy work, you compromise it. It's also dangerous."

He just stared at me for a few moments. He was pretty drunk now, bleary-eyed. He nodded. I thought he finally saw sense.

"I understand you now," he said, far too loudly. He'd been loud all evening, and I wondered if he was even capable of speaking quietly anymore. "Elektros *the Brave* wants me to clam up, everybody. He wants all the spy glory to himself."

"Moron," I hissed, again in a low voice. "There's no such thing as 'spy glory.' You're going to get yourself killed."

"Killed?" he said, words slurring. "Killed? Who's going to kill me? *You*?"

He was beyond reason. How could he not understand that if he spoke out about Themistocles' secret operations, he would become Themistocles' enemy? In Chalkidea, he had done some fine work, but now he seemed to think his work for Athens was done. He could no longer function as a spy now, or even as a soldier—he'd had his ephebe training, but no one would be comfortable in the phalanx if they had to stand next to this bloated oaf.

I got up and began to leave.

"How dare you!" he slurred at me. "You insult my hospitality by refusing my wine, then you threaten me!" He attempted to throw a cup of wine at me, but he was so drunk that from a few feet away he managed only to splash a few drops on my feet. He got more on himself than on me.

I leaned forward. "You sodden twit," I said quietly. "I'm not threatening you. I'm *warning* you."

It was already too late for Persos.

The next day, Damoxenos came to train with me. Something bothered him, and when I asked him about it, he said, "Persos says you threatened him." Damoxenos had not been present at the dinner because he had sentry duty.

"Not true," I said. "I warned him. Spouting off about his spy work will get him killed. I'm amazed he doesn't know this."

"Promise me you won't," he said. "Kill him, I mean."

"I promise," I said. I meant it. What I didn't tell him was that because of Persos' loose tongue, I was also compromised as one of Themistocles' operatives. If Persos was killed—or more accurately, *when* Persos was killed, because it was inevitable now—I would be among the first suspects. Themistocles knew this and would make sure I had an alibi when he assigned the task to someone else.

A few days later, Damoxenos arrived for training ahead of the others. He wanted to talk to me alone. His eyes were red. He hadn't been sleeping.

"Persos has disappeared," he said. I wasn't surprised.

"Off drunk somewhere?" I said.

"Unlikely," he said. "He hasn't left the house in a month."

He drew a sword, a real sword, from a scabbard belted around his waist. He put the tip up to my throat. "Did you kill my brother?" he said.

I admired his courage. He was willing to try

and avenge his brother against a superior fighter. I didn't have a weapon in my hands, but I could easily take the sword from him.

"No," I said. "Nor do I know who did. No one has spoken to me about it."

He just stared at me for a few seconds. He did not initially believe me. He held the sword point to my throat. His hands shook a little.

"Put the sword away, Damo," I said. "It couldn't have been me. I would be too obvious a suspect."

As Damoxenos stood there staring at me, tears welled up in his eyes.

He finally returned his sword to its scabbard. "I apologize for accusing you," he said. "You have to admit, though, it looked bad: you show up for dinner, have a loud disagreement with him, and then a few days later he disappears."

"I'm sorry about Persos," I said. "In Chalkidea, I saw quality in him. I'm also very sorry that he failed to recognize the consequences of his own big mouth."

He shook his head sadly. "He insisted that an Athenian citizen has the right to speak freely."

"Regardless of the law, free speech has limitations, "I said. "It does not include the right to compromise the secret operations of the powerful men who run Athens. When you guys asked to train with me, you all knew about my fight with Firuz. You shouldn't have. I've never told anyone, not even my own brother. Persos was shooting off his mouth long before I came to your house. Even after I warned him, he failed to see the danger he'd put himself in."

"Your warning," said Damoxenos, "was not the first. General Phocas came to the house and spoke privately with Persos. I didn't hear the conversation, but Persos told me afterwards that Phocas told him to shut up about his spy work. Persos was pale and shaken, and kept his mouth shut. Then two days later, he started talking again."

I would not have gone to Persos' house if I had any idea how far he'd sunk. Poor Damoxenos. He watched helplessly as his brother effectively arranged his own murder.

6–ARCHON

Every few days, Phocas stopped by the ephebe training ground to see how all of us were doing. Sometimes he spoke to Phylo or me, sometimes he spoke to other guys, and sometimes he spoke to no one and just watched us train for a while. He had the easy confidence of a born officer. We all admired him and tried to look sharp in front of him.

One day he called me aside and invited me to dine that evening at the house of Themistocles. He invited Phylo too.

This was a rare honour. When our training day ended and we cleaned ourselves up, the envy of the other boys was so thick you could've whacked it with a shovel.

"He's my fucking uncle," said Diodoros, a thin, bony, pimply-faced lad with a long pointed nose aptly nicknamed Stork. "My mom is his sister. But I've never been to his house. Not once." We were all members of Themistocles' tribe, Leontis, and at least a third of the ephebes here were Themistocles' relatives by marriage or blood. Yet only Phylo and I were invited.

"You're family," Phylo said. "He can get away with ignoring you. We're his metic clients. It would be a huge political gaffe to ignore us. Believe me, Themistocles has more important things to do than wine and dine a couple of savage island apes." This got a laugh, because there was nothing savage or apish about Phylo, although the lads probably wondered about me.

"This invitation is an act of diplomacy," Phylo went on. "He wants Skiathos to ally with Athens, and he can't have Lex and me reporting to our father that he ignores us. Skiathos itself isn't large enough to be important, but it's in a strategic spot for sea routes from Athens to Thessaly, Thrace, and the Straits. If Skiathos joins with Athens, then the other islands in the area probably will too. The last thing Themistocles wants is Persian control of the Sporades. I'm surprised he didn't invite us sooner."

* * * * * * * * * *

"Were you raised by baboons, boy?" said the door-steward at the house of Themistocles. "You do not bring weapons into the presence of the Archon."

Themistocles' friends and supporters still called him *the Archon*, even though it had been three years since he'd officially held that office. Archon or not, he was extremely powerful in

Athens. The current archon, Phaenippus, was known to be Themistocles' hireling.

"The streets are dangerous at night, sir," I said to the door steward.

"The Archon's house is not," he said. Two armed guards stood at either side of him. Two more patrolled the perimeter of the house, and we saw others out back. I wanted to ask the doorman, if the Archon's house was not dangerous, then why were there so many armed men present? The man was only doing his job, though, so I took my dagger from under my belt and handed it over.

Themistocles was wealthy but his house was no mansion. It was in one of Athens' better areas, less than a mile from the Acropolis, but it was the smallest house on the street, a simple two-storey building with a small garden. Themistocles knew that the basis of his power rested on the non-wealthy classes. He was as rich as most of the old money aristocrats, but he did not provoke his supporters by flaunting it.

The doorman led us into the dining area. Themistocles' guests were varied. He was particularly popular with skilled craftsmen and their guilds, and they were well-represented here, but there were aristocrats here too. Curiously, one of them was Aristides, nicknamed the Just, Themistocles' most bitter rival. Aristides was known for his unshakeable adherence to the laws of Athens. Themistocles was known to bend the laws, and even break or ignore them outright, when he thought it necessary. It was no surprise that they opposed each other, although they were said to have been friends when they were boys.

Servants brought cups of watered wine to Phylo and me. Before we could mingle with the other guests—or, more accurately, Phylo mingled and I just tried not to say anything stupid—a servant announced in a loud voice that Themistocles had been detained and sent his profoundest apologies. In the meantime, dinner would be served.

As soon as Aristides heard this, he walked out.

It was beyond my ability to comprehend, but Phylo figured it out quickly. Themistocles' mind was a labyrinth, he said, and there were several agendas taking place here, each complex in its own way. Themistocles invited Aristides so he could later claim he attempted to reconcile with him but that it was Aristides who walked out. While I can't say with certainty that Themistocles was intentionally late so Aristides would be insulted, I can't say with certainty that he wasn't. More than once Themistocles said that Aristides was far more useful to him as an enemy than he could ever be as a friend.

* * * * * * * * * *

"Phylo, I must speak to Elektros alone," said Themistocles. Phylo and I had been in his house for several hours. He'd missed dinner entirely, and had just eaten slices of cold pork with bread and some fruit. Most of his other guests had already left.

Phylo, always too smart to ask questions, got up and headed for the door. "See you back at the barracks, little brother," he said.

"A remarkable young man, your brother," Themistocles said after Phylo left.

"Agreed, sir," I said. "He was a remarkable little boy. Quick-witted and great with words as far back as I can remember."

"You want to ask me about Persos," said Themistocles.

"No need to, sir. He's been missing for eight days and his family's worried sick. You haven't sent him on a mission."

"No. He no longer works for me."

I asked no questions. He wouldn't have answered them anyway.

"Answer me this, Elektros," he said. "Why does everyone in Athens know that the Persians captured you and made you fight Firuz?"

I cringed. In the last few days, several brainless hotheads tried to pick fights with me, to prove themselves against the giant-killer. "Persos told his brother," I said. "A lot of other people, too."

"How did Persos know about it?"

"He actually saw it. He was in the area at the time and climbed a tree to see into the Persian camp."

"Who did *you* tell?"

"No one, sir. Not even my own family."

"Because you didn't want them to worry?"

"Yes, partly, but also because my work for you is compromised if people know about it."

"You've told Phylo?"

"No, sir. He found out about it, directly or indirectly, from Persos." Phylo had always been dying to ask me about my mission but never did because he knew I wasn't supposed to talk about it.

"Discretion is crucial in this kind of work," Themistocles said. "You're instinctively discrete. You think before you speak. That's as important to me as your other obvious talents. Phylo is also discrete. He's gregarious, which makes people assume he's not discrete, but it's calculated. When he talks a lot, the people around him do too. Instead of just listening for information, he actually prompts people into spilling their guts. He's a valuable man."

Themistocles just described the working method of Simonides.

"So Phylo works for you too?" I asked, even though it wasn't a question anymore.

I'd had no idea. But when I thought about

it, it made perfect sense.

Themistocles laughed. "Classified information. I cannot confirm or deny."

He stopped laughing suddenly and looked me straight in the eye. "Persos was not discrete. He got drunk every night and blurted things out to anyone who would listen. You're compromised because of that fool. It's not your fault, but you cannot work for me in Athens now. It would have been bad enough if Persos only spoke about his own work. His indiscretion has tainted three men—himself, you, and a third fellow that he also talked about too much. You and the third man are highly effective operatives. You'll both do spy work for me again, but not in Athens."

Persos' family would never see him again. I was certain that he was already dead.

"Is there something I can tell Persos' family?" I asked. "Some of them think I killed him or was somehow involved. His brother Damo is my friend."

"You're doing it again," he said with a smile. "It's a talent you and Phylo share. When I speak, you understand me immediately and then mentally proceed to the next step, sometimes even before I do. Remarkable, two boys from the same family who are so different in every other way."

He stared at his wine goblet, as if he was reminiscing. Then he snapped out of it and said, "Don't worry about Persos' family. I have someone who will talk to them. Such a shame. Persos did great work for me, but when he got back, he figured he'd done his part and would never have to serve Athens again. Let me tell you this, Elektros: as long as you're on this side of the ground, service to your polis *never* ends. Unless you're indiscrete, of course. Then it ends rather abruptly."

He gave me a look that chilled me. He'd always looked out for me, always supported and encouraged me, but he'd have me killed in a second if he thought it would be for the good of Athens.

"As far as talking about your spy work, there is one key exception for you. You can tell Phylo. There may be a time when I'll have a mission that requires the talents of both of you. No one else must know, not even your father."

"Understood, sir."

"And be careful with your Scythian buddies. Discretion isn't their best quality. They all know the Firuz story now, but they think Firuz didn't have a chance simply because you're Scythian and Firuz wasn't. If they ask you what you were doing in my house tonight, what will you tell them?"

"That Phylo and I are your guest-friends—everybody knows that—and you have an obligation to be our host. I spent the evening bored shitless, listening to muckymucks spew drivel they thought was wisdom."

Themistocles laughed hard. "Perfect answer," he said. "One that the Scythians will love. And Phylo's supposed to be the outstanding speaker in the family."

"Sir, you cannot be brother to Phyloctetes of Skiathos," I said, "without learning a trick or two about words."

7–HORSES

As I jogged up the trail to my little grove that overlooked the Ilissos, two horsemen galloped like lightning from the-gods-know-where and charged right at me. It was on a straight but narrow part of the path. There was a wall of rock to my right, and thick trees to my left. I could get clear if I turned around and ran a few hundred yards, but I'd never get there before the horses were on me. My only chance was to stand my ground and try to somehow duck the riders' weapons. I had no time to worry about who these riders were or why they were here.

I expected to die, Ephander. I'd go down fighting, but there was no way out of this. I had no weapon, not even a knife.

The horses charged closer. The hoof beats got louder and louder. When the horses were almost on me, a familiar voice called out.

"Lectoros!" cried Madyes from one of the horses. "Freeze! Don't move!"

I stood straight and tried to make myself as thin as possible. The horses had hellfire in their eyes, like demons in horses' bodies. They passed on either side of me. I smelled their sweat and felt the heat of their breath. Their tails swept across my face as they passed.

Madyes and the other rider, Aki, had big grins on their faces.

They didn't stop right away. I turned around and watched them do something I wouldn't have believed possible if I hadn't seen it myself. Madyes and Aki switched horses at full gallop, and they did it so seamlessly–and with astonishing quickness–that I still doubted my own eyes. Only then did they pull their horses up, turn around and canter towards me. They grinned like children who'd just been given sweets at a birthday party.

"Apologies, Lectoros," said Madyes. "We're a little rusty. We didn't see you until the last second. We would have jumped over you, but we haven't ridden these horses enough to know how well they jump."

"Where'd you get them?" I asked.

"You brother," said Aki. "He borrow to us."

Without horses, Scythians are not entirely themselves. Their duties in Athens did not pay, so they couldn't afford to feed and stable horses here. Without a horse, a Scythian does not consider himself a man. The ones in Athens were, despite their ferocity, sociable men who liked to laugh, but this was the first time I'd ever seen any of them with the head-to-toe full body smiles that Madyes and Aki had as they rode. The horses also seemed happy. Horses know when they're being well-ridden. They instinctively recognize the touch of an expert rider, even if he's never ridden that horse before.

I suddenly had a brilliant idea. I'd just witnessed a trick of horsemanship that Athenians would pay to see, and I knew that Madyes and Aki had a full repertoire. After they continued up the trail with their horses, I ran all the way to Dio's to talk to Phylo. I found him drinking and singing with several other Scythians. I told him about my idea.

"Way ahead of you, little brother," he said with a wink. "Way ahead of you."

* * * * * * * * * *

The wedding feast had barely begun, but the groom was already pie-eyed. The bride, even behind her veil, looked scared and confused. Her father, Epictetos, was the wealthiest man in Attica, and like a true Athenian, he wanted everyone to know it. The feast was held inside a huge tent on his estate ten miles outside of Athens. The tent, like the fortress of a house behind it, was decorated with garlands of laurel and olive leaves. Epictetos permitted the women and men to dine together, which wasn't customary for Hellene weddings. Some of the stuffier Athenians huffed that this was proof of Epictetos' crassness and ill-breeding, although these same snobs still stuffed their faces and drank themselves stupid at Epictetos' expense.

Though not as ascetic as Spartans, Athenians do not regularly gorge themselves. The farmlands around the city could not support them if they did. Meat was expensive in Athens, and most people ate it only a few times a year, on feast days or special events. Beans, lentils, barley bread, olives and fish were the dietary staples of the huge majority of the population. So everyone here was especially eager to taste delicacies most of them had never seen before.

Epictetos wanted to make his only daughter's wedding feast memorable. Behind the feasting tent, twenty wild boars roasted on spits over cooking braziers. It would take years to find so many boars in Attica, so Epictetos had sent teams of hunters abroad to catch them. The boars came from as far away as Macedonia, and had to be captured alive so their meat wouldn't spoil in the time it took to transport them to back to Athens. Dozens of partridges and quails, caught locally by more teams of hunters, were also roasted and brought to table, as well as mutton, clams, oysters, octopus, squid, and the renowned eels from Lake Copais, which most of the guests had never eaten before and, because of their staggering cost, were unlikely to ever eat again.

There were also great varieties of olives, onions, cheeses, nuts, fried vegetables, candied fruits, and honey-sweetened breads and pastries. Epictetos also brought in a boatload—literally--of Chian wine.

As the several hundred guests ate, the entertainments began. The huge tent over their heads was open at its front and sides, which afforded everyone a clear view of the jugglers, dancers, tumblers, and fire-eaters. Lyre-playing minstrels wandered among the diners and took song requests. The Athenians enjoyed these performers, even though they'd seen them often enough.

It wasn't until the main feast was over that the star performers began: the Scythians would display their archery and horsemanship.

Epictetos allowed Phylo and me to eat and drink our fill, even though we had accompanied the Scythians and weren't invited guests. I enjoyed the food, but I only drank one goblet of well-watered wine, and only to toast the future happiness of the bride and groom.

Epictetos was offended. "I barely even know you, boy," he said. "I only fed you because your brother asked me too, then you insult me by refusing my wine."

I explained that wine makes me ill, but he wouldn't hear me. He was even more offended that Aki and Madyes would not take any wine. Epictetos said—loudly—that we insulted not just him but also the gods of hospitality by refusing to drink his Chian.

Madyes bristled under the accusation. This Athenian, who considered Scythians to be uncivilized louts, criticized Madyes for his temperance. To the Scythians, this was the height of incivility—and fighting words. Madyes did not tolerate anyone questioning his honour. He rarely lost his temper. I'd never seen it happen, but the other Scythians told me that it usually ended with someone getting killed. The Scythians agreed that he was their best fighter. If he attacked Epictetos, no one could stop him.

Luckily, Phylo jumped in. "Epictetos, you big dumb sack of goat-shit with feet," he said. "Wine makes my brother ill. Always has, doesn't matter if it's Chian or Dio's donkey-piss. It was difficult for him to drink to the bride and groom, but he did it anyway, to honour the gods and his host. Leave him the hell alone. As for the Scythians, you will soon see why they want clear heads and steady hands. When the show's over, they will be happy to drink as much Chian as you can give them."

Epictetos listened to Phylo, even though Phylo didn't say anything to him that I didn't say, apart from the *big dumb sack of goat-shit with feet* part. Phylo was a master at using crudity to command a man's attention. If anyone else had spoken that way to Epictetos, there would have been a fight, but Phylo got away with it. He always did.

Epictetos was loud, opinionated and now drink-emboldened, but a man doesn't rise to his position without diplomatic skills. "Gentlemen," he said to Aki and Madyes, "I apologize if I said anything inappropriate. If you join me later for a cup of wine, I will consider myself honoured." Then he bowed to the Scythians. Madyes and Aki, like most Scythians, are quick to anger but also quick to forgive. With broad smiles, they shook hands with Epictetos.

As the dining drew to an end, Epictetos rose and stood up from his place at the head table and made a wedding speech. He was a fine orator. He flattered the bride and groom, got laughs with his randy predictions about what would happen in their wedding bed later, then called for yet another toast to their happy future. The groom was thoroughly sodden by this time, barely conscious, and Epictetos joked about that too. But he also had the good sense to keep his speech short. He called for all of his guests to rise and walk over to the area in front of the tent, where a tiered wooden grandstand had been built, so they could see the flat field where the Scythians would show their skills.

"The Scythians are wild men, savages, barbarians," said Epictetos, "but they claim to be the best horsemen alive. Shall we give them the chance to prove it?"

The assembled guests roared their approval. Madyes and Aki were not offended when Epictetos described them as savages. They knew that such showmanship would increase interest in their performance. Besides, they'd long accepted that this was how most Athenians already thought of them.

Madyes and Aki started with some target shooting. There were twelve targets, made of wood and bundled straw, placed at ten-foot intervals on the field. Each target was roughly the size and shape of a man and had a large muskmelon for a head.

Aki, bow in hand, charged at one of the targets. He rode a fine black stallion. He appeared to have made a mistake: he charged past the target. But as his horse galloped away from it, he held his bow behind his left shoulder and loosed an arrow. There were *oohs* and *aahs* as the arrow hit the target square in the melon. He didn't even look at the target as he shot.

It was Madyes' turn. Instead of charging past his target, he stopped about ten feet in front of it. He sat astride his horse and aimed his bow at the target's head. This couldn't be right: it was a shot so easy that most people present, drunk as they were, could have made it. Madyes then turned his bow skyward and shot an arrow straight into the air. People thought he was being funny, and many chuckled, but they applauded mightily when the arrow came down and plunked dead centre into the top of the melon.

Some of their shots were more subtle but no less extraordinary for their precision, although the Athenians clearly preferred the spectacular ones. Madyes and Aki simultaneously charged a target at full gallop and each man shot an arrow at the target. Both arrows struck the torso of the target at exactly the same moment. If the target was a real man, he'd have an arrow in each of his nipples. I was amazed, but few in the audience appreciated it. Applause for this trick was modest.

Madyes and Aki did a few other precise target shots, including shooting two arrows into same melon that were so close to each other that they actually touched.

When they saw that the audience was unmoved by this, the Scythians merely shrugged it off and moved on to the next trick. Madyes did the same backwards shooting trick that Aki had done earlier. Aki stopped in front of the same target and aimed an arrow straight up in the air. Everyone thought Aki was repeating Madyes' earlier shot, but when the arrow came down, it missed the melon completely. That was because it had hit a bird. The arrow had passed through its neck, a good clean hit. It was a particularly impressive shot because it was a nightjar, a small bird nearly impossible to see at night. The field area was lit with torches and lamps, but the sky was not. How Aki even saw the nightjar, I'll never know. It was a precision shot that was so impressive that everyone clapped and hooted with pleasure. Epictetos beamed.

The Scythians did more shooting, and the crowd was well pleased. Few knew that the best was yet to come.

Some Hellenes think themselves skilled horsemen. Compared to other Hellenes, they are. But a Scythian rides his first horse when he's three or four years old. By the age of eight he can use only his knees to steer at full gallop. By that time, he's probably spent more time on horseback than a Hellene cavalryman will spend in his entire life.

The wedding guests expected to see some fancy spins and twirls and maybe a jump or two. This would have entertained them. They rarely saw Scythians on horseback, so they did not understand that when it came to horses, the Scythians were superhuman.

Madyes rode his black stallion at a soft gallop. Then he stood on the horse's back. There was polite applause. Then he stood with one leg. The crowd cheered. They'd seen it before but still appreciated the skill it required. Madyes' horse circled back to where Aki waited on his grey gelding. As Madyes approached, still standing on his mount, Aki swung a sword at Madyes' legs. Madyes jumped over the sword before it made contact, and landed, in perfect balance, on his feet on the horse's back. Aki applauded as Madyes turned around and approached him again. Madyes stopped his horse, as Aki took his turn. He stood on the gelding's back, then stood on one foot, then he stood on his hands as the gelding went into a full gallop. The crowd howled. They'd seen a handstand on horseback before, but never at full gallop. As the horse circled back towards Madyes, it didn't slow down, but after the pass, Madyes was riding the grey gelding and Aki was standing on his hands on the back of the stallion.

"What in Hades just happened?" one astonished guest said to his buddy.

"Unbelievable!" said the buddy. "They switched horses so quickly that if you blinked, you missed it." The crowd was hooting and hollering, even though a significant number of them probably missed the rapid switch.

For their next trick, they sat astride their mounts about two hundred yards apart, facing each other. Then they charged. They looked like they would collide head on, then swerved slightly just before they would have made contact. But they'd switched horses, again in an eye blink. Now each man sat astride his horse but faced backwards, looking out over the horse's rump.

"Holy shit!" cried out Aki. "Where my horse head go?" The crowd screamed with laughter. As he stared in mock perplexity, Madyes circled behind him until they were both side by side and facing in the same direction, with each man still looking out over his horse's rump. Then they raced. Each horse ran backwards, and surprisingly fast. The guests guffawed and cheered the comic spectacle. Each rider pretended to steer his horse by pulling its tail. Few knew that they actually used their knees to guide their mounts. Horses like having their tails brushed, but absolutely hate having them touched when they run. That they allowed the Scythians to do this was a measure of the trust they'd developed in such a short time. The horses circled the field backwards, and when they returned to their starting point, both horses stopped and reared up on their hind legs. Madyes and Aki used their horses' momentum to easily leap off and land on their feet. Then they bowed to the crowd.

The applause was like thunder. When it finally died out ten minutes later, Madyes addressed the crowd.

"My Hellene friends," he said. "I must apologize for the brevity of our performance tonight. These are wonderful horses, but we've only been using them for about ten days. Some of our more complicated routines require extensive training. Give us a couple of months and we'll *really* show you something. In the meantime, let's have a round of applause for our generous host Epictetus, and thank him for letting us perform for you tonight."

The crowd was on its feet, clapping and cheering. Epictetus then embraced both of the Scythians. He was wide-eyed, giddy with joy. "And to think," he said, "that I wanted you guys to have a few drinks beforehand. I'm an idiot! Please forgive me."

"Already forgive," said Aki. "Forgive even more if give few drinks *now*."

Epictetus laughed, and said, "Of course, of course. As much as you want." He signaled for the slave girls to bring wine to the Scythians.

"I know a little about horses," Epictetus said. "These horses will now be hard for anyone else to ride. You Scythians have spoiled them. They'll have to be retrained before a Hellene can ride them again."

"Is true," said Aki.

"You have a fine eye, Epictetus," said Phylo. "I borrowed these horses from Pamphilos. He's furious with me now, because he tried to ride the stallion a few days ago, and it wouldn't let him. It bucked and bit and snorted and kicked until Pamphilos gave up. He wants me to buy them outright, which I'm afraid I'll have to do now."

"I'll lend you the money, if you need it," said Epictetos. "I'll even get Pamphilos to accept a fair price." Wedding or not, Epictetos pursued money-making opportunities whenever he sniffed them out. He and Phylo headed off to a corner to talk business. It wasn't the first time, and wouldn't be the last.

Later, the Scythians sat at a table with Epictetos and toasted his health, and the health of the bride and groom, and the health of every deity that ever graced the earth. The feasting and drinking was still going strong when a man came running up to Epictetos. The man was dusty from the road. He'd ridden his horse many miles and looked exhausted, but his message could not wait.

He hesitated. His message was for Epictetos alone. "Well, out with it man," said Epictetos irritably.

"Sir, you may want to hear this message in private," said the man.

"My friends here," said Epictetos, referring to Phylo, the Scythians, and me, "can hear anything you have to say to me. Speak up, boy."

"As you wish, sir," said the slave. "Eritrea has fallen."

The messenger's hesitation was now understandable. This news could cause panic.

The colour drained from Epictetos' face. He turned white so quickly it was like someone had just dipped his head into a barrel of chalk dust. We knew the Persians were on their way, and that they'd taken Karystos, but no one thought Eretria would fall so quickly.

The Persians' next stop would be Athens. They'd be here in a matter of days.

8–RAIDERS

After they took Eretria, the Persians encamped at the plain of Marathon. All of Athens' fighting men were there to face them. This left Athens itself vulnerable. The strategoi risked it because they needed every available soldier to face the Persians.

But what if Athens was attacked by someone else?

The Scythians could not defend the city from an attack. They were too few and they weren't even here. The Persians brought Scythian cavalry with them, so some Athenian strategoi reasoned that the Scythians in Athens might defect or open the gates to the invaders. This showed how little they understood Scythians, who would rather die than violate the oaths to Athens that had been sworn to Hippias so many years ago. Our Scythians also considered the Persians enemies. The Scythians who came with the Persians were a different nation from the ones in Athens, but the strategoi took no chances and sent the Scythians from Athens to Plataea to sit out the battle.

All the ephebes were at Marathon too,

except for the forty-eight men—boys, really, when it came to battle–in my troop. We'd been left behind to guard against brigands and pirates, and also to assure the women and children and old men in Athens that they weren't completely undefended. Nobody considered us soldiers. If an army attacked the city, we were, pardon my Phoenician, fucked.

The morning after the troops departed, we got the news that a force of raiders had landed at the Phaleron and were headed to the city. As we assembled outside our barracks, there was latent panic in the eyes of most of us.

Proxenos didn't help. As soon as he broke the news to us, he puked his guts out, then muttered something about some bad mutton he'd eaten. He fooled no one.

When he recovered enough to speak, he said, "March out the Itonian Gate. The raiders are coming from the Phaleron, so that's where they'll come at us. Go a half-mile up the road and wait by the Temple of Dionysus. I'll meet you there, but first I need to make a few inquiries."

We marched out and waited, then waited some more. Proxenos didn't show. None of us was surprised.

Krites rode a horse up to us. The Scythians had already turned him into a passably good rider. He'd scouted the raiders and told us there were over a hundred of them, and that they were big and hairy and headed our way.

I took command. Someone had to. I had more fighting experience than any of my fellow ephebes. They all assumed it included fighting in a phalanx.

It was not the time to tell them it was my first time too.

I could not show fear. These young men looked up to me now. They acted bravely so far, but it wouldn't take much to break them. We were raw and outnumbered. If we turned and ran away right now, we might claim a tactical retreat. Young as we were, we might be forgiven. But could we forgive ourselves if we ran from our first fight?

We stood in five rows of nine or ten, tightly packed. In a hoplite phalanx, each man is protected partly by his own shield and partly by the shield of the man to his right. You present a wall of shields and spears to the enemy. As the fighting progresses, the phalanx will usually veer slightly to the right, as each man tries to get that extra bit of protection from the next man's shield. The men are not always aware that they do this. If they veer too far to the right, their left flank becomes vulnerable to an attack from the enemy's right.

I took the most important position in the phalanx, the rightmost place in the first rank. If I could stabilize the first row, keep it from breaking up or veering to the right, then the rest of the phalanx would hold firm. If I wavered, we'd collapse and run. Then we'd be slaughtered.

Simeon stood to my left. A steaming puddle formed at his feet. "I'm only pissing myself," he said to me, "so you won't feel so bad when *you* do it."

I laughed. It was a good sign that he could joke despite his fear. Simeon would hold his ground today.

"Everybody does it their first time," I said, pretending authority on the subject. "Some do it every battle, but it is your courage that must hold. Your bladder doesn't matter."

"'Your bladder doesn't matter,'" Simeon parroted, and the men behind us chuckled. "You just composed my favourite poem."

As commander, I had to address the men. I'm no rhetor. Public speaking is probably my greatest fear. My mouth was dry as ashes, and I shook a little. Then I laughed to myself when I realized I was more afraid of addressing the men than I was of the hundred hairy raiders coming to kill us. This realization helped me relax a little and get the quaver out of my voice before I spoke.

I stepped out of the phalanx and stood in front of it. "Okay, listen up, you worthless goat-fuckers," I growled nasally. This is what Proxenos would have said to us, and the boys laughed at my little impression of him.

Then I spoke seriously. "I have no sacrifice

to make to the gods. We did not expect to see battle today, and I did not expect to command, so I do not even have a cup of wine for a libation. So I ask the gods to accept my promise to sacrifice later, after the battle.

"Our enemies will be here soon. They are fierce, big, and strong. They have us outnumbered, they stink like the harpy-holes of Hades, and they're unspeakably hairy." Some of the men chuckled, but nervously. All I'd done so far was scare them. I changed my tone.

"Yet we are the ones with all the advantages this day. They walk five miles to us while we rest. According to our scout, they do not have proper weapons for infantry battle. They have clubs and a few axes, and maybe a sword here and there, while all of us have spears and swords. Only a handful of them have shields. A few have armour, but every one of us has a full panoply, and our armour is of better quality than theirs. So we're more rested and better equipped than they are.

"These advantages alone could turn the battle in our favour, but our greatest advantage is tactical. These big hairy fucks are plunderers, not soldiers. They've come to rob and rape civilians, not fight hoplites. If they had any sense, they'd turn around and get back on their ships right now. We are *disciplined.* They are not. We will hold our formation. They have no formation to hold. Their battle plan, if it can be called a plan, is to break us on their first charge. This we must not let them do. Make no mistake, their first charge will be deadly, but once we withstand it, we will defeat them. We have drilled and drilled and drilled. We could rotate men in and out of the phalanx in our sleep. Remember that in a phalanx you fight not only for yourself, but for your brother beside you.

"There's also one other thing, perhaps most important of all: these hairy savages fight for plunder. They'll only fight so hard before they cut their losses and leave. We fight for our homeland, for our mothers and sisters and sweethearts. We will not give up, will not back down, will not let them defeat us.

"Got that, goat fuckers? There is no 'I' in 'phalanx.'"

I'd finished with another imitation of Proxenos' favourite homily. All the men chuckled, but I still heard nervousness from them. Then from the middle of the phalanx a voice called out, "Your bladder doesn't matter! We're with you, little brother!" It was Phylo. He was with us because he'd taken ill a few days earlier, vomiting and diarrhea, and was unable to march to Marathon with his own ephebe troop. When he recovered, Proxenos placed him in our troop rather than have him go alone to Marathon.

Phylo's timing was perfect. Without any prior signal, the guys laughed, then cheered in unison, and then sang the war paean to Apollo. I returned to my place in the phalanx and felt much better about our chances.

We could now see the enemy approach. We didn't know where they came from, but whoever they were, they were smart enough to raid Athens when most of our troops were at Marathon. Most of the raiders had long hair and thick beards. They wore animal skins. They were *huge*. What did their mothers, if they had mothers, feed them to grow them so big? It looked like we were about to be attacked by a hundred bears.

When they were two hundred paces away, we saw that Krites was right, they were a mob, with no formation at all. From fifty paces, we could actually smell them, a sickly reek of animal feces and rotting flesh. A few of us vomited at the smell. I almost did too.

"Remember, men," I yelled out. "Hold off that first charge."

You've fought enough battles, Ephander, to know that it's impossible to see the whole battlefield, and foolish to even try. Once the fighting starts, all you really see is what's immediately in front of you. If you stop to look around, you will die. You have to give your full attention to the foe in front of you. So you only ever see a small percentage of the action in any battle you fight. You hear and smell as much as you see. You hear swords hitting shields, grunts, war cries, shrieked orders, the sick sound of a spear ripping into a man's guts, howls of pain, the crunch of iron against bone, curses, prayers, the moans of the dying. You smell the piss and shit of the men around you as their bowels and bladders evacuate in the terror of battle. But even with these potent competing smells, you still smell the blood.

The raiders' first charge was the blood-storm I'd expected. Their biggest man screamed his war cry, waved his battle-axe and charged right at me. Before he reached us, I saw arrows coming at us from behind the raiders. There were only a half-dozen arrows, but that could be enough to make inexperienced hoplites panic.

"Arrows incoming!" I bellowed as loudly as I could. "Shields up!" I saw an arrow coming straight for my head, so I ducked quickly. This saved my life. The arrow would have hit me in the face. I found out later that it killed the man directly behind me, went right through his eye socket into his brain. One other man was killed by an arrow, and a man at the rear of the phalanx took an arrow through his foot.

I could no longer watch for arrows because the big axe-man came at me. The arrows distracted me, so I was late with my spear. When I tried to push it into the axe-man's guts, he side-stepped it. Holding the spear would only prevent me from reaching my sword, so I hurled it into the man behind the big axe-man, putting it through that hairy bastard's chest and stopping him dead—literally. The axe-man swung his weapon at my head. I blocked it with my shield. Xenocrates had taught me a trick to defend against an axe. I twisted my shield slightly at the moment of impact, which caused the axe-head to cut into the edge of my shield and get stuck there. The big axe-man then made a fatal mistake: he used both hands to pry it loose. He got it out, but not before I took the spear that had been passed to me from behind and plunged it into his undefended side. As he collapsed, I quickly pulled the spear out so he wouldn't take it down with him.

The next raider came at me with a club. What an idiot. Before he'd gotten anywhere near me, my spear was in his guts. He actually seemed surprised.

"Change up!" I yelled. I felt but did not actually see Simeon beside me roll back as a fresh man took his place. I was not tired so I held my place. I snuck a quick peek to my left and saw that the entire front row had held firm and changed over flawlessly. I was relieved to see the bodies of a dozen raiders and only two dead hoplites. The enemy's clubs were no match for our nine-footers.

The raiders still came at us, but they took casualties and began to lose their will to fight. "Change up!" I yelled again, and once again I felt the men to my left rotate seamlessly in and out of the front line.

The raiders now identified me as the leader, so three of them came at me at the same time, two armed with clubs and one with an axe. The hoplite to my immediate left—I didn't know who it was and this wasn't the time to stop and find out—put his spear into the groin of the axe-man. This saved my life. Now I could concentrate on the other two. I jammed my spear into the neck of one of them, then quickly pulled out my sword, hacked at the second man's right arm, and almost severed it at the elbow. He shrieked, dropped his club and held his mangled arm, as a hoplite further down the line jammed a spear into his side to finish him off.

The big hairy raiders abruptly lost all desire to fight. They turned and ran. At least thirty of them lay dead, and a dozen others were wounded too badly to run away. They'd expected an easy battle against a bunch of ephebes, but our basic infantry tactics were so superior to theirs that, in the end, our inexperience didn't matter.

The young Athenians were no longer afraid and began to chase the enemy. I had to stop this. The raiders were still numerous enough to turn and make a stand. If we broke formation, we'd lose our greatest advantage. We also had to consider our panoplies: our armour was made for fighting, not chasing, and we'd soon exhaust ourselves if we ran after men who had no armour.

"Halt!" I bellowed. "Finish off the enemy

wounded. Be careful, make sure none of them is playing dead. If you find one coherent enough to speak, unarm him and bring him to me alive."

Most of the Athenians obeyed my commands, but five men kept on running. This wasn't insubordination in the usual sense. They were so caught up in battle frenzy—what Grandfather called *the Black Mist*—that they probably weren't capable of even *hearing* my command to halt. They wanted only to kill and kill and kill. I grabbed a spear from the ground and chased after the Athenian who'd run the farthest away. I used the spear to trip him. He fell flat on his face. I then broke the spear over the helmet of another of the runners. It did not hurt him much. He stopped and looked at me with murderous confusion in his eyes. The others stopped too, and looked at me, dazed.

"Back in formation! *Now!*" I screamed. "Or I'll fucking gut you right here."

All five of the runners sheepishly jogged back to the other men. "We're better equipped for fighting than they are," I explained more gently as I jogged back with them, "but their lack of armour makes them better equipped for running. If we chase, we break formation. We've won this battle, but there are about sixty of them left. They could still band together and turn on you. By yourself, you wouldn't have a chance. We'll follow them, but in formation and at a pace we can maintain. Remember our objective here is to defend the city. Right now, driving them off is just as good as wiping them out."

When we got back to the rest of the phalanx, Phylo was chattering excitedly. He had a dent in his helmet and a slight slash on the bicep of his shield-arm, but was otherwise unharmed. Years later, he would confess that the slash on his arm was made with his own sword, when he waved it a little too excitedly. In this battle, he'd killed his first man. When the three raiders came at me, he was the man to my left who put his spear into the axe-man. I thanked him for saving my life, and he laughed and beamed with pride. "It was the least I could do, little brother," he said. "You saved all of our lives when you took control and wouldn't let us panic."

"You kept calling the order to rotate," said Simeon, "but you never rotated yourself. Is that what the corner-man does in phalanx fighting?"

"No," I said. "I planned to rotate out but never saw a clear opportunity." This was, in fact, untrue. I remained in my place because I was the only one who could hold the line effectively. I would have rotated out if I'd become too tired to defend myself, but in this short battle it never happened. Don't want to brag, Ephander, but all that running had given me the stamina of a ploughman's mule.

The men joked that the best place to be

during a battle is behind me—in this battle, the men directly behind me didn't get into the fight, apart from the poor fellow killed by the arrow. "Next battle, if I have to line up behind Lex," said Phylo, "I'm bringing a chair. Might as well sit down and have a drink while Lex kills everything in sight."

The raiders who were too badly wounded to run away were all incoherent or unconscious, so we finished them off. I would have liked to find out where they'd come from. We marched to the Phaleron to either kill the rest of them or just make sure they'd gotten back on their boats and left our shores. We had seven dead, so I ordered four men to commandeer a wagon from the nearest farm or shop and bring the bodies into the city for proper burials. We marched at a brisk but unhurried pace back to the Phaleron.

When we reached the docks, the raiders were gone. Proxenos, miraculously recovered, showed up shortly after we did. He'd ridden his father's horse from the city and now tried to maintain an air of superiority. He resumed command.

"So you goat-fuckers fought a battle," he sneered. "Don't think for a second that it makes you real soldiers." He glared at me, and me alone, as he spoke. As if he didn't hate me enough, I'd shown him up. I did what he could not. I led raw recruits into battle and won, with minimal casualties. It unmanned him. We, for our part, would not forget that he left us to fight the raiders without a commanding officer, and now he taunted us because we'd survived. The stones on the man! Before this battle, I had little respect for him. Now I had none at all.

Later, after Proxenos dismissed us, Phylo acquired two goats—the gods know how he did it, acquiring things on short notice was one of his conspicuous talents—and we returned to our little battlefield, where the blood of friend and foe still stained the ground. We sacrificed the goats to Athene, to thank her for giving us the wisdom and courage to survive the battle with so few casualties. I supervised the rites and made another speech to the men. I'd avoided public speaking for my entire life, and here I had to do it twice in one day. I wasn't nervous this time.

"Proxenos is dead wrong," I said, after the rites had been performed. "We *are* real soldiers. We fought in the phalanx against a terrifying enemy. We were outnumbered but stood our ground. We were scared shitless but never backed down. Not one man among us wavered, not one. We remembered our training when it counted most, fought as a unit, protected each other, and routed an enemy that would have slaughtered us easily if our courage failed. We now know the elation of surviving battle, but we also know the deep grief of losing treasured comrades. To me, that's the *definition* of a real soldier. Be proud, men of Leontis, and know that you honoured your ancestors and your city with your bravery this day."

9–TO WAR

After the sacrifice, our day was far from over. Proxenos was useless to us, so we did what needed to be done without his guidance. We posted sentries at the Phaleron and at every gate to the city, in case the raiders returned or other ones came. Hyperion, deft at organization, quickly drew up a sentry schedule that was thorough, fair, and covered every gate. He took one of the first shifts himself. The more I got to know Hyperion, the more I liked and respected him.

We also had to make sure the bodies of our fallen comrades were received by their families.

If I'd known how unpleasant this would be, I would never have taken command.

Alexandros, the ephebe with the bad leg who worked so hard to be a soldier, was the guy behind me in the phalanx who was killed by an arrow. When we got back to Athens, the first thing we saw was Alexandros' mother at a public fountain. She wailed and tore out her hair. Alexandros was laid out on a wagon, the arrow still sticking out of his eye socket. His mother had blood on her face where she'd scratched herself, and her slaves and family members could not restrain her. She was suicidal. She'd lost her husband a few years earlier, and now she'd lost her only son. Tears came to my eyes too.

We saw similar scenes when we returned the other bodies to their families. Afterwards, I went to bed but did not sleep. The sight of the bereaved families took more out of me than the battle. Others in the barracks had lain awake, either from lingering battle adrenaline or from their own grief over friends lost today, but eventually they all drifted off and I was the only one awake.

Maybe we should have run from the battle. We could have formed up at a city gate and fought the raiders there. I chose to stand and fight. Seven ephebes had died because of that decision. Seven mothers were devastated because of me. Seven families grieved.

I never again wanted the responsibility of command.

I never again wanted men's lives in my hands.

I was alone with these black thoughts when an officer entered the barracks. This was unusual. No one came into our barracks after lights out, not even officers.

He saw me looking at him and came over to me. "Elektros of Skiathos?" he said in a quiet voice.

I stood up. "Yes, sir," I said.

He motioned for me to follow him outside. My first thought was that I was going to be disciplined for taking command of the ephebes without authorization. The penalty for impersonating an officer was death.

A second officer stood outside with a torch. By its light I saw that both men were dusty from the road. They had two horses with them. The horses were sweaty and tired. The first man introduced himself as Eurymachos. The man with the torch was Milo.

"We know you've had a long day," said Eurymachos, "but Themistocles has ordered us to bring you to Marathon. Get your armour. We'll help you put it on."

"Permission to speak frankly, sir," I said.

"Okay," said Eurymachos. "Keep it brief."

"Sir, this unit of ephebes is currently without effective command," I said. "What if there's another raid?"

Both men nodded. I didn't need to say anything else. They were of the tribe Leontis and knew all about Proxenos.

"Who would you recommend to command?" Milo asked, with a quick glance at Eurymachos. He was testing me.

"Hyperion, sir," I said. "He's quick-thinking, courageous, and understands the gravity of command."

The two officers looked at each other and smiled. "That's who Themistocles told us to put in command in your place," said Milo. "Where is he? I didn't see him in the barracks. We'll talk to him before we leave."

I told them that Hyperion was currently on sentry duty at the Dipylon Gate.

Milo nodded. "I'll go," he said.

A slave brought us three fresh horses and took the two tired ones away. Milo mounted up and rode to the Dipylon Gate. After he spoke to Hyperion, we were to meet him at the Acharnian Gate, which led to the road to Marathon.

Eurymachos helped me get my armour on. "We leave immediately," he said. "Can you ride a horse?"

"Yes, sir," I said.

"Good," said Eurymachos. "We need to get to Marathon before daybreak."

As Eurymachos and I rode towards the Acharnian Gate, I asked him if he knew how Themistocles planned to punish me.

"*Punish* you?" said Eurymachos. "For what?"

"I took command, sir, without authorization," I said.

"That's insane, lad," he said. "Your battle with the raiders is the talk of the army. You're a hero. Every man at Marathon wants to buy you a drink. Themistocles is so impressed with your quick thinking that he wants you around when we fight the Persians. I don't know his exact plans, but he'll probably use you as a scout or a messenger. So get the idea of punishment out of your head right now."

"I got seven ephebes killed, sir," I said. The image of Alexandros' mother, as she wailed uncontrollably over his pale corpse, still tortured me.

"You kept your men in formation," he said. "That's extremely difficult with first-timers. In fact, our practice is to *never* use a phalanx that consists entirely of new men. It's too much pressure for them. We always mix in experienced men to steady them, and we don't put new men in the front line for their first battle. You did so because you had no choice, and somehow they didn't panic. Frankly, my friend, there are damned few officers in the entire Athenian army who could have done that."

"Sir, if you don't mind me asking, how do you know so much about the battle?"

"Linos," he said. Old Linos was the shoemaker who trained us for a few weeks when Proxenos was laid up with his pestilential rash. "He was on his way to take command of you boys but didn't get there in time. He was close enough to see the whole battle, and as soon as it was done, he sent a messenger to Themistocles. Linos was particularly impressed with the way you kept your men from pursuing. That's never easy for a young commander, because there's always a good chance he'll have the Black Mist himself and will also want to chase."

"I still feel terrible, sir," I said. "Seven men died under my command." I told Eurymachos about the death of Alexandros, which haunted me the most. I could have blocked the arrow that killed him. Instead, I ducked, and he was dead because of it.

"You can't torment yourself about that, kid," said Eurymachos. "You made the sensible decision to duck from an enemy arrow. If you tried to block it, it might've killed *you.* Did you shout a warning that arrows were incoming?"

"I did, sir."

"That's all a commander can ever do. I'll never say this around his family, but Alexandros should have put his shield up. He didn't, so he's responsible for his own death, not you. Grieve for him as you would any worthy comrade, but do not blame yourself."

"If we chose to fight at the city gates," I said, "which was where the raiders were headed, we might not have lost anybody."

"You might also have lost *everybody,*" Eurymachos reasoned. "You would have had to race back to the city to get there ahead of the raiders. That would only have tired out your men. No, the decision to stand and fight was the best one. The road narrowed there and funneled the raiders right into you. They couldn't go around you. It's the easiest spot to defend on that entire road. You fought with your men well rested. Remember too, Elektros, that the longer you put off the decision to fight, the harder that decision becomes. Waiting gives young men's minds time to find excuses to avoid battle. The longer you wait, the more time your new men have to overthink things and let panic creep into their thoughts."

"Thank you for your kind words, sir," I said, "but I still feel bad about Alexandros and the others we lost."

"What do you want me to say? There are no magic words that will make everything okay. You led your men effectively and minimized casualties. In war, men die. Linos said those raiders were *fierce*. Nobody would've been surprised if half of you died, but you had only seven casualties, and that is simply amazing. So instead of beating yourself up over it, consider how many more casualties there could have been. You're feeling commander's remorse. It's normal. All officers feel it. It's actually a good sign. When you lead men into battle, you should *always* feel responsible for their welfare. If you don't care if your men get killed, then you shouldn't be leading them."

By this time, we'd reached the Acharnian

Gate. Milo must've ridden quickly, because he was waiting for us there.

When the three of us were through the gate and on the road to Marathon, Eurymachos continued the conversation.

"The fact that these things occur to you tells me that you understand the responsibility that comes with command," he said. "Any moron can give orders, but a good officer always considers the consequences of his orders before he gives them. Our best commanders—Themistocles, Miltiades—do it, although they do it so quickly that it's not noticeable. The men under their command know it. The best young commander I ever fought for did this better than anybody."

"Who was that, sir?"

"Proxenos."

Proxenos? Was this even possible?

"Sir, may I speak frankly about Proxenos?" I asked.

"No, Elektros, because I know what you want to say," he said. "Proxenos is such a fuckup that you're wondering if I'm teasing you about his skill as a commander."

"True, sir," I said. "He holds pointless grudges and becomes enraged over trivial things. None of us respect him. He abandoned us today."

Eurymachos was silent for a few moments before he spoke again. "Everything you just said is true," he said. "In today's battle, he'd have been worse than useless because he would have panicked. You didn't see it today, lad, but panic, even when it's unspoken, spreads like wildfire on dry brush. Once it starts it's almost impossible to stop. Proxenos trains ephebes because it's all he can do now.

"He wasn't always like that. He was an excellent soldier, and he kept his head so well that he commanded a phalanx before he was twenty-five. Neither Themistocles nor Miltiades did it so young. Proxenos commanded men twice his age, yet they respected him because he was so effective."

"Is that why he's so bitter, sir?" I asked. "Instead of leading men into battle, he trains a bunch of snot-nosed kids."

"Yes, he's bitter, but he was once a confident, calm, quick-thinking war leader. He'd led a dozen successful battles. In a border skirmish with the Megarans, he was leading his men to victory. I was in that phalanx. The battle was all but won. We were fighting in a field. The Megaran phalanx had begun to fall back. We expected them to collapse and run at any moment. There was a short furrow in the ground. The Megarans knew about it and avoided it, but we didn't see it. When Proxenos ordered us forward, four of our front men stepped into the furrow. They fell forward. Then the men behind them, who were pushing forward at a trot, fell on top of them. The Megarans, who'd been on the verge of breaking, regained their confidence and charged at us. The first four men who'd fallen were killed by Megaran butt-spikes.

"Proxenos did everything right. He rallied us and got our formation back in order immediately. Our back ranks filled the vacant spaces left by our dead. The Megaran resurgence was short-lived. We routed them. It was one of the finest pieces of commanding I'd ever seen. Proxenos was a hero.

"Then we realized that the four men who died in the furrow were Proxenos' father, both of his brothers, and his closest friend. It was as if a god punished him, because no other Athenians died that day. Proxenos could never shake the feeling that he'd gotten those men killed. He considered himself guilty of patricide and fratricide. From that day on, Proxenos was a wreck. When the mourning was done and it was time for him to resume command, he couldn't hold himself together. The battle traumatized him for life. Out of respect for the commander he was, and for the losses he personally suffered, we made him the ephebe trainer. It's all he can do now."

"Even that's debatable, sir," I said.

"Yes, I know he plays favourites and turns molehills into mountains, but consider the battle you just fought. Did your men hold formation?"

"Flawlessly, sir," I said.

"That's because Proxenos drilled and drilled and drilled you guys. You kept them calm, but it was Proxenos' training that made you rotate in and out of formation so well. You wouldn't have won today without that preparation. As much as you hate the endless drilling, it saved your lives today."

"We should pick up the pace," said Milo. We were a half-mile out of Athens. The road, which would normally have farmers and merchants heading into the city at this time of early morning, was deserted. We were just about to prod our horses into a trot when we heard rapid hoofbeats approach us from behind.

"Off the road," said Eurymachos quietly. "Quickly."

We froze at the side of the road. The terrain here offered no place to hide, so we had to hope the night would hide us. The rider could be an Athenian messenger or a Persian spy, although I doubted that a spy would ride down this road so noisily.

As the rider approached, we saw in the pale moonlight that he carried a Scythian bow and arrows in a gorytos, but he was too small to be a Scythian. The horse he rode was a fine black stallion.

"Freeze!" roared Eurymachos with his spear raised and ready to throw. "Identify yourself or die."

The rider, who hadn't seen us at all, pulled up. "Don't shoot!" he said. "I'm unarmed!"

"A man with a Scythian bow," said Milo, "is hardly unarmed."

"I know this guy," I said. "He's Krites, a slave from Skiathos. I can vouch for him."

"He's your slave?" Eurymachos asked me.

"No, his owner is Xenocrates," I said. "He's currently on loan to the Scythians and me."

"Why are you chasing us, boy?" Milo said to Krites.

"To offer my services to Elektros in the battle, sir," Krites replied.

"Elektros will be a messenger," said Milo. "He won't need a battle squire."

"Maybe not," said Krites, "but I can run errands, serve as a scout, and I have some skill at archery."

"That's an understatement, sir," I said. "He's the best Kretan-style archer I've ever seen. The Scythians were so impressed that they gave him the gorytos, and they *never* give those to non-Scythians. But Krites, aren't you supposed to look after the Scythian barracks?"

I realized the absurdity of these words the moment they left my mouth. The Scythians had been sent to Plataea. There was nothing for Krites to do in the Scythian barracks.

"Sirs, I want to do my part," said Krites, "Please let me come with you."

Milo and Eurymachos walked a few feet away from Krites and me, and spoke in low voices that we couldn't overhear.

Half a minute later they came back and Eurymachos said, "We can use all the help we can get at Marathon. Elektros, you will take full responsibility for Krites. That includes feeding him. If anything happens to him, you're the one who makes amends to his master. There's no way in Hades that Milo or I are going to get on Xenocrates' bad side."

It was agreed. I would serve Themistocles. Krites would help me. Off we rode. To Marathon. To war.

10–STRATEGOI

He seemed more hog than man, and he wouldn't let go of my hand. The armour on his chubby little body made him look like some swinish clown rather than a soldier. He reeked of sweat and onions. He was the first man to notice us when we entered the Hellene camp at Marathon at sunrise, and when he realized who I was, he grabbed my right hand and pumped it like it was a well-handle and he was dying of thirst. My hand started to hurt.

"The gods bless you, son," he said over and over. "The gods bless you."

I was tired and hungry and ready to smack this fool, but Eurymachos read my thought and shook his head, no, I was to suffer pig-man for a while longer.

When pig-man finally let go of my hand, he embraced me. This also seemed like it would never end. The man was sunken-eyed, like he hadn't slept in the two nights the Hellenes had been camped here.

Finally, Eurymachos grabbed the man by the shoulder and pried him off of me—Apollo's balls, Ephander, if he hadn't, I might still be there.

"That's enough, Dromeos," Eurymachos said, laughing. "The kid's had a long ride and a longer night."

"I cannot thank Elektros enough, sir," said Dromeos. "He kept my wife and daughters safe. I didn't mean to offend."

"That's okay, Dromeos," I said, "but give credit to the ephebes who fought beside me, and the seven who died."

"When this is over, you're coming to my house for dinner," said Dromeos. "I'd like you to meet my eldest daughter."

We headed for Themistocles' tent in the centre of the camp. The sun had just risen and the men who weren't on sentry duty stood or sat in front of their tents eating breakfast, mostly hard bread and harder cheese.

"Dromeos is a good man," Eurymachos said when we were out of earshot. "Since he got here, he hasn't stopped worrying about his wife and three daughters in Athens. He's not the only one. Every man here knows that we don't have enough men to fight the Persians *and* properly defend our city."

As if on cue, another Athenian soldier came up to me and shook my hand. "I'm buying you a drink when this is done, Elektros," he said. Unlike Dromeos, though, he just smiled and walked on. Other men also shook my hand or patted me on the back as they passed us.

I understood. When I was four years old and all the men of Skiathos were off fighting a battle, raiders killed my mother. If anyone had prevented it, I would've been at least as grateful as Dromeos.

"As you can see," Eurymachos continued, "Dromeos' opinion of you is not unique here. The story of the battle with the raiders has made the rounds, and it's lifted morale. Every man here is proud of you. Relieved, too, because most of them doubted that a single unit of ephebes could protect Athens. Now we can all worry less about our families and focus on the Persians."

"But sir," I said, "do I really want to meet Dromeos' daughter?"

Eurymachos laughed. "Are you ready to take a wife?" he asked. "That's what he has in mind. If you are, his wife is surprisingly attractive and the daughters, fortunately, take after her."

We found Themistocles in front of his tent. He sat at a canopied table and ate his breakfast of bread, dates, and sausage. He conferred with another man over a map. Early as it was, he'd already been up for hours.

"Ah, our hero arrives," he said when he saw me. He came and shook my hand. "So you've received an offer of marriage?"

"Strategos," I said, "how could you possibly know that already?"

"It's my job to know things, kid," he said.

"Plus ever since Dromeos heard about your fight with the raiders, he's told anyone who'll listen that he wants you to marry his daughter."

There were chuckles all around. The older man next to Themistocles nodded at me and said, "Dromeos is my cousin, lad. You could do a lot worse."

He was Miltiades, the most experienced general on either side. His beard was snow white, as were the last holdout strands of hair on his head. He was past sixty but wore his armour like he was born in it. He was known for his easygoing manner both on and off the battlefield.

Themistocles told one of his men to find Krites and me places in the tent with the other runners—in this case, 'runner' meant messenger or errand-runner, which would be my role during the battle. Themistocles told me to store my armour and kit there, get some sleep, and come back to see him late that afternoon.

Krites and I slept for a few hours. Themistocles' task for us was to scout out the slopes of Mount Stavrokoraki, north of the Hellenes' camp. We were to look for caves large enough to conceal ambushers, and also for a trail large enough to let us sneak a few hundred hoplites behind the Persians.

On our way to the mountain, which was about three miles from the camp, the land rose and afforded us a great view of the entire encamped Hellene forces. The Athenians had about eight thousand hoplites, another two thousand light-armed troops and a small force of cavalry. The Plataeans had sent their entire army of a thousand hoplites and a few hundred light infantry.

"About twelve thousand men, mostly hoplites," I said to Krites. "Looks like a pretty big army to me. Why don't we attack?"

"The Persians have three times that many," said Krites. "No hoplites, but their cavalry would kill us. They have over a thousand Scythian horsemen, we have less than two hundred. Ours are *not* Scythian."

I once heard Scylurus say, "Hellene ride horse like fucking baby! Hundred Hellene riders not last minute fight ten Saka rider!" He exaggerated, but not by much. Our Athenian cavalry, overmatched in numbers and skill, would mostly scout. If they fought the Scythian cavalry, they'd be slaughtered.

"So what's the Athenian plan?" I asked Krites. The Hellenes' camp blocked off the only two land routes the Persians could take to Athens. The Persians, camped near the beach, had an impassable swamp to their left and an equally impassable mountain to their right. If they wanted to march on Athens, they'd have to go through our army. Our infantry was outnumbered but superior. Most of their soldiers were armed with short spears, wicker shields and very little armour. Most of ours wore iron and bronze armour, and our hoplite tactics were well-practiced. If the Persians attacked, they'd also have to charge slightly uphill. The Persians might try to invade Athens by sea, but their infantry was all on land now. If we saw them load troops onto their ships, we'd have time to get back to the city to defend it.

"The plan is to wait for the Spartans," said Krites. "They'll be here in five or six days."

"They'll *be* here?" I said. "Why aren't they here now? It's not like this was a last minute surprise."

"You know what those grim fuckers are like," said Krites. "They're observing the *Carneia*—they won't leave Sparta until the next full moon, the day after tomorrow. Then it'll take them three days to get here."

The Carneia, Ephander, is a religious festival. The legendarily pious Spartans refused to take up arms during the Carneia—if they did, they believed next year's harvest would fail—although I wondered how pious they'd be if the Persians were camped twenty miles outside of Sparta. They would bring only five thousand hoplites, but they were the best soldiers in all Hellas, accompanied by twenty-thousand light-armed helots. It made sense, militarily, to wait for them.

Delaying battle was to our advantage for another reason. In our homeland, our supply lines were short. We could reprovision easily. The Persians had to bring all the food for their men and horses by sea. With their recent conquests, they could now get supplies from Eretria and Thessaly, and from the medized Thebans. Eretria was two days' sail from Marathon, and Thessaly was four days overland. Our spies reported that the Thebans had jacked up their grain prices, claiming—falsely—a poor harvest.

Krites and I, when we got to Mount Stavrokoraki, found two goat trails, both long unused. Neither trail was large enough to hide more than a handful of men, but would be perfect if Themistocles wanted us to sneak to the edges of the Persian camp at night and kill sentries or poison food supplies. The trails were treacherous in the dark—in fact, Krites and I almost got lost trying to pick our way home after the sun started to sink—but this meant it would also be tough for any Persians to pursue us.

We saw no caves. There was a lot of mountain to explore and only two of us, so after a few hours, with the sun sinking fast, we started back. A few minutes later, we spotted a rock partridge on the trail ahead of us. It had a broken wing. Quick as the wind, Krites had an arrow nocked in his bow, but the bird ducked under a bush before Krites could shoot. I chased after it. It ran into a small thicket and got trapped there, its useless injured wing caught in the underbrush. I quickly wrung the poor creature's neck.

"We'll eat well tonight," I said to Krites. "You ever eat partridge?"

Krites said no, but he wasn't looking at the bird. I now saw, directly behind me, what had caught his eye, a small cave in the side of the mountain. It hadn't been visible from the trail. It had been lived in, though not recently. A small spring flowed beside the entrance, and it was so well hidden that you could even light a fire inside it without anyone seeing it, although the smoke might be visible in daylight.

We headed back to camp smiling. We had dinner and good news. We'd walked only a few minutes more when Krites suddenly grabbed my arm. He put his finger to his lips. I heard nothing at first, but after a few seconds, there were voices. I drew my sword as quietly as I could. Krites already had an arrow nocked in his bow.

Three men came up the trail. Krites and I had kept our voices as low as possible, barely above a whisper, even if there were no enemies nearby, but these three showed their inexperience. They spoke in normal voices. We knew about them long before they knew about us. It was their death. Two of the men were Persians, an officer and an infantryman. The officer spoke thickly accented Hellenic. The third man was a scrawny old guy with grey hair. He had the local Hellenic accent.

He was showing the Persians the trail.

Krites put an arrow through the officer's throat, and before the other two men were fully aware it had happened, he fired another arrow through the infantryman's heart. I charged and smashed the butt-end of my sword into the old man's face. He collapsed, moaning, bleeding. The infantryman was already dead. I plunged my sword into the officer's chest to finish him off.

The old man babbled in terror. He knew the area well, and maybe he could guide us around the trails, but we couldn't trust him. I hauled him to a spot off the trail, slashed his throat and left him to the kites and crows. Traitors deserve no better.

We found twenty gold darics on the Persian officer, probably the traitor's payment. I told Krites to take all of it—he would be freed soon and would need it—but he insisted I take half. We pushed the bodies of the Persians over a cliff that faced away from the Persian camp. They wouldn't be found for days, if they were found at all.

Not a bad day's work: we scouted the trails, found the cave Themistocles wanted, killed two enemy soldiers and a traitor, pocketed ten gold darics each, and we'd dine on partridge tonight instead of just hard bread and harder cheese.

* * * * * * * * * *

Hysteria in the Persian camp: the Hellenes had sprung a night-attack! The clamour drew every last man out of his tent in the dark. Some tents were on fire, and panicked horses charged through the camp. Confused soldiers thrust spears and swords at shadows, and accidentally killed a few of their own men. Then the prevailing rumour changed, shifting like the autumn winds that blew so unpredictably across the Bay of Marathon: the Hellenes weren't attacking, but Commander Datis has been assassinated! More panic, more confusion, more phantom-chasing, and a few more accidental deaths.

Then the whispers in the wind changed yet again: there was an attempted assassination of Datis, but his bodyguards had fought it off. Datis yet lived.

I have no idea how Themistocles wrought such panic in the Persian camp so suddenly. He obviously had men inside. The Persians had only been here for three days, not enough time for a Hellene spy to gain their trust enough to infiltrate their camp, so Themistocles' agents must have been with the Persians long before they reached our shores.

Krites and I had to act quickly, with the confusion still close to its peak.

Before the tumult, Krites and I had carefully

observed a Persian officer. He was a *hazarapatis*, a commander of a thousand infantry, high enough in rank to know the Persian battle plan.

"Hazarapatis Tammuz!" I bellowed. We were in the trees just outside the Persian camp. Our task was to capture an officer and bring him back to the Hellene camp alive. Before the panic broke out, Krites and I spent an hour on the edge of the Persian camp listening to their conversations. We had to make sure we had the man's name right or our ruse would fail. "Tammuz! Here! NOW, damn you!"

My Persian was clear and authoritative, and I could speak it without an accent, at least in short bursts. I tried to sound like Tammuz's impatient superior. Our biggest fears were that he might not respond to my command, or that he'd bring other soldiers with him. If either of these things happened, Krites and I would have had to flee without capturing him.

My simple ruse worked. Convinced that a superior officer was in distress, Tammuz immediately ran over to where Krites and I hid. "I'm here, sir!" he said into the darkness.

I jumped him before he knew I was there. I twisted his arm behind his back to make him drop the sword he'd drawn. I put my dagger to his throat. "One peep out of you," I said in Persian, "and you die right now." Krites quickly stuffed a rag into the man's mouth and used another rag as a bandana to hold the first rag in place. A third rag blindfolded him.

We bound his hands and feet with leather thongs and slung him over one of the horses we'd ridden here, which we'd concealed a hundred yards further into the woods. Then we took him back to our camp. Interrogation would be somebody else's job.

At dawn the next day, the strategoi breakfasted quickly and then met in Kallimachos' command tent. The tent had a room big enough to hold a large table, eleven generals, and their attendants. As Themistocles' attendant, I was permitted inside the tent during the debate, although I'd probably be chained and flogged if I opened my mouth.

The Athenians were commanded by ten strategoi, one elected from each of the ten tribes, and an overall commander, the *polemarch,* or war archon. The Athenian assembly had elected Kallimachos as polemarch. He was the titular commander of the Athenian army and highly regarded as a soldier, but everyone knew that once the battle started he'd defer to Miltiades. Of all the strategoi at Marathon, Miltiades was the only one who had significant experience fighting against the Persians. Miltiades had also fought *alongside* the Persians. He knew them inside and out. Kallimachos freely acknowledged this. The battle hadn't started yet, so Kallimachos was still given his dues as overall commander. They conferred in his tent, not Miltiades'.

On the first day at Marathon, the eleven generals voted on whether or not to attack. Only Miltiades and Themistocles had voted in favour. The other nine wanted to wait for the Spartans. Themistocles and Miltiades were both persuasive, though in very different ways. Themistocles convinced through rhetoric and logic. It was not Miltiades' words that convinced—in fact, he spoke relatively little during these meetings. His *reputation* persuaded. On the third day, one of the strategoi changed his vote solely on the belief that if Miltiades favoured attacking, then it must be the right thing to do. The tally now was three strategoi in favour of attacking, eight against.

Grandfather once said, admiringly, that Themistocles could talk the scales off a snake. Themistocles made his plea to the others yet again. "The *last* thing the Persians expect us to do is attack. If we do it just before dawn, they won't be ready. The element of surprise will more than make up for their advantage in cavalry, which they won't be able to deploy in time. Our infantry will cut theirs to pieces. Plus, delay is not good for our troops. I'm confident in their ability to fight, but they're not professional soldiers. Few have ever had to wait for days before a battle. The more time that passes, the more their morale can waiver. Right now, morale is high." As he said this, he nodded towards me. Several of the other strategoi looked my way and nodded too. I now understood why I was there instead of one of Themistocles' usual attendants: the sight of me reminded the other generals that our men could defeat an enemy when badly outnumbered. If ephebes could do it, then there was no doubt that fully trained hoplites could too.

"Now is the best time to attack," added Miltiades.

"Now is the *worst* time to attack," said Brontes, strategoi of the tribe Pandionis. "The Spartans will be here soon. They'll even up the odds. Plus, we can surprise the Persians after the Spartans get here just as much as we can before they get here."

Themistocles glared at Brontes. He despised the man. Brontes, whose name meant 'the thunderer,' was aptly named. He was a blusterer, an all-talk-no-action kind of commander. He'd never admit it, but he probably hoped that if we waited long enough, the Persians would just leave.

"What's coming out of your mouth right now, Brontes," said Themistocles, as he struggled to control his rage, "is what normally comes out of other men's assholes. The Spartans will not leave Sparta for two more days. It will take them three days to get here. After that long march, they'll need at least one day to rest. So that's another six or seven days for our men to sit idle and get nervous. We cannot surprise the Persians *after* the Spartans get here, because firstly, it won't be a surprise, and secondly, *the fucking Persians will not wait!* They know the Spartans are coming. They will attack us *before* they get here!"

"You know this for certain?" said Aristides. "That they'll attack before the Spartans get here?"

"I do not," said Themistocles. "It's the smartest thing for them to do, though, so they'll surely think of it. We court catastrophe, gentlemen, if we take the Persians for fools. They have spies between here and Sparta. They know as well as we do when the Spartans will get here."

"Another thing to consider," added Miltiades, "is that the Spartans will not fight under our command, or even under a joint command. It is their custom, when fighting with allies, to take overall command. I don't doubt their courage or skill, but can we count on them to do what's best for Athens? To remain masters of our own fate, we must take the initiative."

Kallimachos pointed out that we should wait for the Persians to attack us, because to do so they'd have to charge us slightly uphill. Themistocles quickly countered that if we attacked, we'd still have the gravitational advantage because our men would charge downhill.

The strategoi voted again. One more strategos, swayed by Themistocles' logic, changed his vote, but that still meant only four strategoi favoured attacking. The meeting was about to break up when Eurymachos stuck his head inside the tent flap and tapped me on the arm. He needed to talk to Themistocles immediately. I bent forward and whispered to Themistocles that Eurymachos was here.

"Gentlemen," Themistocles said. "Before we break up this meeting, I ask you to indulge me a few moments longer. Late last evening, we captured a Persian officer. Captain Eurymachos interrogated him, and he is here now to report on it. You'll want to hear this."

Aristides looked irritated. "What are you playing at, Themistocles?" he said. "You capture a Persian officer, but you don't think it's important enough to tell the rest of us?"

"In such matters," said Themistocles, "it is common practice to inform as few people as possible." I recognized the trace of sarcasm in his words: there were several men here, Brontes in particular, that Themistocles did not completely trust. "I also didn't mention it because I don't know if the prisoner has anything useful to tell us."

"Let me guess," said Aristides. "Your man here will tell us that the Persians' are about to attack."

"No, Aristides, I don't know what the prisoner said," said Themistocles. "Eurymachos interrogated him, not me. I'll be hearing it for the first time, just like you. So rather than bickering, let's let the man speak."

Kallimachos agreed. "Themistocles' ethics," he said, "can be debated another day. Let's hear what the captain has to say."

Themistocles nodded to Eurymachos. "Report."

"Sirs," Eurymachos said. He stood stiffly at attention in front of the strategoi. "The prisoner has revealed that the Persians plan to evacuate most of their cavalry. They will put their cavalry on ships with two thousand infantry. Their intention is to besiege Athens with half the infantry and use the cavalry and remaining infantry to attack us here from behind."

There was a collective gasp around the table. Everyone, including Themistocles, was stunned.

"When do they plan to do this?" asked Kallimachos.

"Tomorrow night," he said. "They'll load the troops on the ships in the dark. By dawn the day after tomorrow, they'll be halfway to Athens."

Miltiades, ever the strategist, asked, "What about siege equipment?"

"It will be transported from Eretria to Athens by ship," said Eurymachos, "and has already left. The majority of their infantry will engage us here, but only as a diversion."

"We need to get back to Athens!" said

Brontes, who jumped to his feet.

"No we don't," said Miltiades. "Their biggest advantage in battle is not their numbers but their cavalry. As soon as their cavalry gets on the ships, we attack."

"What's the point of defeating their infantry," said Kallimachos, "if we don't have a city to go back to afterwards?"

"We have time," said Miltiades. "Against a siege, Athens can hold out for a few days. We can send a few men back today to organize the defenses. We can defeat the Persian infantry here in a few hours and still have time to march back to Athens without exhausting our men."

Themistocles spoke next. "I propose that we send three hundred men back to Athens immediately. Did we not upgrade the city walls last year for this exact purpose?"

The strategoi debated like this for another hour. Then they voted again. Only one more general changed his vote. Surprisingly, it was Themistocles' greatest political enemy, Aristides. He was nicknamed the Just because he always did what he believed was right, even if it was unpopular or politically disadvantageous to him.

The vote still remained six to five against attacking. The six who did not want to attack also did not want to remain at Marathon. They wanted to rush back to Athens. Themistocles was so frustrated that he kicked over a chair and stomped out of Kallimachos' tent. I would've liked to hear what the others would say next, but I could not remain there without Themistocles.

As we headed back to his tent, Themistocles walked quickly, as he always did when he was angry. "I gambled and lost," he said. "I honestly did not know what Eurymachos would say, but I was certain our prisoner would tell us that the Persians planned to attack us here. I had no idea they'd besiege Athens. It's a smart plan."

"The Persians supply their troops by sea, sir," I ventured. "Their supply lines are long but we lack the capability to break them. If we sent all our troops back to Athens, they'd just starve us out, even if it took a year."

He looked at me with a mixture of irritation, because I'd offered an opinion without being asked to do so, and admiration, because what I said made perfect sense. He stopped walking, put his hand on my shoulder and smiled.

"A seventeen-year-old kid who has fought one battle in his life understands this," he said, "but some of these fucking ladies have fought fifty battles and just don't see it. The only way to avoid battle with the Persians is to surrender. If we let them attack us here, or if we cower inside the city walls, we fight on their terms, not ours. If we attack them, especially after their cavalry departs, we'll destroy them."

We walked back to his tent in silence.

When we got there, he said, "I have another small job for the two of you." He meant Krites and me, of course, and almost as soon as the words were out of his mouth, Krites arrived without being summoned. He had a habit of doing that.

* * * * * * * * * *

"You've got the wrong man!"

The man was hooded and hogtied and draped over the back of the horse that Krites and I led.

"Shut it mouth!" I said, as I faked a Persian accent and punched him in the kidneys. We were headed for the cave we'd found two days earlier on Mount Stavrokoraki.

"I don't know anything!" he wailed. "I'm just a foot-soldier. If you're working for the Persians—unnnh!"

I punched him in the kidneys again, harder this time. "Shut it mouth," I said, "or next time is knife, not fist!"

I hoped he wouldn't notice that my fake Persian accent sounded like a fake Scythian accent. Luckily, it fooled him. Themistocles told us to do this. Our prisoner was an Athenian named Korinthos. He was not to know that he was being abducted by fellow Hellenes. Themistocles said Korinthos was part of a plot to open the gates of Athens to the Persians. We were to hold him in the cave, keep him blindfolded and smack him around a little, but not to kill or maim him.

We could not use the road to Mount Stavrokoraki. Our soldiers patrolled it, and it would be impossible to satisfactorily explain to them why we'd just kidnapped an Athenian. So we were off-road. We tromped through marshland where there was no trail. The midges and mosquitoes were particularly happy to see us. It was late summer, so parts of the marsh were bone dry, which made it easier for us to pass through. The marsh eventually gave way to rocky scrubland. We left most of the mosquitoes and midges behind, but now we had to watch for snakes.

When we got our prisoner back to the cave, we beat him a little—a traitor deserves no better. He whimpered quietly but made no attempt to cry out or escape. Krites guarded him while I returned to the camp to report to Themistocles. When I got to his tent, he wasn't there. His slave told me that the generals were conferring in Kallimachos' tent. They could be in there for hours, the slave said, so he suggested that I go to my tent and get some sleep, and someone would be sent to wake me when Themistocles returned.

I slept for maybe an hour before Themistocles himself came and woke me. He was tired but oddly elated. He motioned for me to get up and accompany him. I shared the tent with others and what he wanted to say was not for their ears.

Out of earshot, he spoke in a low voice. "There's been a mistake," he said. "Korinthos is the wrong man. Let him go, but don't let him know you're Hellenes. It will be better for everybody if he continues to think the Persians abducted him."

"Yes sir," I said. "May I ask why you seem so cheerful?"

"Yes, but keep it to yourself," he said. "One more strategos changed his vote. We attack tomorrow at dawn."

* * * * * * * *

I was too excited to sleep, so I walked around the camp a little.

At one campfire, a dozen men quietly passed a jug of wine. One of them, who had a face that probably embarrassed his own mother, jumped to his feet when he saw me.

"Elektros! Join us!" he said. It was Dromeos. "I promise not to be an idiot this time."

"No harm done, friend," I said.

He shook my hand, calmly this time. "Sit here, lad," he said, indicating the empty stool beside him. Before I could sit, every one of the men here got up and shook my hand. They thought I would bring them luck. Once I sat down, they passed me the wine-jug. I took a perfunctory sip. The attack the next morning had not been officially announced to the soldiers yet, but they all seemed to know. Veteran soldiers can smell battle coming. Insomnia is not unusual the night before a battle. As often as not, it is excitement, not fear, that prevents sleep. The men all spoke quietly. No one sang. This wasn't a party. The men around me were not particularly frightened at the prospect of battle. They were all much older than me, though, and maybe they'd just learned to conceal fear convincingly.

Dromeos asked me if it was true that the Persians had battle elephants.

"No chance, Dromeos," I said. "We can see into their camp. If they had elephants, we'd know. Even one elephant is too big to hide. They're also impossible to transport by sea. I'd hate to be the poor fucker whose job it is to coax an ornery elephant onto a ship."

The men laughed. I hoped they believed me. They had many worries and I wanted them to have one less. To be honest, Ephander, I almost wished the Persians *had* brought elephants because I'd never seen one before. Grandfather had told me they were unpredictable and often as dangerous to their own army as they were to the enemy. A rampaging battle elephant can easily kill two hundred men before it is brought down. Its bellow is louder than a lion's roar, and it terrifies the piss out of the men who stand against it. Their one great disadvantage, Grandfather said, is that they're too intelligent to rush into pain and danger. Arrows bounce off their thick hides, and swords don't do much to them either, but they won't charge into fire or a mass of spears, and if they do not like how the battle is going, they'll bolt from the field, and they won't care if the men they trample are friend or foe.

"Any idea where those guys are going?" one of the men asked me. He referred to the troop of hoplites who were about to leave the camp and march back to Athens.

"Special assignment," I said. "Best not ask."

The man nodded. He understood that commanders kept secrets as a protection against enemy spies in our camp. If the men knew about the Persian plan to besiege Athens, they would only worry about their families. Some would desert and rush home. The ones that stayed would be distracted during the battle. Even the men headed back to the city did not yet know their destination.

It was past midnight. We would muster in three hours. We would move quietly, in the dark, advance to the Persian camp, then attack as the sun rose.

Just then, two of the other men had a conversation that made my hair shiver.

"You hear about Korinthos?" said one man.

"Yes," said the other. "The Persians took him, roughed him up a little, then let him go."

"I heard he escaped."

"I heard that too. The fucking Persians had him in a cave somewhere, took him outside so he could take a shit, then just left him there. He was squatting somewhere on the mountain, blindfolded, waiting for the Persians to kill him, but they never came back for him. Doesn't make a lot of sense."

"Sounds like the Persians didn't know what they were doing."

"True. Maybe the Persians fell over a cliff or something and that's why they didn't come back."

"Fuckers might've just got lost on the mountain. So where's Korinthos now?"

"In the med tent. Alive but pretty fucked up. Broken ribs and his face is a mess."

"How's his dad taking it?"

"Old Kallimachos? You know him, calm as a clam."

So Korinthos was the son of Kallimachos, the last general who changed his vote.

There had been no mistake. Korinthos was never involved in any plot with the Persians.

I was furious. Krites and I might have been the only people in all Hellas who didn't know that Korinthos was the son of Kallimachos, and Themistocles took advantage of us.

I left the fire and went looking for Themistocles.

"You're dangerously close to insubordination, boy," Themistocles said when I confronted him. He sat on the cot in his tent and sipped wine before he slept for a couple of hours.

"So what if I am, sir?" I said. "Do you plan to kill me?"

"No," he said. "I just want you to sit the fuck down and let me explain a thing or two." He indicated the stool next to his cot. I sat.

He drained his unwatered wine and stared into his cup for a moment. Then he spoke. "You are right. Korinthos was never involved in a plot. I could not tell you the truth. You have many skills, Elektros, but lying isn't one of them."

"How in Hades would you know that, sir?" I said. "I've never lied to you before."

"No, you haven't," he said, "but I'm rarely wrong about a man's character. You're a man of integrity—almost as bad as fucking Aristides sometimes. Deceit does not come easily to you."

"If this gets out, sir," I said, "Kallimachos and Korinthos and their entire tribe and circle of friends will be my enemies."

Themistocles looked at me and guffawed.

"I'm sorry to laugh, Elektros, but when it comes to politics, you're such an innocent," he said. "The moment I sponsored you as an ephebe, your name became associated with mine. My friends became your friends and my enemies became your enemies. Make no mistake, boy—Kallimachos was already your enemy."

"If he finds out I kidnapped his son, he'll want to kill me," I said.

"True," he said. "So you and Krites better keep your fucking mouths shut about it."

As I turned to leave, feeling no better, he spoke again. "Look at it another way. I did what was necessary to get our strategoi to make the right decision. They were a flea's fart away from running back to Athens. You never win a war if your actions are dictated by panic. As things stand now, we *will* win this war because of what I did—and what I got you to do. Since I kept you in the dark, I'm the only one morally or ethically tainted by this. The gods will despise me, not you. Now get the fuck out of here so I can get some sleep. You should too. In a few hours, we're going to kick the fucking Persians' asses halfway back to Susa."

11–DAY OF BLOOD

I wasn't close enough, Ephander, to see the looks on the Persians' faces, but even from a distance, their postures showed shock. As the first rays of sun crept over their camp and they emerged from their tents to take their breakfasts, they saw us and stood sculpture-still for a few moments. The entire Hellene force stood about a stade away from the Persian camp, just out of bowshot. The Persians gawked like they thought they were still asleep and only dreamt us.

Their sentries did not see us earlier. The Persians concentrated their night-time sentries on the side of their camp that was closest to the Hellene camp, but after the first few nights here they stopped venturing more than a few dozen yards beyond their camp. That's because the ones who did never came back. Krites' bow and my sword made sure of that.

Themistocles and Miltiades were immediately proven right. The Persians did not expect us to attack without the Spartans. Their intelligence about us was spectacularly wrong. Themistocles expertly used *dis*informants, spies who took Persian gold, then told them that we were terrified by their cavalry and wouldn't budge until the Spartans got here.

We left our own camp in the murk of night and waited in silence. Some of the strategoi suggested we attack while it was still dark. Miltiades would not even consider it. He'd night-attacked with an army years earlier, when he conquered the Thracian Chersonese, and knew well the disadvantages of this tactic. While there would initially be many enemy casualties, it was impossible to control your own forces in the dark. They would quickly lose formation. Our first assault might eliminate as much as a quarter of the Persian troops, but the rest of their forces would still have us outnumbered. They would regroup and counter-attack when we were out of breath and out of formation. The initial damage we'd do to them would not make up for our many casualties that would follow. The only way to avoid such casualties was to either wipe out the enemy completely on that first assault, impossible against such a large force, or have the attackers withdraw immediately after first contact, which meant we would never again have the advantage of surprise. So we waited for rosy-fingered dawn.

We were rested and relaxed. The sight of the disbelieving Persians gave our troops a huge morale boost, and won over the strategoi who still had lingering doubts about this attack. Even

Brontes, standing in the front line with his men, grinned when he saw the confused enemy. Once the Persians had seen us and there was no more point in concealment, twelve thousand men sang the war paean to Apollo. The loudness of it gave me chills.

Miltiades devised our formation the night before. Our centre, which consisted of the hoplites from two tribes, Leontis, led by Themistocles, and Antiochis, led by Aristides, stood four rows deep. The troops from the other eight tribes and the Plataeans stood eight men deep on the flanks.

Brontes was confused. "That's a formation to defend against cavalry attacks on the flanks!" he protested. "They have no cavalry here."

"We know that," said Miltiades, "but *they* don't know that we know that."

"You leave our middle weak," Brontes harped on.

Miltiades smiled and put his arm around Brontes' shoulders and spoke to him like he was a cherished but dull-witted child. "I *want* them to think our middle is weak," Miltiades said.

"Why?" Brontes asked.

Miltiades smiled indulgently at Brontes, winked, and said no more. I'll be honest, Ephander: I also didn't understand how a weak centre could be to our advantage. But I had faith in Miltiades as a strategist. He wouldn't form us up this way without a good reason.

I was armoured and ready. I wanted to fight in the Leontis phalanx, but Themistocles wouldn't let me. "I need you as a messenger," he said, "and as a second set of eyes. Besides, I promised your father I'd train you, not get you killed."

The forces across from us were a smatter of colours. Some of the Persian infantrymen, armed with axes, had red and gold crescent-shaped shields, and wore purple tunics with red and white striped trousers. The enemy soldiers directly in front of us were sparabaras. They wore white slippers—they would not stay white for long—with black-and-white patterned tunics and black-and-white striped trousers. Their shields, striped in black, white, and red, were rectangular and could cover a man from knee to crown. Brilliant as this display was, I thought it was ridiculous. This wasn't a parade or a festival. Were they planning to bedazzle us to death with their splendid colours? Did they think we'd be intimidated by their fashion sense?

As the Persians hastily formed up in front of their camp, infantry in front, archers in back, Miltiades had another surprise for them.

We charged.

Nowadays, Ephander, some people claim that our hoplites sprinted half a mile to meet the Persians at Marathon, but they're either misinformed or they deliberately exaggerate our soldiers' abilities. If they'd sprinted that distance, they'd have been too tired to fight well. The Hellenes jogged towards the Persians. If any of the men tried to run faster, their commanders ordered them to slow down and keep formation. So the bards gild the asphodel: *the Hellenes slowly jogged towards the foe* does not sound particularly heroic, so they sing of sprinting hoplites. That doesn't make it true, though.

Our men only sprinted the last twenty-five yards to the Persian line, as twelve thousand men shrieked "Elelelelelelu!" at the top of their lungs. Even this was risky. The men in our front line would be at a slight disadvantage once battle was joined, as they'd be a little winded, but the effect that the charge had on the Persians made it a risk worth taking. Miltiades had earlier ordered the Hellene commanders to put their most fit men in the front ranks, the men who could best handle a fight after a short sprint in armour. These men also had orders to rotate out of the front line quickly.

When the two sides clashed, the Persians weren't ready. Their front line was ragged, with visible gaps. I stood behind our shortened centre and could only see what was going on immediately in front of me, but I spotted something crucial in the eyes of the Persians.

Doubt.

It was not yet fear, not yet panic, but in battle, doubt can become fear or panic in moments.

I have a theory about the doubt, Ephander.

The sparabaras were armed with short swords and wicker shields. They wore no armour and had felt caps instead of helmets. They were much more vulnerable to our weapons than we were to theirs, but they were far more mobile than we were. They carried much less weight than we did and would be less affected by the summer heat. They had us outnumbered three to one, so there should have been absolutely no doubt in their minds. I believe the source of the doubt was the wicker shields. A wicker shield has advantages, the foremost being its lightness: it's no strain on the arm to hold in battle, even for hours, but if the enemy across from you is armoured in bronze and steel, and has a nine-foot spear and a thick wooden shield coated in bronze, how safe would your wicker make you feel? A half-dozen solid blows from a steel sword would shred a wicker shield. The sparabaras were equipped to strike quickly and withdraw, but in this battle, they had to go toe-to-toe with heavy infantry. This was a grievous error on the part of the Persian high command. Wicker shields are not completely useless—I've seen more than one hoplite get his spear stuck in one, only to have a Persian cut him down as he tried to pull it loose—but if I had to stand against an enemy armed with bronze and steel, I would want bronze and steel too. Not wicker.

I now understood why Themistocles and Miltiades were confident enough to attack a numerically superior enemy: *our foes were not properly equipped for the battle they were about to fight.* They could not strike quickly and withdraw because with so many men behind them, they had nowhere to go. They'd never practiced rotating in and out of the front line as we'd done. When the Persians put their cavalry on ships to Athens, they lost their main advantage.

The Persians, despite what our bards say, fought bravely. When the Hellenes crashed into their hastily formed line, they stood their ground as well as they could and died like soldiers. They fought on even after the charging Hellenes devastated their front rank. Themistocles himself fought like ten demons. Years later, when Themistocles had some vocal enemies in Athens, some of his detractors claimed that he did not actually fight at Marathon and commanded from the safety of the rear. I tell you here and now, Ephander, that this is pure horseshit. He was in the front line on the first charge. He was the first man of Leontis to make contact with the Persians, and the first to kill one. He was frighteningly fierce: I did not watch him every moment of the battle, but I saw him kill no less than eight enemy soldiers. His ferocity did not surprise me, but his skill with sword and spear did. During all of my time in Athens, I never once saw him train. Yet he must have done so. While he was physically strong and had natural stamina, no one could fight like he did without a great deal of practice. When he rotated out of the front line and came to the rear to rest, he was barely even breathing hard.

"Roll out smoothly, men of Leontis," he roared. Then he said to me, more quietly, "Report."

My height was an advantage because I could see over the enemy front ranks. This is why Themistocles wanted me here instead of one of his other runners. "The Persians in front of us are at least sixteen rows deep, sir," I said, "possibly seventeen or eighteen. They're still in some disarray, so it's hard to tell for sure. Their archers are just forming up and will shoot any second now."

The superiority of our infantry was already obvious, but the Persians could still wear us out through sheer numbers. Eighteen lines against our four? Even with frequent rotations in and out of the front line, our men in their heavy armour would soon become exhausted. How long could we keep this up? I was worried. Themistocles was not.

"Their numbers," he said, smiling, "will be their downfall."

I didn't know what that meant, and I couldn't ask because I saw movement overhead.

"Arrows incoming!" I shouted as loudly as I could. "Shields up!" Themistocles would have been hit if I hadn't warned him. He raised his shield at the last second and two arrows stuck into it. He nodded his thanks to me.

The Persian archers formed up late because our attack had surprised them. They probably wanted to drown us in a sea of arrows while we were still charging, *before* we engaged their infantry. Our last three rows got their shields up in time and suffered no casualties from the arrows. Our front line men had to keep their shields in front of them, as they were engaged with the Persian infantry, and several times I heard the sickening *ffffttt!* sound of an arrow tearing through flesh, followed by a cry of pain, but most of the arrows bounced off shields or armour, and our casualties were few. That first volley also hit some of the front-line Persians in the back. Since the sparabaras wore so little armour, and none of it on their backs, that first volley killed more Persians than Hellenes.

Behind their lines was an officer on horseback. He harangued the infantry and shrieked at the archers to keep firing. The archers did not follow his orders as crisply as he wanted them to. They'd just hit their own men and were hesitant to do it again. I could not hear the officer's words, but he was furious. He was tensed up, his face red with rage. He grabbed a spear from an infantryman's hands and used it to skewer an archer who'd been slow to follow orders.

Seconds later, the Persian officer was knocked clean off his horse by an arrow shot from beyond our flanks. The arrow had struck him in the forehead, just under the protection of his magnificently plumed helmet. I was sorry to see him die—he caused tension amongst the Persians, so it might have been better for us if he lived—but only a Scythian compound bow would have the force to kill him so cleanly, and it was no lucky shot. Krites was still with us. I prayed to every god that he shot from a safe place.

"Report to Miltiades," Themistocles told me. "Then wait there for further orders from him."

Miltiades was about sixty yards away, as he fought in the phalanx of his tribe Oineis, to our right. He'd just rotated out of the front line and caught his breath in one of the back rows of his phalanx. There was blood on his face, but it wasn't his own. When I told him about the Persian depth, he nodded and smiled but said nothing.

He would not let me join his phalanx, either. "No chance, kid," he said with a laugh. "I know what Themistocles promised your father." He was so calm, like he and I were chatting in a wine shop on a pleasant spring evening, not standing in the middle of a great battle. This only improved my confidence in him.

I couldn't fight as a hoplite, but I still tried to help. I wore my full panoply, including helmet, sword and shield, but instead of my nine-footer, I'd brought a brace of javelins, six in total. I hurled them one at a time at the Persians, from our rear, over our men and into the mass of sparabaras. The hoplites at the rear saw me do it and cheered. The men in the front were uplifted by the cheers—when you're fighting in the front line and the men behind you cheer, it picks you up, even if you don't know the cause. I didn't hit anyone with my first javelin, but I aimed the others more carefully and took a Persian out with each of them.

I did a lot of running. I ran to each tribe's strategos and got reports of how they were holding up, then returned to inform Miltiades. The heat and the battle wore down the old man, but he smiled every time I reported that our front lines were steady. The Persian archers caused casualties, but our armour limited them. One of our mounted scouts told me to report to Miltiades that the Persians did not have reserves. The news made him laugh loudly and slap me on the back.

"Best news I've heard all day, lad," he said. "They're all in. When we win this battle, their survivors, if they have any, will leave our shores."

After an hour of fighting, only a handful of men from the entire Hellene front ranks had been killed, while the Persian body count rose steadily. There were so many enemy bodies on the ground in front of us that they hindered our advance. We outfought the enemy, but each new line of Persians was fresh. Our men tired, even with frequent rotations in and out of the line. It was late summer, and though it was still morning, the heat rose continuously and took its toll on men in armour. We outfought the Persians but could still lose because of their sheer numbers. No matter how many we killed, they always had more, an infinite wave. It seemed like we couldn't even make a dent in their forces. I didn't share Miltiades' joy at their lack of reinforcements. They didn't appear to need any.

Then Miltiades unveiled his master stroke. At the time I didn't fully understand it. He ordered our centre ranks to withdraw. "Tell Themistocles and Aristides to fall back," he said to me.

I hesitated. We were winning in the centre. Surely we must continue to advance, and drive the fucking Persians back into the sea. All momentum was ours. Withdrawal looked foolish. I wasn't sure I heard him right. I just gawked.

"Run, boy, damn you!" he yelled at me. He looked like he would kill me if I failed to follow this order. So I ran and passed the order on to the two strategoi.

Both Themistocles and Aristides followed the order without question and ordered their men to withdraw. They were both in their front lines.

They walked backwards slowly, as the men behind them guided them over the fallen Persian bodies that now hindered their withdrawal.

I saw in Themistocles' face, for the only time ever, uncertainty. The Persians now looked sure of themselves. They howled war cries and surged forward, finally believing they'd worn us down and victory was within their grasp. They killed only a few of our men—our lines retreated in order, walking backwards in formation, shields up, always facing the enemy, giving them precious few places to do damage with their short swords—but, undeterred, the Persians advanced, and now it was their turn to be impeded by the dead bodies at their feet.

When we'd retreated a few dozen yards, doubt returned to the enemy's eyes. Some of the Persians noticed that the front ranks of our centre had withdrawn, but the front ranks of our flanks hadn't budged. The Persians suddenly realized their advance had been too easy.

"They're up to something!" one Persian soldier shouted to his mates.

"It's a trap!" said the man next to him. "If we don't fall back, we'll be enveloped!"

Some of the sparabaras tried to stop but were pushed forward by the mass of men behind them. Some were knocked down and trampled by their own men.

The retreat had been a ruse. Themistocles

had only pretended to be uncertain.

Miltiades relayed the order for our centre ranks to advance again. Themistocles whooped and charged forward. The men around him resurged with energy and jumped in too. The Hellenes on our flanks were eight rows deep to give the appearance of defending against cavalry. The first four rows would hold the line against the Persian infantry, but the fifth to eighth rows, with no cavalry to worry about, fell in on the Persian centre once it had over-committed against our centre.

The front-line Persians saw they were now being attacked on three sides and tried to retreat, but could not. Their commanders, behind their lines, could not see exactly what was happening and assumed the front ranks retreated from cowardice. Officers with leather whips lashed at the sparabaras' backs, and drove them forward with curses and threats. As the Hellenes on the flanks closed in on the Persian centre, it had already begun to fall apart.

The battle turned. As our reinvigorated hoplites advanced, the Persians dropped like cornstalks to a scythe. The sparabaras wanted only to get out of this field of blood but could not because their own rear ranks blocked their escape. Their retreat had no order.

Themistocles' primary task now was to control his troops. Caught up in the Black Mist, they wanted to chase the Persians. He stopped them because the Persians still had enough men to defeat us if we broke ranks.

"Hold the line!" roared Themistocles. "Steady, men of Leontis! Steady! Rotate out! Advance slowly. No need to rush. They're not going anywhere! They've got nowhere to go!"

It was true. The harder the Persians struggled to escape, the less progress they made. Our hoplites then advanced slowly, almost leisurely, killing men who could no longer defend themselves properly. Many of the Persians had dropped their shields and swords in their panic to escape and died from wounds to their backs.

"Don't kill them all!" bellowed Themistocles. "Let a few survive so they can spread panic to the men behind them!" This was a difficult order for our men to follow. In battle, when you get a chance to kill an enemy, you do it. The enemy you spare could be the one who kills you later. Few of our men actually followed the order, as most just killed and killed the retreating Persians, but some of the panicked sparabaras made it to their rear ranks, which also fell apart now. When the Persians who fought against the front-line hoplites on our flanks saw what was happening to their centre, they too collapsed and retreated.

The battle turned first into a rout, then a massacre. The ground beneath our feet was dry at the start of the battle, but now there were large patches of mud, made not by water but by Persian blood. There were spots where the blood-soaked mud was almost knee deep. I do not exaggerate.

You know the rest, Ephander. The Persians fled to their ships and did not even try to take the booty and supplies they'd left in their camp. They never came back for their dead. Their ships pushed off quickly. Some Persians, who'd tried to scramble onto ships that were already overloaded, were killed by Persian shipmasters. Any Persian who did not make it onto a ship was slaughtered where he stood. We could have taken hundreds, possibly thousands, of prisoners, but we did not. The Hellenes' blood was up, and Miltiades decided that the men needed what he would later call a 'therapeutic massacre.' No enemy wounded were spared.

One hundred and ninety two Athenian and Plataean mothers lost sons that day. But this is nothing compared to the six and a half thousand Persian bodies we found on the battlefield, in the Persian camp, and in the marshes behind it.

After the battle, and after the adrenaline of combat had worn off, our men sagged visibly. They were exhausted and wanted to drift into sweet dreams–for many, their first restful night's sleep in days–but we could not stop yet. The Persians had sent troops by ship to besiege Athens. Miltiades ordered three hundred men to rest for two hours and then deal with the bodies on the battlefield. The rest of our troops were also told to rest for two hours, and then march back to Athens to relieve the siege. Miltiades knew that two hours rest was hardly enough for men who'd been awake most of the previous night and then fought a long battle in summer heat, and the gods know he was himself exhausted, but he had no choice.

The fallen Hellenes would be buried with honour right where they fell. Some of the strategoi wanted to just leave the Persians to rot where they died, but Miltiades refused to consider this. "So many rotting corpses," he explained, "will spread disease to the local population. Last thing we need now is a typhus epidemic." The Persian bodies would be thrown into huge pits and burned.

Krites and I returned to our tent. Krites slept for two hours. I did not. I was still wound up from the battle. I was wide awake when Miltiades summoned Krites and me to his tent.

12–HIPPIAS

Were we insane? The battle was won. The Persians didn't besiege Athens, never even got there. Once the Battle of Marathon was lost, they sailed to shores friendlier than ours. Yet we followed them, Krites and me. We snuck off our little skiff onto the beach on Lemnos in the rain and the dark and the cold, then slithered into the woods like a pair of wet whip snakes. Bone tired, too. Couldn't remember the last time I'd slept. How I felt mattered little. This final task could not wait. It had to be done while the Persians were still close. The Persian commanders planned to rest overnight on Lemnos before they sailed away from this embarrassment. Old Hippias still travelled with the Persian general Datis. Our mission was simple. Hippias must not leave Lemnos alive.

The bards had already begun to exaggerate Hellenic courage and Persian cowardice at Marathon. The Hellenes had united magnificently against a mighty foe, but with this victory their aggressive impulses now lacked an external target. The Athenians resented the Hellenes who did not fight beside them, particularly the Thebans, who sided with the Persians, and the Spartans, who strutted to Marathon the day after the battle, inspected the battlefield, saw the pit filled with burning Persian corpses, and then sent an embassy to Miltiades to say that they approved of the battle. Did they think their approval mattered to the rest of us? Miltiades laughed in the Spartans' faces and said he approved of them kissing his wrinkled old ass. The Spartans just shrugged and marched back to Sparta.

The Hellenic poleis would soon fight each other again. It was our grand tradition. The question was *when*, not *if*.

If troop numbers were all that mattered, the Persians still had a great army. Even with all their casualties, they still outnumbered us, but they were broken, a spent force. It showed in a hundred little ways. On Lemnos, Datis had sentries posted around the house where Hippias spent the night, but even from a distance Krites and I could see that the sentries shuffled like they didn't care. They just wanted to go home. They didn't give a rat's ass about Hippias. We'd heard the rumour that back in Susa, the Great King himself had lost faith in the old man, and only honour prevented him from executing his guest. How could the Persians trust him now? Betrayal is addictive. Hippias had betrayed his countrymen to the Persians and would just as easily betray the Persians to his countrymen. Darius wouldn't lose sleep if someone took the old man out of his immaculately coiffed hair. It was also not lost on Krites and me that Hippias' house warranted only four sentries. Datis had twenty sentries around his small command tent. Hippias' safety was much less important to the Persians now than it had been before the battle.

After the battle, most of our soldiers rushed back to Athens to fight the Persians again, only to find that the Persians had changed their minds and headed back home. We'd also heard rumours that Hippias' health was failing. Miltiades said maybe we should just wait for the old man to die. "He's already told the Persians all he has to tell them," he said to the other strategoi. "If the Persians invade again in a few years, Hippias won't be around. He's eighty-three. How long can the old bugger possibly live?"

Miltiades was not himself when he said this. It was the fatigue talking, and perhaps the elation of victory had given him an impractical sense of clemency. Hippias, the former tyrant of Athens, advised the Persians about the best ways to defeat Hellenes. He betrayed us in the hope that the victorious Persians would reinstall him as the tyrant of Athens. He could not be forgiven. He had to die, and soon. If we let him live, the other Hellene leaders would be outraged. Miltiades, a great commander, was a man of action. It was never his style to wait for a problem to go away.

Sure enough, once he'd had a cup of mulled spiced wine and a couple of hours of sleep, he summoned Krites and me to his tent. Themistocles was there too.

Miltiades said only one word to us: "Hippias."

Krites and I understood.

"The ship is ready now," said Themistocles. Off we went to Lemnos, to slither onto the beach in the rain and the dark and the cold.

An hour after rosy-fingered dawn, when the rain had lightened to a soft drizzle, a man brought a tray of pastries to two Persian sentries who guarded a house. The man, a beggar with grey in his beard and rips in his tunic, babbled to himself before he got anywhere near the amused Persians. A local lunatic. Harmless enough. "Sweet cakes for brave soldier!" the man said in battered Persian. "Sell cheap! Two cake, one obol. Good businesses!"

"No thanks, old man," said one of the soldiers, not unkindly. The soldiers were probably hungry, and the price was good. They just had no appetite for anything this filthy beggar had handled.

"You no get price more good!" the old man insisted. "Cheaper than cheaps!"

The soldier growled at the old man.

"We've told you nicely that we don't want any," he said. "Now fuck off before you get hurt."

The old man wouldn't let it go. "Sweet! Cheap! Four cakes, one obol! How you no like?"

The soldier lost his patience and knocked the old man's tray out of his hands. The cakes scattered on the ground. The old man bent over to pick them up.

That was the signal.

Before the soldier knew anything had happened, an arrow ripped through his throat.

The second soldier's eyes had barely widened in surprise before his blood stained the ground: the old man, with impossible quickness, had slashed his jugular with a hunting knife in a single deft motion. Neither of the soldiers had made a sound to alert the two sentries on the other side of the house. It was right after the sentries' morning shift change, so the bodies might not get noticed right away.

Krites had shot the arrow, of course. Ashes in my hair and beard, and a few rips in my tunic, had turned me into the old man. I bought the cakes from a local baker. I did not worry about the accuracy of Krites' shot. He *always* hit his target. The hard part for me was that I had to pretend to speak pidgin Persian, because my Persian is actually pretty good.

We dragged the guards' bodies into the house. Security was so lax that the door wasn't bolted. The guards' blood outside the door would soon be washed away by the drizzly rain, and we'd be long gone before anyone found the blood and mud we'd tracked inside.

The house had two floors and a cellar. Old Hippias would not want to climb stairs, so we looked for him on the first floor. We found him quickly. He was asleep in the main bedchamber. A pretty black-haired slave girl slept beside him. Her presence proved that Hippias had enough vigour to live on for years. It would have been a mistake to just wait for him to die. The girl woke with a start as I pulled her to her feet and put my hand over her mouth.

I twisted one of her arms behind her back. "I will not hurt you if you don't make a sound," I whispered into her ear, in Persian. "I will take you to a room upstairs and leave you there. You will not attempt to leave or cry out until the Persian soldiers call for you. Do this and you live. Understand?"

Terror still widened her eyes, but she nodded. I would spare her. Miltiades and I did not see eye to eye on this. He insisted I just kill anyone I encountered on a mission. Slaves and bystanders were expendable, he said, and less trouble to us dead than alive, but it did not sit right with me to kill this girl. It served no purpose. She'd done nothing, and it's not likely that she even shared the old man's bed voluntarily. She would not die by my hand. And yes, Ephander, I knew that the Persians would probably kill her. We would kill Hippias, the Persians would be embarrassed, so they would eliminate anyone who witnessed that embarrassment. The two sentries on the other side of the house would also be executed. Then the Persians would report that Hippias had died of natural causes.

I quickly dragged the girl into an upstairs room, left her there, and blocked the door with a chair so she couldn't get out easily.

Krites stood silently outside Hippias' bedchamber. Good as he was with the bow, he didn't like knife-work. That was my job. Hippias woke up as soon as I entered the room.

He smiled, even though he knew why I was there.

"A Hellene who looks like a Scythian," he said, his tone slightly mocking. "I am honoured, Elektros of Skiathos. I'm also surprised it took you so long to get here."

He knew that he had only seconds to live but didn't seem worried. He'd probably been close to death so many times during his long life that once more wasn't going to shake him.

I stepped over to him with my knife.

He put up his hand and I paused. "Kill me, Elektros," he said, "and do it right. But I'm not the only person in this room who has taken Persian gold."

I slit his throat before he could say another word, wishing only that I'd done it a few seconds sooner.

As his blood gushed over his blankets and bedclothes, I swear he had a smile on his face.

"Persian gold?" Krites asked me. "What's he talking about?"

"He was old and confused," I said. "He's either making it up or he's mistaken us for someone else."

Krites and I disappeared like a smoke whiff in a windstorm. No one saw us enter or leave the house. No one pursued. The dead old man and the dead sentries were the only signs we'd ever been on Lemnos. We got our skiff from where we'd hidden it, in a mulberry thicket close to the beach, and rowed to the dark ship anchored in a nearby cove.

When I told Krites that Hippias lied when he said one of us had taken Persian gold, as a tactic to sow doubt between us, I truly believed it. As we crawled over the railing of the trireme that would take us back to Athens, however, I suddenly realized that Hippias had spoken the truth.

I'd taken Persian gold. Until now, I hadn't known it.

If Hippias knew, who else did?

13–OUTCOME

A day and a half later, Krites and I were back in Athens. Still wet, tired, cold, and hungry, we walked through the Itonian gate and saw a city in chaos. But it wasn't panic or despair. It was the exact opposite, the celebratory havoc of victory, of boundless relief. The great enemy who'd sworn to kill or enslave us all had been soundly beaten. It was early afternoon, but almost everyone we saw was drunk. Men rutted openly with whores, bending them over on hands and knees and plowing them right there in the street. This was unusual behaviour–Athenians are naturally prudish, at least in public–but these were unusual times. The Persian threat, which had hung over all of us for so long, was over, at least temporarily. Euphoria was everywhere. (In fact, a large percentage of the girls born in Athens in the next few months would be named Euphoria.) Who could begrudge the people of Athens a little wild behaviour?

Two women approached Krites and me. They were cheerful, a little drunk, and topless. They were both past thirty–ancient for the hard life of a prostitute—but both were still pretty. One was fair-skinned and blonde, the other African, black-haired with skin as dark as Anatolian oak.

"Special today for soldiers," said the blonde. "Two for the price of one. How 'bout it, boys?"

I was tempted. Hey, Ephander, I was seventeen. I was *always* tempted, but we had to report to Themistocles before we could indulge. "Dear ladies," I said, "there's nothing I'd like more than a good hard fuck and ten hours sleep. Maybe later, when we're off duty."

"Maybe later we'll still be here," said the dark one, laughing. The two women headed towards a group of men up the street.

Most Athenians thought the Battle of Marathon was the end of our struggle with the Great King. This was wishful thinking that bordered on delusion. The Persians had left for the season but they'd be back, and they'd bring an even larger force next time. Few Athenians understood that the great army we defeated at Marathon was only a small percentage of the Persians' armed forces, and easily replaceable. They'd lost the last battle but their campaign was successful overall. They'd taken control of the Cyclades, including Naxos and sacred Delos, they'd crushed Eretria, and they'd asserted their control of our seas, where their three hundred warships would not be challenged, or even mildly inconvenienced, by the grand total of eight warships the Athenians had at the time. The loss at Marathon did no harm to their empire. The people of Athens had just survived a year of stress, duress, and distress, so I wasn't going to trample their begonias by telling them that we'd probably have to do it all again next year. Cruel reality could wait until the party was over. That could take days.

Most of the troops had returned to Athens. The ones not required for sentry duty returned to their homes. Krites and I found Themistocles at his house. He sat at a table, still in his blood-spattered armour, and dictated a letter to a slave who jotted it down with a stylus and wax tablet. Themistocles looked like he hadn't slept since we'd last seen him.

Themistocles stopped talking when we entered, and merely raised his eyebrows.

I nodded once.

He grinned broadly and told the slave to go get himself something to eat.

"You're back sooner than I expected," he said as soon as the slave left.

"The task was easier than expected, sir," I said. "Hippias is no longer the apple of the Great King's eye. He was guarded by four apathetic men. We got in, did the job, got out quickly. No one saw us, and no one pursued."

"Any chance he survived?" asked Themistocles. He had to ask me this, to make sure we hadn't left him wounded with a chance of recovering.

"If you want to know if he's still alive, sir," said Krites, pulling Hippias' head out of his knapsack, "ask him yourself!"

Themistocles guffawed. He clapped his hands and beamed at us. "Well done, Elektros and Krites," he said. "I knew I could count on you guys. Give me the head. I'll show it to the other strategoi, then dispose of it privately."

Krites handed it over. Themistocles was ready to dismiss us, but I asked to have a private word with him. He agreed, so I sent Krites back to the Scythian barracks to get some sleep. Before he left, Themistocles tossed him a silver drachma. "Get yourself a whore later, boy," he said. "You've earned it. They're in a generous mood today, you might even be able to get two."

Krites left, grinning.

"So what's on your mind, Elektros?" Themistocles said.

"A minor domestic problem, sir," I said. "It's about the money you sent me last year, after I scouted Mardonius' forces in Thrace."

"Yes," he said. "What of it?"

"I never properly thanked you for it, sir," I said.

"No need, lad. You earned it. That's thanks enough."

"Exactly how much did you send me?"

"A half talent of silver. Why do you ask? Surely you trust your father to safe-keep it for you."

"Yes sir, I trust my father. I'm not so sure about a couple of our slaves. Father was not at home when the payment arrived, and I just wanted to make sure they didn't pocket any of it. So it was exactly a half-talent of silver and nothing more, right?"

"Exactly a half-talent of silver," he said, "and nothing more, although I'll give you and Krites more than the price of a whore for the job you just did."

This proved Hippias' claim that I'd taken Persian gold. When I got home from Thrace the previous year, there was a half-talent of silver *and* a quarter-talent of gold waiting for me. If Themistocles sent only the silver, then who sent the gold? Mardonius, most likely. Even though I'd done it unwittingly, I had taken a sizeable payment in Persian gold. I was as tainted as any traitor who'd been paid off by the enemy. If word of this got out, no Hellene would completely trust me for the rest of my life. It would have been different if we'd taken it as plunder—no one squawked about the gold darics Krites and I had taken from the two Persians and the Hellene traitor we'd killed on Mount Stavrokoraki—but the quarter-talent was delivered right to my home. I admired the cunning of whoever thought of this. They knew I'd think the gold came from Themistocles, and that from Skiathos I wouldn't be in close communication with him.

Who else knew about the gold? Themistocles? He never mentioned it, but based on the depth of his intelligence about everything else, he probably did.

"Anything else, Elektros?" he said.

"No, sir, just that," I replied.

"Then you are dismissed. Get some sleep. Take three days leave, too. You've earned it." He then called for another slave, who he sent to inform the ephebe commander that I was on leave.

I left. We'd just accomplished a great victory, so I shouldn't have felt as demoralized as I did. I guess I'd hoped that Themistocles would tell me that he sent me the gold. But I was cheered up by a familiar voice as soon as I stepped out of Themistocles' house.

"Lectoros is back!" the voice said. "Men of Hellas, lock up your daughters!"

"Lock up daughters?" said another voice. "Lock up *goats*!"

Madyes and Scylurus always made me laugh. "So you guys left me some girls and goats?" I said. "Thank the gods for that!"

We embraced. When a Scythian hugs you, it's always a bone-crushing constriction that makes your lungs shut down for a few seconds. The more he likes you, the harder the hug.

"You do us big fuck favour!" said Scylurus. "Fucking Hellenes want put us in prison! Not do because of you. We thank!"

This was true. There had been Scythians among the Persian forces. Even though they were northern Scythians, who were usually at war with the southern tribes that the Scythians in Athens came from, the Athenians were worried that the Scythians here might take up the Persian cause. Scythians had been present in Athens for several decades now, but the Athenians still did not understand them. The Scythians in Athens considered the Great King an enemy—they would've wanted to fight *alongside* the Athenians. They'd also sworn loyalty to Athens, but the Athenians also failed to understand how seriously the Scythians took oaths. If they'd been imprisoned during the battle, they would have considered their oaths voided, and when they were eventually released, they would be extremely hostile to the Athenians. One thing you don't want, Ephander, is Scythians angry at you.

Before the Athenian forces left for Marathon, I told Themistocles of Kallimachos' plan to imprison the Scythians. He'd been so busy with the million other details of war preparation that he had not even been aware of it. Themistocles, to his credit, immediately understood what a mistake this would be and quickly arranged for the Scythians to be sent to Plataea for the duration of the battle. With all of Plataea's soldiers at Marathon, the Scythians would be needed to guard the polis from bandits and raiders. More importantly for Athens, though, was that the Scythians saved face. They came back to Athens relaxed, cheerful, and ready to police the polis with their usual aplomb.

"We have feast tonight," said Scylurus. "You come." It was a command, not an invitation.

"I'll be there," I said, "as long as I can get some sleep first. I've been awake for three or four days."

"You good!" said Scylurus. He then slapped me on the back so hard he almost knocked me over.

"What's the occasion?" I asked.

Scylurus turned away. There were tears in his eyes. He wouldn't speak.

"Scylurus is leaving Athens," Madyes said. "His term here is done, so he'll head back to the land of the Saka in a few days. We also have a ceremony we want you to witness."

I headed to the ephebe barracks. I was almost there when I was met by Hyperion and Krios. They openly hugged me, which neither of them had ever done before.

"Careful, guys," I said. "Proxenos could see us."

"We don't need to worry about him

anymore," said Hyperion.

"Did that asshole finally lose his job?" I asked.

"Come with us," said Krios. "We have something to show you."

"Can it wait?" I said. "I'm dead on my feet. I must sleep."

"This won't take long," said Hyperion. "You'll sleep better after you see it."

We walked over to the agora. The butt of a spear had been stuck into the dirt between the agora paving stones. A man's head was on the spearhead. The bloodied face was surrounded by a thick mop of red hair and a matted beard. The front teeth had been knocked out. There was no spot on the face that wasn't bloody or bruised. It wasn't decomposed, so it hadn't been there long.

"Anybody I know?" I asked.

"Actually, yes," said Hyperion. "You've seen him before. He was one of the raiders we fought. His brother was their leader, the big guy."

"They were *all* big guys," I said.

"The leader was the biggest of them," said Krios, "the one you killed after his axe got stuck in your shield."

"So this guy was looking for me?" I said.

"Yes," said Hyperion, "but you were his secondary target."

"Who was his primary target?" I said.

Before either of them could answer, a

mule-wagon rattled past us. It was headed out of the city. Hyperion made the driver stop. There was a body in the back of the wagon, wrapped in a filthy brown sheet.

"I carry a traitor," the driver protested. "Best let me get him out of the city as soon as possible." Athenians denied funerary rites to traitors. The driver's task was to take the body ten miles out of the city and dump it there for the kites and the dogs and the crows.

"We won't delay you more than a minute, good sir," Hyperion said as he pressed a coin into the driver's hand. He took the coin but still made the sign to avert the evil eye.

"The barbarian killed his primary target," said Krios. He reached into the back of the wagon and pulled the sheet back.

It was Proxenos. His throat had been cut so deeply that his head was almost severed.

"The raiders came," said Hyperion, his face taut as he tried to control his rage, "because Proxenos told them the city would be weakly defended. You were supposed to die in that battle. Proxenos wanted you dead so badly that he didn't care if the rest of us got killed too. Did you notice that the raiders targeted you? We won the battle, which wasn't supposed to happen. Proxenos promised the raiders an easy skirmish against a bunch of boys, after which he would've opened the gates for them, so they could rape and loot at their leisure."

We sent the wagon driver on his way. We did not speak. What was there to say? It was a depth of treachery we couldn't comprehend. To get me killed, Proxenos would sacrifice innocent lives, possibly hundreds of them, because who knows how many women and children the raiders would've killed if they'd gotten into the city? They'd given Proxenos gold, but he came from a moderately wealthy family, so it's not like he needed it.

Hyperion was right. I would sleep better knowing that when our ephebe training resumed, it would not be with Proxenos. As Hyperion and Krios walked me back to the barracks, where with the gods' sweet blessing I would finally get some sleep, they gave me more details. The dead barbarian was a warrior but no plotter. He saw Proxenos in the agora in broad daylight, and just walked up to him and slit his throat. There were a few soldiers present, and they subdued the man quickly. Hyperion saw it all, and was present later when Miltiades interrogated the barbarian, who spoke some Hellenic. After the man was kicked and punched almost senseless, Miltiades offered him a choice: if he talked, he'd have a quick and painless death. If he did not talk, he'd be tortured for several days, after which he'd still die. He chose to speak.

I went to the barracks and slept for seven

hours—that's a lot for me, I usually get by on three or four hours a night—then went to celebrate with the Scythians.

*   *   *   *   *   *   *   *   *   *

In the piercing harvest moonlight, Scylurus and Krites emerged red-eyed from the small tent. Normally, the other Scythians might make bawdy comments about what they were doing in there, but this was a sacred occasion, so they said nothing. Scylurus and Krites were in the tent to take *dreamsmoke*, as the Scythians called it. The Scythians considered it sacred. Only their priestesses and holy men used it more than a few times a year. They claimed it opened the mind, brought clarity, and induced spiritually meaningful dreams. The smoke came from the dried leaves of the cannabis plant, which was common in the Scythians' homeland. The fumes, when inhaled, were a euphoriant and had medicinal uses. That sodden twaddler Herodotus claims that the dreamsmoke came from burning cannabis seeds on a brazier. He was right about the brazier but wrong about the seeds. Madyes told me that it was the leaves and resin around the seeds that gave the smoke its power. The seeds themselves had no effect.

We were in my ash grove that overlooked the Ilissos. The solemn occasion this evening was the blood-brother bonding ritual of Scylurus and Krites. I'd just spent two days alone with Krites, and he never once mentioned it. I admit, Ephander, I was jealous. I'd known the Scythians longer than Krites did. I was half-Scythian and even related by blood to one of them, but none of them offered the blood brotherhood to me. Make no mistake, the Scythians always treated me well, like I was one of them. They would defend me to the death, as I would for them. We were guest-friends, which was as sacred to them as it is to Hellenes. Even so, it was to Krites that they'd taken a liking in a way they did with no other Hellene.

Scylurus said he felt a powerful bond to Krites the moment he laid eyes on him. It did not matter that Scylurus was twenty-two years older than Krites, or that Krites was a Hellene slave. To the Scythians, blood brothers were equals. An insult or injury to one of the blood-brothers would automatically bring the vengeance of the other. A Scythian considered his blood-brother as important as his family, and the ritual was not undertaken lightly. While a king might have several blood-brothers, most Scythians had only one. They would take another only if the first died in battle.

I was truly happy for Krites, so I swallowed

my envy. The day I first met him, he was a tiny sad slave child that Xenocrates ordered me to kill with a sword. I refused to do it, even with Xenocrates screaming at me. Now here he was, still a slave but befriended and respected by the greatest warriors in the known world.

After the blood-brothers-to-be emerged from the dream-smoke tent, they stood by a bonfire hand-in-hand. Before you jump to your usual lewd conclusions, Ephander, I'll tell you right now that the blood-brother bond was not sexual. Such activity between blood-brothers was permitted but not common. The bond was more spiritual than anything else.

The incantations began. The Scythians paid me a huge compliment by allowing me to be here. No other outsiders were, and two Scythians guarded the pathway to the grove to prevent intrusion. We linked arms in a circle around the blood-brothers and the fire. Aki's mother was a priestess, so he was familiar enough with the ritual to lead us. He chanted and the rest of the Scythians responded. This took two hours.

Then the blood-brothers chanted oaths of loyalty to each other, which according to custom bound them together in this world and the next. Krites enunciated the Scythian phrases perfectly. He started to learn the language the day he got to Athens, and after only a couple of months could converse in Scythian. "They have over a hundred different words for 'horse,'" Krites once told me. "No exaggeration."

Aki brought forward a special cup of wine. Scylurus pulled out a dagger, opened a vein in his wrist, and let several drops of his blood drip into the cup. Krites took the dagger and did the same. Aki held the cup in front of him as Scylurus and Krites dipped the points of their swords, the ends of their bows, and the tips of their daggers and spears into the blood and wine. They chanted together for a few minutes. Then they drank the cup together. They did not take turns: they both drank at the same time, putting their mouths close together and tipping the cup so that each man drank the same amount at the same time. They even swallowed in unison. They did this three times and drained the cup on the last one.

Then Scylurus and Krites hugged each other heartily as the rest of us cheered. Gifts were given to the blood-brothers. Krites, who'd already been given a Scythian compound bow by Scylurus, was presented with a magnificent leather and bronze gorytos.

My gift to the blood-brothers was that I would purchase Krites' freedom from Xenocrates. When Scylurus returned to Scythia, he'd want to take Krites with him. It was a crime in Athens to knowingly taking another man's slave, even when the slave was owned by a non-Athenian. So I would formally purchase Krites from Xenocrates, then manumit him. It would take some time—I could not return to Skiathos until my first term as an ephebe finished in two months—but it would make everything nice and legal.

Once the gifts were given, everyone got roaring drunk. They danced. They sang. Aki played up-tempo tunes on his bird's foot-bone flute, while others clapped hands or tapped a spear against a shield to keep the beat.

After a couple of hours of watching Krites and the Scythians dance and stumble around and get progressively drunker, I left. On the trail back to Athens, I heard voices, women laughing.

It was Phylo and ten prostitutes.

"You sure you want to go up there, big brother?" I said. "They're pretty plastered and they don't take kindly to visitors."

"They know I'm coming, little brother," he said. "They told me I couldn't witness the ritual but could join the celebration afterwards. These, uh, *additional entertainers* are my gift to the blood brothers. Think they'll be glad to see me?"

"I know they will," I laughed.

14–JUSTICE

The next day, I was summoned to Themistocles' house. He'd finally taken off his bloody armour. He'd bathed, had his hair combed and curled, and wore a deep red tunic.

"I'm sponsoring games," Themistocles said to me. "I'd like you to compete."

"I'd love to, sir," I said, "but I'm not freeborn."

"These are not the Delian games," he said, "or the Olympics. Post-battle celebration games have more relaxed rules. As sponsor, I can permit slaves and freedmen to compete. You are known to most Athenians, so it would do them good to see you run a race. Your slave birth is still an issue for some people, though, so you should compete in only one event."

Along with boxing, wrestling, javelin, and discus events, Themistocles' games would include the *dolichos*, a two-and-a-half mile footrace, and the *diaulos*, a four-hundred-yard sprint. I would run the latter.

The races would be in two days in the fields outside the Diochares Gate. I spent the time resting.

The diaulos was the first event. As I limbered up, a man approached me.

"Elektros of Skiathos?" he said. He was in his thirties, blonde and fit, with a scar on the left side of his face that started above his eye and ran down his cheek. Whoever gave him the scar probably did not live to tell about it. There was an air of menace to this man. His hair was cropped short and he wore a breastplate. He was not as tall as me, but was muscular and outweighed me by twenty-five or thirty pounds. This was a fighter.

"I am," I said. "Who are you?"

He ignored that. "Interested in buying a slave?" he said.

"You don't look like a slave dealer," I said.

"Hey, pal, are you interested or not?" He was actually trying to intimidate me. I was trained by Xenocrates. I was not easily intimidated.

"Get the fuck away from me," I said.

I looked him straight in the eye. I thought one of the other sprinters sent him to disrupt my concentration. He held my gaze for a few seconds, then shrugged and left.

A couple of minutes later, he returned. "We got off on the wrong foot, Elektros," he said. He still looked menacing, but I saw now that it came so naturally to him that he couldn't *not* do it.

"Give it up, asshole," I said. "It's counterproductive to rile me up. Just makes me run faster."

"I don't give a shit about the race," he said. "My name is Anakletos." He held out his hand for me to shake. I didn't.

After a few awkward seconds, he pulled his hand back and said, "I'm looking for my nephew Agapios."

Something wasn't right about this guy. With his blonde hair and green eyes, he resembled Agapios a little. But I still didn't believe him.

"Agapios," I said, "is a name I haven't heard in a long time." This was no lie. He was Krites now. I'd almost forgotten his original name.

"I heard that he might've come to Athens," he said. "Did he happen to contact you?"

I understood now. Anakletos first asked me if I wanted to buy a slave because he wanted to find out if I already had one, namely Krites.

"You don't have a slave for sale, do you?" I said.

"No," he admitted. He forced a laugh. Intimidation didn't work, so now he tried friendliness. He wasn't very good at it. Menace was natural for him. Charm was not. "I spoke to Xenocrates a few days ago, and he thought Agapios might've come here."

Now *this* was startling. When Krites first got to Athens, he told me that Xenocrates had sent him here to serve as my slave. Now Anakletos just told me that Xenocrates did not actually know where Krites was.

"My race is about to start," I said.

"We'll talk later," said Anakletos.

"Not if I can help it," I said. "You're not Agapios' uncle and everything else you've said is horseshit. Go bother someone else."

Anakletos frowned and walked away. I put him out of my mind. After the race I'd go and talk to Krites about the situation.

Of the race itself, Ephander, there is little to tell. I was well rested, but all the other runners spent the last few days drinking and whoring. For some, the race was an inconvenient interruption of their revelries. As we lined up to start, one of the other runners said, "Let's get this over with. Moira's pussy's getting cold!" Everybody laughed. Moira was a well-known hetaera.

I won easily but can't claim a great victory. I smelled wine on the breath of the men nearest to me. Some came directly from the brothel to this race, and returned there immediately afterwards. When the race started, one man took off like a burnt jackrabbit and led for the first twenty yards, but he immediately struggled with the pace. I passed him easily. I didn't go all out and still crossed the finish line twenty feet ahead of the guy who came second.

"No fair!" one of the others shouted. "How can we possibly beat the Scythian? He's not shit-faced like the rest of us!" I laughed with everyone else. Few if any of the spectators had bothered to place bets.

Despite the lack of seriousness by the other runners, the spectators—all men, as no proper Athenian would allow his womenfolk to watch naked men run—were in good spirits, probably because they were as drunk as the runners were. "True son of Belkos!" they cried out, and "The Scythian of Skiathos!" They cheered me, and at that moment I would have been willing to swear to all the gods that my slave birth was not an issue in Athens anymore.

How little I knew. More about that later, Ephander.

After the race, I went to see Krites at the Scythian barracks. I made sure Anakletos didn't follow me. I saw him go into a brothel. Did he think he'd find Krites in there?

When I got to the Scythian barracks, Krites had just finished packing his few belongings in a gunny sack.

"You could've told me," I said.

Krites had tears in his eyes. "You would've turned me in," he said.

"Apollo's balls I would have!" I said. "Slave or not, you're my friend."

"I didn't mean it like that."

"Then how did you mean it?"

"I trust you with my life, Lex, you know that," he said. "But you're not a good liar. You might've given me away unintentionally."

There was some truth to this. "So why did you leave Skiathos?"

"Do you remember the day you and I first met?" he asked me.

I did. I was eight years old. Krites was six. Xenocrates had tied him to a post behind his shack and ordered me to kill Krites with a sword. I refused. Xenocrates screamed abuse at me, and again ordered me to kill Krites. Again I refused. Xenocrates did this to test my judgment, to see how readily I would kill a helpless person I had no reason to kill. Xenocrates was terrifying when he yelled like that, and I never told Krites how close I actually came to sticking a sword in his guts.

"Xenocrates took on another student," he said. "A rich man's son, a sniveling prick named Diocles." I knew of Diocles and agreed with Krites' assessment. Krites pulled down the top of his tunic to show me a three-inch scar on his stomach, just under his ribcage. "Xenocrates ordered Diocles to kill me, and the fucker ran me through without a second thought. Xenocrates refused to train him, told him to leave. 'My slave is useless now,' he said. 'Your father owes me a new one.' Then Xenocrates left me to die in the dirt by the goat pen. Didn't lift a finger to help me. I was lucky Ling was home, because she carried me inside, treated my wound and nursed me back to health. It took three months, and every day

Xenocrates yelled at her to just let me die. I was totally insignificant to Xenocrates. I always did everything he told me. He never once disciplined me because he never once needed to. This is how he rewards me. After I recovered, he took on another student, another pampered son of a rich man. I ran away because the sword test was coming up again."

"So who's this guy who says he's your uncle?" I asked.

"No relative of mine," he said. "Anakletos is a mercenary, and sometimes he tracks slaves. Xenocrates fought with him in Persia."

"I figured him for a liar the moment I met him," I said. "Plus he's not much of a slave tracker. If you want to avoid him, just stay out of the wine shops and the whorehouses."

"He's not particularly smart," said Krites. "he's sneaky, though. He can be dangerous."

"So where will you go?" I said. I was getting teary-eyed too.

"Can't tell you," he said, "for the same reason I couldn't tell you I escaped. You'll figure it out."

In fact, I already had. He would go, eventually, to Scythia. Scylurus was leaving Athens in a few days, so Krites would probably wait for him somewhere east of here. The further east Krites went, the harder it would be for a slave tracker, even a competent one, to find him. Once he reached Scythia, he'd be safe. No slave trackers ever went there.

I hugged Krites and tried to give him my pouch full of coins. He refused it. "I've still got my share of the gold darics we took from the Persians," he said, "and the silver Themistocles gave us." Themistocles had paid us nicely for the Hippias job. Krites saved his share because he'd anticipated this day.

Later, Krites rode a horse through the Dipylon Gate, which led *away* from the Phaleron. He assumed that Anakletos, once he pulled his dick out of a prostitute long enough to think of it, would watch the port. Krites was probably headed west to Megara, to take a ship from there to Ionia, or wherever Scylurus would meet him. The Scythians regarded Krites so highly that they'd given him one of their two precious horses. The next day, I used some of my silver to buy them another.

I resumed training with the other ephebes. In less than two months, we would complete our first year. Old Linos trained us again. He worked us hard, punished slackness more severely than Proxenos did, and would not tolerate a lack of effort from anyone. He was unerringly fair, though, and we all liked and respected him.

Four days after we resumed training, Linos called me into his office, which was a tiny room in the barracks that was so cramped that he could not sit at the desk and close the door at the same time. So he left the door open, sat on the table, and told me to sit on the chair.

"What's this I hear," he said, "about you training in secret with some of the others?"

I cursed to myself. Idiotic Proxenos never found out, but Linos was on to us in a few days.

It was pointless to deny it. "Sir," I said, "please don't make us stop. The boys really benefit from it, and they're teaching me to dance, and—"

He put up his hand to shut me up and actually laughed. "Make you stop?" he said. "Why would I want ephebes not to train in their spare time? That doesn't make a lick of sense, boy!"

"Our previous trainer, sir, ordered the other ephebes not to fraternize with me. If he found out about this, he would've punished us and ordered us to stop."

"Well, I don't want you to stop," he said. "Nobody told me who the other boys are, but I can guess. Krios, Damoxenos, Capros, Philostratos, and you are better swordsmen than the others. Same with the hand-to-hand fighting."

"Is that a bad thing, sir?"

"Fuck no! You think I called you in here to punish you, boy?"

"Sir, I've never been called in here for any other reason."

Linos laughed again. "I'd heard you were a fiend for training. Until now, I never understood how much. So know this: you don't have to keep it secret anymore. I don't give a honeyed fuck about who fraternizes with who. If you guys train in your spare time, then you have less time to get drunk in the wine shop."

Linos then took a wine jug from his desk, offered me a cup.

"No thank you, sir," I said. "I'm no drinker."

He poured himself a cup and sipped it. "Did you know that some of the others have followed your example and sworn off wine?"

I'd heard this. "Is that a bad thing, sir?" I said.

"No. Wine is good for easing your sorrows at the end of the day, but ephebes are fitter if they avoid it."

Linos wanted to see some of the drills we were doing on our own. I demonstrated them to him on our training ground outside the barracks. He approved of all of them but cautioned me not to over-emphasize the importance of sword-fighting. "In the phalanx, you fight with the spear," he said. "You're part of a team. Never forget that. You use your sword only if your spears are broken, or your formation falls apart, or if the enemy's phalanx collapses and you're pursuing them. In many battles, your sword stays in its sheath."

Linos told me if I'd let other ephebes train with us, we could use the barracks training ground. I would still go to the grove sometimes, mostly because it was good hill training to run there and back, but now most days I drilled outside the barracks.

At first it was just me and my 'sword buddies,' Krios, Damoxenos, Capros, and Philostratos. The second night, Hyperion and Simeon asked if they could join us. The next night, several others joined. Within half a month, every guy in our troop had joined us.

Linos even joined us sometimes, but he insisted that I lead the drills, up front like an officer, while he stood in the ranks. "Keeps me in shape, lad," he said. It showed. He was, despite his age, one of the fittest men in Athens. Sometimes he joined us when we ran the five miles to the Phaleron and back, and the old bugger had no trouble keeping up.

My original sword buddies continued to work me hard on the Pyrrhic dance moves. It seemed hopeless. Even after months of extra practice, I still had the finesse of a gutted hog. I frustrated my teachers so much that they decided to teach me only the most basic steps. Anything more would only mess up the little I'd managed to learn. I could compensate, they figured, if I did the basic steps at double the speed they were normally done.

One evening, a few days before our first ephebe term was over and we were doing our extra training, we had visitors. Four slaves carried a litter, which another man walked beside. The litter stopped a few yards away from us. An old woman got out of the litter and just stared at me for a few minutes. Her face was twisted into a scowl.

She made Linos uncomfortable, which was unusual for him. "Keep drilling, boys," he said. He left our formation and went to speak to the old woman, but she had no desire to speak to him. As he approached her, she got back into the litter and ordered the slaves to take her home. The man left too.

"Nothing good will come from that," Hyperion said to me. "That's Euphrosyne, Proxenos' mother. Even after her son's treachery, she still has enough clout to cause you a lot of grief. The man is her brother Menodoros."

Euphrosyne was legendary in Athens as an example of matronly strength in the midst of personal tragedy. Her husband and her other sons all died in battle–the battle that Proxenos commanded–yet she persevered like a Spartan, knowing that their deaths were all on behalf of Athens. Her last son, Proxenos, did not seem destined to die young. He was an ephebe trainer, not an active soldier, but he still died. She looked at me like she held me responsible–not the first grieving mother to ever deviate from rational thought. The name Euphrosyne, ironically, means 'joy.'

The day came for us to do our Pyrrhic dances. For first year ephebes, there was less emphasis on group dance formation than on individual form—the opposite was true for the second-years. We did our dances on the training ground, observed by the elders of the tribe Leontis who would evaluate us and decide if we were fit to continue training. A long table and chairs had been set up for the elders. Themistocles, though far from elderly, was among them because he was the current strategos. Dozens of benches had been set up for the boys' families and friends.

I'd practiced and practiced and practiced, but I still had my mental block about unnecessary movements. I did not overcome it because, in my heart, I did not want to. I knew that excess movement in a battle just tired you out faster. Compact movements could save my life, which was far more important to me than some stupid dance.

We danced before the elders one at a time. Three hired flautists played, as two other men drummed swords against shields to keep time. A dozen ephebes danced before I did. All passed easily. Before I began, I requested that the musicians play twice as fast as they'd been playing for the others. The elders were shocked to hear this, discussed it animatedly, but finally allowed it. "You may dance twice as fast," said the oldest one, Gennadios, a crag-faced ancient with a rusty door-hinge voice, "but that does not mean you can dance for half as long. Understood, boy?"

"Understood, sir," I replied.

The music began. I did not try anything difficult. The other ephebes twirled numerous times. I considered it ludicrous to present your back to your opponent, even in a stylized dance a world away from the battlefield, but it was deemed such an important move in the Pyrrhic dance that I had to include it. I twirled once, and only once, near the beginning so I could put it out of my mind and, with luck, never have to do it again for as long as I lived. I focused on basic moves, which required less extraneous movement than the more complex steps. I crossed one foot over the other to move sideways, backwards, and forwards in time to the music. These were things that the average Athenian five-year-old could do, except I did them so quickly that some of the elders struggled to follow my movements. I added moves that were not normally considered part of the Pyrrhic dance. I did several shoulder rolls—in full armour—and flawlessly landed on my feet each time. I used the sweep-kick that Madyes had taught me, crouching low and swinging my left foot to trip up an imaginary opponent, in time to the music. A couple of the judges smiled when I hit my spear against my helmet in time to the music. Then came my big finish: I tossed my shield in the air, shifted my nine-footer to my left hand, then reached down and grabbed, with my right hand, a javelin I'd placed on the ground earlier. While the shield was still airborne, I threw the javelin at it. When shield and javelin crashed to the ground, the javelin was stuck into the front surface of the shield.

The crowd applauded. I bowed to the elders. Not all of their faces were readable. Two of them looked like they wanted to applaud my finish, but knew it would be inappropriate for this rite. Gennadios, frowning, clearly disapproved of what I'd done, as did the two old codgers on either side of him. Themistocles smiled at me and nodded slightly. This gave me hope.

The elders had immediately and unanimously approved the ephebes who danced before I did. In my case, there was angry discussion. Krios told me to expect this, because I was doing a variation of the Pyrrhic dance that they'd never seen before. We always knew that one or more of the elders might hate it. Some of them clearly did.

After a few minutes of debate, Gennadios called for silence and stood up to speak. "We are not amused, *ephebe*," he said, emphasizing that last word like he was mocking me, "by your decision to ignore most of our traditions and introduce *barbarian* movements to the sacred dance. Several of us believe your dance was inadequate, bordering on sacrilege, even though you performed it at a speed few could emulate. We have good reason to repudiate your dance and dismiss you from our Ephebic College.

"At the end of your dance, you were not even breathing hard. This has impressed us all. A boy so fit should be permitted to continue his training. Your fitness has saved you, boy. You have passed."

Cheers erupted from the audience. More than a few Scythians were present, judging by the number of times I heard the name 'Lectoros!' from the crowd.

After the cheers died down, Gennadios continued. "Know this, Elektros of Skiathos: if you stand before us next year, you will perform with your entire phalanx. Such individualism will serve you ill. You will be expected to dance properly, in deference to the gods and traditions of Athens. Next dancer!"

After each of us danced—all of us passed, I was the only one who even came close to failing—we assembled in front of the elders and recited the ephebic oath in unison.

I will not disgrace these sacred arms, nor ever desert a comrade in the ranks. I will guard the Temples and the Centers of Civic Life, and uphold the ideals of Athens, both alone and in concert with others. I will at all times obey the Magistrates and observe the Laws at present in force as well as those the Majority may hereafter enact. Should any one seek to subvert those laws or set them aside, him I will oppose either in common with others or alone. In these ways it shall be my constant aim not only to preserve the things of worth in Athens, but to make them of still greater worth.

It was time to celebrate. Hyperion's father hosted a banquet for all of us. We would go to his house after the second-year ephebes danced—most of us wanted to watch because we had brothers and friends among them.

I admit it, Ephander, I was worried. Phylo was no soldier. I'd seen him train. He always did the bare minimum of work required. He was indifferent about athletics, but he was never the absolute worst at anything. When the second-year ephebes competed in the javelin, Phylo had no hope of winning, but there would always be two or three boys whose throws were worse than his. Even though he'd probably inherited some of Father's athletic ability, running bored him. Yet when his troop sprinted, he was never the last across the finish line, and in the long runs in armour, he would also plod along well enough to finish ahead of a few others. When the second-year ephebes wrestled, Phylo sometimes won. He would make his opponent laugh just enough to let his guard down, then Phylo would pin him. It would not work against an enemy soldier, but Phylo did not care. His aim was to pass his ephebe training.

I worried needlessly. During the second-year Pyrrhic dance, Phylo fit in perfectly. He did not share my problem with the illogic of some of the dance moves. At the end of it, he may have been breathing a little harder than most, and sweat flowed down his face, but he'd acquitted himself well. There were a few minor missteps by the second-years, but none was serious and none was made by Phylo. After the dance, the second-years repeated the same ephebic oath that we did. They too were headed for a banquet put on by the father of one of them—in Athens, men actually competed for the right to show off their wealth on this occasion—but before they headed off, I hugged him long and hard.

"I'm proud of you, big brother," I said.

"As I am of you, little brother," he replied. "Now that it's over, I'm never running in fucking armour again."

"So will you go back to Skiathos?" I asked.

"Yes, but just to visit," he said. "I have ventures here. I love Athens."

Athens loved him too. Phylo made money easily. He arranged the Scythians' horsemanship exhibitions and took a percentage of their fees. When he first got to Athens, about a year before the Battle of Marathon, he convinced Epictetos to invest with him in a factory that used slaves to assemble weapons and armour. His timing was brilliant. Demand for weapons and armour had never been higher. With the Persians temporarily stalled but by no means defeated, demand would remain high for years to come.

We headed off to our respective banquets.

I never got to mine.

As I left with Hyperion and the others, Themistocles said he had to talk to me. I told my mates that I'd catch up later. Themistocles led me into the first-year barracks. Linos was there, with several of the elders, including Gennadios. None of them looked happy. Gennadios, who had no trouble looking me in the eye when he spoke so spiritedly against my Pyrrhic dance, would not do so now. None of the elders would.

Themistocles broke the silence. "There's no gentle way to put this, so I'll just say it," he said. "The Leontis Council of Elders has revised its ephebe eligibility policy. Ephebes must be freeborn. The Council has decided, against my advice, Elektros, that you cannot return for the second-year training."

I wasn't as stunned as I thought I'd be. I'd

been around Athenians long enough to know how much importance they placed on trivial things like birth status. I was more pissed because if they'd told me sooner, maybe I wouldn't have risked my life defending their polis—and I definitely wouldn't have wasted time practicing that idiotic dance.

"Are you fucking kidding me?" I said, looking at Gennadios. "Did Euphrosyne talk you into this?"

"Watch your mouth, boy," said Gennadios. "You're in the presence of your superior officers."

"Wrong, asshole," I said, standing face to face with the old man. "I'm no longer an ephebe. You just said so yourself. I'm a civilian, so you're not my superior officers anymore. Right now you're a withered old turd who has pissed me off!"

A wave of fear splashed over Gennadios' face, like he thought I was going to slug him. I won't deny that it crossed my mind.

"Elektros!" Themistocles said. "I know you're upset, but talking to us like that will do you no good."

Linos was red with rage. At first I thought he was angry with me because I'd just called Gennadios an asshole.

"This is a horseshit decision, Gennadios," Linos said, "and you know it. Elektros is one of the best young men I've ever trained. He's an expert with sword and spear, and I've seen him run ten miles in armour and barely break a sweat.

His discipline is superb and sets a standard for the others. Have you forgotten how he led a bunch of recruits against an attack on our city? He works hard, does not panic under pressure, and has proven himself in battle. He's first-rate officer material. Do you honestly think he's not fit to train as an ephebe?"

"It is his birth that disqualifies him," said Gennadios, "not his abilities. I don't make the rules."

"No, you don't," Linos said. "A traitor's mother does."

"You also speak insubordinately," said Gennadios, "to your superior officers."

"Wrong again, asshole," said Linos. "I agreed to train the ephebes only until completion of this term. When the last one danced tonight, this term ended and you ceased to be my superior officers. And if this is how you run things, I will never train your ephebes again, or even stand in your fucking phalanx. In fact, all of you can go suck a dead dog's ass!"

Linos raged towards the door, but stopped just short of it. "Fools," he turned and said. "When the Persians come back, we want this guy on *our* side, not theirs. How can you halfwits not see this?" Then he left, slammed the door behind him. He probably wanted to say something like that to Gennadios for a long time. His refusal to take up arms was not a revocation of his rights as a citizen, as Athenians were not obliged to fight in the phalanx past the age of sixty. Linos would still be missed, though. He was fitter than men half his age and was a superb trainer.

Gennadios and the other elders shuffled out of the barracks. They were not proud of what they'd just done. They looked cowed. The decision to kick me out was forced on them.

Themistocles stayed behind. "I tried," he said, "but I was outvoted and couldn't change their decision. These old men do not realize that the Persians will be back soon, with an even bigger army, so we need to train every fighting man we can. Their birth status will be the least of our concerns."

"Were any of those old farts at Marathon?" I asked, even though I knew the answer.

"Of course not," he said. "They're too old. Gennadios is past eighty. They were here in Athens."

"So they cowered behind the walls while I fought raiders outside their gates," I said.

Themistocles gripped my shoulder. "Forget those old fools," he said. "They don't know your worth. But I do. Come work for me. I'll pay you well."

"No, Themistocles," I said, calling him by name for the first time ever. It sounded odd coming out of my mouth, but he was not my commander anymore. "I think I've had enough of

Athens for a while."

"Going home?" he said.

I nodded. "I miss my father."

"Give Belkos my regards," he said. "Don't stay there too long, though. I don't see you as a farmer. My offer to you stands. Any time you return to Athens, you can work for me." Then he left.

At the agora, I ran into Madyes and Aki. They'd already heard. "Just when I start to like this fucking city," said Madyes, "they pull something like this. Pettiness is ingrained here."

"That why," added Aki, "no Saka stay here after to live. Many like city but not like it bullshit."

I told them I was going home for a while. "Have you ever noticed," asked Madyes, "how similar the words 'Scythia' and 'Skiathos' are? It's no coincidence, Lectoros." Madyes was the only Scythian who could pronounce my name correctly, but he chose to call me *Lectoros* like the others.

He went on. "My term here is done in less than a year. When I return to the lands of the Saka, why don't you come with me? Your uncle Borysthenes and your aunt Gia would love to meet you. So would your cousins. Scylurus will tell them all about you."

"Won't they hate me for being such a crappy horseman?" I asked.

Aki laughed loudly and slapped me on the

back. "You Saka, Lectoros," he said. "You learn fast."

"Might take you up on that, Madyes," I said. I meant it, too. I was more than a little curious about Scythia and my relatives there.

Madyes and Aki were on duty, so they resumed their patrol. I headed back to the ephebe barracks. I couldn't sleep, so I packed my trunk. The next day, I'd see if I could find a ship back to Skiathos. It was early autumn, late in the sailing season, so it wasn't a sure thing.

I did not go to the celebration at Hyperion's house. If I did, I'd only spoil the party. I walked around Athens for few hours. The streets could be dangerous at night, so I kept my armour on and took my sword and dagger with me.

As I passed a tavern, I heard laughter. Noises and voices came from inside, but the laughter came from outside.

I was in no mood to be mocked. A man leaned against the wall beside the door to the tavern. It was dark and I couldn't see his face.

"You wouldn't be laughing at me, would you, sir?" I said.

"I most certainly would, *Lectoros*," he said. "Half savage, half island chaw-bacon. Fucking barbarian trash."

I stepped closer. "You apologize for that right now!" I said.

Even from ten feet away, I could smell the

wine on him. He took a step forward.

It was Menodoros, Proxenos' uncle. "You got something you want to do about it, sonny?" he said, smirking. He was a little glassy-eyed. Another man that I hadn't seen at first was leaning on the wall on the other side of the tavern door. He also stepped forward.

They moved towards me. "You'll be long dead," said Menodoros as he pulled out a dagger, "before your horse-fucker buddies can save you."

I don't know what these fools were thinking. Drink had made them bold but, as always, it hadn't made them any smarter. They both had daggers but no armour. I had all of mine, apart from my helmet and shield. I had my sword in my right hand and my dagger in my left.

As they got closer, Menodoros grinned like he knew something I didn't. I was lucky he did that: if he hadn't, I wouldn't have known about the third man who tried to sneak up behind me. I quickly spun around and hacked his right hand off. He clutched his bleeding stump and screamed. His severed hand fell to the ground, a dagger still gripped in its fingers.

I spun around so efficiently because it was almost identical to the move I'd practiced for the Pyrrhic dance. So I was wrong. The twirl *wasn't* completely useless.

Then I turned back to face Menodoros and the other man. Menodoros, paralyzed with surprise, didn't smile anymore. I charged. I feinted to Menodoros' left with my sword, feinted to his right with my dagger, then stomped on his foot as hard as I could. As the pain in his toes distracted him, I hit him in the mouth with the hilt-end of my sword. Teeth flew. Then I stabbed him in the thigh. His drinking buddy turned and ran.

Menodoros tried to speak, but with his bloodied mouth, which had already begun to swell, I couldn't understand what he tried to say. He looked terrified.

"Best you just shut it, old man," I said, "and listen. I could kill you, but won't because I want you to live with your family's shame. Just know that there are no traitors in my family."

Then I did something I'd never done before. I hiked up my tunic and pissed all over Menodoros. I made sure I got some on his face and into the wound on his leg. To the man with the severed hand, who whimpered on the ground and clutched his bleeding stump, I said, "You're lucky I don't need to shit right now."

I'm not proud of this, Ephander. Menodoros deserved to be pissed on, but I let him drag me down to his level. Afterward, I thought how disgusted Grandfather would have been. He always said that my behaviour should be determined by my own sense of right and wrong, and not by anything else.

I had the barracks to myself that night. The

ephebes had some time off before they'd begin the second year training, so after the party at Hyperion's house they'd all stay with their families. I did not sleep. I laid on my bunk and contemplated my time in Athens, the friends I'd made, the enemies too, and the things I'd done. I would actually miss this place. As an ephebe, I'd immersed myself in my training, which helped me avoid thinking about Kandra. I still ached for her.

When the sun rose, I headed over to the Scythian barracks to say my goodbyes. More bone-crushing bear-hugs and hard slaps on the back. They offered to beat the shit out of Gennadios for me, but I told them that as much as I liked the idea, it would do no good. They all invited me to come back to Scythia.

As I left, Madyes walked out with me. "Tell me about the little altercation last night," he said. "A man had his hand hacked off, but he wouldn't tell me what happened."

"Will he live?" I asked.

"I think so."

"Too bad. Three guys tried to kill me last night. Proxenos' uncle was one of them."

"Menodoros. A very bitter man. You messed him up pretty good too."

I told Madyes what happened. He just shook his head. "They hate us because we're barbarians," he said, "then they do barbaric things that none of us would ever do. Then they forget we're better man-to-man fighters than they'll ever be."

Madyes thought it was a good idea for me to leave Athens, at least for a while. "Don't underestimate Euphrosyne. She can still make trouble for you, even though her brother was clearly at fault."

When I got back to the barracks to pick up my trunk, most of my fellow ephebes, hung over to a man, waited there for me.

"We just found out," said Hyperion, shaking his head sadly. "Athens is a democracy. Any man who wants to fight beside us should be allowed to do so, but old traditions die hard. For aristocrats like Gennadios, birth status is everything. Don't take it personally."

As true as Hyperion's words may have been, there were some among the ephebes who agreed with Gennadios, even though they would never say it to my face. They too wanted all ephebes to be freeborn Athenians.

Several of the guys invited me to come and stay with them at their homes for a while, but I had to get out of Athens. I said my goodbyes and hired a carter to haul my trunk down to the Phaleron. In the Scythian manner, I walked beside the mule-drawn cart and chatted with the driver, a fat old man named Lasthenes, who told me tall tales about his own time as an ephebe. Before we were halfway to the port, I heard running footsteps approach us from behind. I had my sword with me and unsheathed it to face this new problem.

It was Phylo. "Whoa, slow down," he said. After he caught his breath, he added, "No way is my little brother leaving without me seeing him off. Plus Lasthenes here will need someone to protect him when he heads back to the city."

Lasthenes laughed. Phylo, not being Scythian, had no qualms at all about sitting in the cart. I still walked beside it.

"Little brother, I was afraid this would happen," he said. He referred to my dismissal from the ephebes.

"Seems awfully petty," I said, "to kick me out over a technicality."

"It's petty, all right," he said, "but it's not really about birth status."

"No? Then what is it about?"

"Your crime, little brother, is excellence. If you were a half-assed soldier like me, no one would care about your birth, but you're the best fighter in the barracks, the best athlete, and men will follow you on a battlefield even when you don't hold official rank. This scares the shit out of the people of Athens. You're a threat because you're a hero. Heroes always have more enemies than friends."

As I pondered this, and wondered what I could have done differently, we passed a wine shop. It was morning but the place was still open because the previous night's revelers hadn't left yet.

Several drunks sat against the wall outside the doorway, sound asleep. Another bunch of sodden twits sat at a table outside the shop. "Hey!" one of them shouted. "Elektros! Hold on a second!"

It was Anakletos. When he'd first arrived in Athens, he was lean and fit. Now he was bloated and bleary-eyed, and had gained a few pounds. Drink and inactivity does that to a man.

"Piss off, Anakletos," I said. "I don't have time for you."

"Just need a second, Elektros," he said. "Any sign of Agapios?"

What an idiot. Agapios—Krites—had left Athens two months ago. Anakletos' slave-tracking method was to hang around wine-shops and brothels in the hope that Krites showed up at one of them.

"Haven't seen him," I said. No lie there. "Have you spent all the money Xenocrates gave you?"

"Not yet," he said. "But rest assured, I'll catch Agapios sooner or later."

"Good luck," I said.

I turned to go, but Anakletos said, "Almost forgot, I have something for you." He pulled a small scroll out of his tunic. It was worn and brown. It had been in his pocket a long time.

"Kept forgetting to give you this. Brought it from Skiathos."

"Are you serious? You've had it all this time and you're just giving it to me now?"

"Like I said, I kept forgetting. An old woman gave it to me. I told her I'd give it to you, but I never told her *when* I'd give it to you, and she never told me it was urgent."

He held the scroll out to me. I knocked it out of his hand. "Don't bother me with this shit, Anakletos."

Anakletos just shrugged, picked the scroll up off the ground and handed it to me again. "I told her I would give it to you," he said, "and that's what I'm doing. If you don't accept it, that's not my problem."

Anakletos held the scroll out to me. I was about to knock it out of his hand again but froze when I saw my name written on the outside of it.

It was written in my own handwriting.

I didn't write it myself. So it must have been written by the only person I'd ever taught to read and write.

Kandra.

I slugged Anakletos, knocked him flat on his ass.

"Oww!" he moaned from the ground. "What was that for? I delivered the letter like I was supposed to."

I pulled out my sword and held it to his

throat. "I don't like you much, Anakletos," I said. "Every time you speak to me, you lie, but if you lie to me now, they'll be the last words you ever say. Who gave you this letter?"

"I-I—I told you, some old lady," he said. "A slave. She came down to the port and handed it to me just before I got on the ship to Athens."

"What did she look like?"

"Like all old ladies do. Grey hair, short, stooped over. She wore a hood, so I didn't get a good look at her face. Had an old burn scar under one eye."

Adina. Father's housekeeper. Father wanted me to forget Kandra for the rest of my life, so Adina went behind his back to get this letter to me. It must have been delivered to our house when Father wasn't home. If he'd known about it, he would have destroyed it. Adina couldn't read, so I'm not sure how she knew it was from Kandra. Perhaps whoever had delivered it told her.

I read the letter.

I was alarmed.

Change of plans. I would still leave Athens. But Skiathos would have to wait.

I would write to Father and tell him I was going to Halicarnassus.

To my Kandra.

HALICARNASSUS

15–KRATISTO

"Stand aside, imbecile," the armed guard growled as he gave the old man a straight-arm shove. "Important lady comin' through."

The old man fell backwards. The *important lady* was in a green-curtained litter carried by six slaves, accompanied by two armed bodyguards, headed for the Temple of Artemis. The lady went there almost every day. The guard who'd spoken, Mastropos, had the tact of a speared boar. He was dumb as stone, too. He didn't know that he'd just shoved Boreas, a city leader, much more important to most Halicarnassans than the lady in the litter. Boreas chose to walk rather than use a litter, so Mastropos assumed he didn't have bodyguards with him. The moment after Mastropos shoved old Boreas, one of Boreas' men quickly grabbed Mastropos' wrist and twisted his arm behind his back. There was a sick dull crack as Mastropos' arm was wrenched out of its socket. His howls drowned out the laughter of onlookers. Boreas' guard released Mastropos, who collapsed in agony.

The lady's other bodyguard, Orestes, drew his sword, but with his partner now incapacitated, he was outmatched by Boreas' two guards, who had also drawn their swords.

"I have no quarrel with you," said the guard who'd just incapacitated Mastropos, "but your partner manhandled our master. Get him out of here and this is over."

Orestes agreed. I knew their names, Orestes and Mastropos, because I'd been watching them for almost a month.

This was the chance I'd been waiting for.

"Sir," I said to Orestes, "allow me to help."

"Who the fuck are you?" said Orestes. He had to choose: abandon Mastropos on the street or leave the lady's litter unprotected. A vein pulsed in his forehead as he tried to decide. He didn't like my looks. Not too surprising. I was a stranger. In his place, I probably wouldn't have trusted me either.

"My name is Markos, sir," I said. "For a couple of obols, I will see your friend safely home." I didn't need money, but I asked for it because Orestes would never believe that a stranger in Halicarnassus would help him for nothing.

"This idiot," said Orestes as he glared at the moaning Mastropos, "is no friend of mine today."

"Orestes," said the lady from inside the litter, her voice slightly muffled by the drawn curtains. "Everything all right out there?"

"A minor problem, despoina," said Orestes. "Mastropos has been injured and needs to be taken home. A stranger says he'll do it but I don't trust this guy."

The lady opened the curtain and looked right at me. It was Kandra. Until this moment, I hadn't known for sure. I watched this litter leave the house every day, and there was always a lady inside it, but she was always veiled and there could have been other ladies who lived in the same house. Her lower face was still veiled. All I could see were her eyes and a few dark ringlets of her hair, but I'd recognize those eyes, greener than spring grass, anywhere. She stared at me without emotion. If she was surprised to see me, she didn't show it.

"Give him these," she said after a few seconds, and handed Orestes some coins. "Have him take Mastropos home while you accompany me to the temple."

"Despoina," said Orestes, "we know nothing about this man."

"True," she said. "We don't. But all we stand to lose is Mastropos. He's proven again today that he would be no great loss."

"As you say, despoina," said Orestes.

He gave me the coins. "If you don't get our man home," he said to me, "by the gods, I'll hunt you down and gut you like a dinner pig."

"I am a stranger to you, sir," I said, "so I can understand that you don't trust me yet. But once I complete this task, you will not question my honour again."

"And if I do, sonny," Orestes smirked, "what might you do about it?"

Before I could answer, the lady spoke again. "Orestes!" she said. "Forget this guy and forget Mastropos. Just get me to the temple. When we get back home, Mastropos will either be there or he will not be. I don't care much one way or the other." It was not like Kandra to be indifferent to the pain of those around her. She played the role of ruthless matron rather well. At least I *hoped* it was role-playing.

Orestes ordered the litter-bearers forward. I held Mastropos up as we walked in the opposite direction. Every step pained him, and it hurt him so much that he almost lost consciousness.

"Stay awake, friend," I said. "Don't pass out on me. You haven't told me where you live yet." I knew where he lived, of course, but had to pretend I didn't. Like I said, I'd been watching these people for a month.

"Street of the Apple Blossoms," he gasped. It hurt him to talk. "Second house from the end. Biggest house on the block."

The house was only a few streets away. I propped Mastropos up under his good shoulder and we hobbled along. He didn't pass out, but now I almost hoped he would. He'd be harder to carry unconscious, but at least he'd stop whining.

"The guy suckered me," he said several times. "You saw it, right?"

"Best not talk," I said. "You need to save your strength."

"I coulda took 'im," he said. "He suckered me." The fool didn't want to admit that the man who hurt him was only doing his job, and wouldn't have needed to if Mastropos had just been a little less reckless.

"We'll talk about it later," I said. "The man you work for–what's he like?"

"Kratisto?" he said. "He's the best. A hard man, but he loves wine and pussy, and makes sure his men get their share."

Kratisto–the name meant *the strongest*–was well known in and out of Halicarnassus. Mastropos was the first person I'd ever heard speak well of him. The rumours were nightmares. In a tavern, Kratisto once beat a serving-girl to death because she spilled wine on one of his friends. Another time, in a temple of Apollo, he cut out the tongue of a priest who'd sacrificed a lamb and then gave an unfavourable omen. He sliced off the ears, nose and lips of one of his slaves, an attractive young man, because he wanted to maintain his claim as the handsomest man in the household. Some of Kratisto's house slaves were reportedly missing body parts that he'd cut off either for punishment or for fun.

And I wanted to work for this man. I *had* to work for him. It was part of my plan to get Kandra away from Kratisto. I hoped these wild rumours were just that, rumours, or at least exaggerations.

Months earlier, Kandra wrote a letter that found its way to me in Athens. I knew her father Simonides had married her off, but I didn't know who the husband was or where he lived. He turned out to be a very nice man, she wrote, a fifty-one year old widower named Kyrios, although many people called him Midas. He had a rare metallurgical talent: he knew how to find underground gold deposits by analyzing the dirt and stone on the surface. It was a secret no one else knew. He didn't do the mining himself. It was always rocky land, usually close to a mountain and no good for farming or grazing, so he'd buy it cheap, then sell it to the highest bidder. Whenever he claimed there was gold or silver on a plot of rocky land, he was always right. He was wealthy, and the men who bought land from him ended up wealthy too. The Great King himself was a happy customer.

Kandra liked Kyrios. She knew that she could have done much worse. He was too old to be the love of her life, but she'd become fond of him. He was kindhearted, considerate, cheerful. He treated her well, made her laugh and didn't make many demands on her. When he came home every evening, she was genuinely glad to see him. His great flaw? He indulged his son too much.

Then Kyrios died. At a chariot race, just as the racers crossed the finish line, he collapsed. He died at home a few hours later. Kandra grieved. He was a good man. It was a Hellenic tradition for a young widow to return to her father, so he could arrange another marriage for her, but no one, not even Kandra, knew where Simonides was. He moved around constantly. So she stayed in her late husband's house. Kratisto, Kyrios' son, claimed Kandra as his wife. He had no legal authority to do so, with her father still living, but his own father's death made him wealthy enough to disregard any laws he found inconvenient. He wanted Kandra. She had no place else to go, and as a foreigner and a woman, no legal status in Halicarnassus to challenge Kratisto in court. She was a prisoner in his house. In her letter, she also told me that I could not just sweep into Halicarnassus and steal her away. Kratisto was simply too powerful to let that happen. Plus his enemies had a tendency to disappear suddenly. So I figured I had to get into his household somehow without arousing suspicion. From there I could observe, plan, and pick the right time and method to get Kandra out of there.

When I finally got Mastropos to the biggest house on the Street of Apple Blossoms, he was barely conscious. The house was huge. It was four stories high and half a stade wide. When I opened the gate, two big armed guards charged out the front door. One of them immediately took Mastropos under the shoulder and led him into the house.

The other put his sword to my throat. "What the fuck did you do to Mastropos?" he demanded.

"He was hurt in an altercation," I said. "I had nothing to

do with it. I was nearby, and the despoina gave me six obols to bring him home. So put your sword away." I had learned that armed men respect you more if you don't act intimidated. The guy with the sword, a red-bearded fellow with a huge paunch, smiled. He was amused by me but still held the sword to my throat.

"I say his *altercation* was with you," he said. "Where's his sword?"

I noticed then that Mastropos' scabbard was empty. "I don't know," I admitted. "Orestes probably picked it up." That was optimism I didn't actually feel. If Mastropos dropped his sword on the street, it was long gone by now.

"You have a partner," Redbeard said. "He took the sword."

"You're inventing things, buddy," I said. "I don't have a partner. I didn't take anybody's sword. The lady gave me a few coins to bring this guy here. So that's what I've done. He's your problem now. Goodbye and fuck you."

Redbeard kept his sword to my throat, but there was nothing behind me, so I quickly rolled backwards and came up on my feet a few yards away from him. He was about to come at me—he wouldn't have reached me, I could outrun him easily—but a woman suddenly appeared in the doorway.

"Briareus!" she said. "You simpleton. If he was a thief, he would have taken Mastropos' helmet and armour instead of bringing him home." She rolled her eyes as she spoke, a habit that she probably developed from having to explain the obvious to Briareus so often.

"Sir, I thank you," she said to me. "If you left Mastropos on the street, he would have succumbed to his many enemies.

My brother will want to reward you for bringing him home. Are you hungry?"

"Yes, lady, I am," I said.

"Come in, I'll give you something to eat," she said. "I apologize for Briareus."

"No need," I said. "I would think that vigilance is a good thing in a guard. No hard feelings, buddy?"

I held out my hand for Briareus to shake. He looked at me like I had leprosy.

"Briareus," said the lady, rolling her eyes again, "shake the man's hand."

Briareus grunted, took my hand, gave it a moist limp get-it-over-with squeeze. The lady brought me into the house, sat me at a table and brought me cheese, bread, olives, dates and cool water. She was past thirty, brown haired and green eyed. Her name was Nysa. With her wide forehead and large jaw, she wasn't pretty, except when she smiled.

I told her my name was Markos and I was from Athens. I'd spent enough time there that I could convincingly fake an Athenian accent. An Athenian speaks as if his testicles are in a clamp that will snap shut if he fails to clearly pronounce every syllable of every word, and believes that this somehow makes him intellectually superior to all other Hellenes. Even Athenian slaves talk like this. Now I did too. I told Nysa that my father had made some bad investments and died bankrupt, and that I was in Halicarnassus seeking employment. I had some experience as an oarsman, as well as enough skill with a sword to be a bodyguard.

"Mastropos will be out of commission for a while," I said. "Would your brother consider me as a temporary replacement?"

Naked horror passed over Nysa's face, and she sputtered before she said, "No! You don't want to work for my brother!" Then she recovered and said, "You can ask him. He generally wants older men as his guards. Trust me, though, you'd be better off on a ship."

Nysa asked me about the Battle of Marathon and was thrilled when I told her I was there. She wanted to hear everything about it. All she'd heard were rumours and bards' songs, almost none of which were accurate. She asked many questions. Were the Persians cowards? No, they fought bravely, but Miltiades was a better tactician than Datis, and the Persian light infantrymen were badly equipped to fight Athenian heavy infantry. Did the Hellenes really sprint a mile at the Persians? No, if they did, they'd have been too tired to fight in the August heat and would have lost the battle. They only sprinted the last few yards. Did Phaedippides really run all the way from Marathon to Athens to report the victory, then drop dead immediately after saying 'We won!?' No, another man delivered that message, but he rode a horse and was alive and well when I left Athens, as was Phaedippides. Was it true that the Persians lost over six thousand men and the Athenians less than two hundred? Yes, that was actually true. I knew guys who had to burn the Persian bodies.

Nysa was initially confused by the Athenians' strategy of attacking at dawn before their reinforcements arrived. "Wouldn't it have been better to wait for the Spartans?" she asked. "Their contingent would have doubled your numbers."

"We had intelligence that the Persians planned to put their cavalry behind us and attack us front and rear before the

Spartans arrived," I said, "so we took the initiative away from them."

She understood. In fact, her ready grasp of military tactics would have made her a natural general. We spoke for several hours. I was interested in how Cyrus the Great had begun the Persian Empire, and Nysa knew every general and every strategy in every battle. We might have talked all night, Ephander, if her brother and Orestes hadn't suddenly burst into the room.

Her brother Kratisto was an extremely handsome man of thirty who wore the type of long moustache you'd normally associate with the barbarians of the far north. The dark blonde moustache was so long that it drooped down the sides of his mouth and below his clean-shaven chin, which had one of those chin dimples that I think looks like a deformity but the ladies all seem to love. He was smiling when he entered the room. I would learn that he always smiled, even when he was angry.

A man who smiles when he's angry is not only dangerous but usually deranged.

He did not seem angry now, though. He walked to the table like he was driven, like he was in a footrace and I was the finish line. He shook my hand. "I am Kratisto," he said. "I thank you for bringing my injured man home, and I am honored to be your host."

"My name is Markos, sir, of Athens," I said, "and the honour is mine. Nysa has fed me well and entertained me with her impressive knowledge of military history."

Nysa did not smile when Kratisto came in. In fact, her shoulders tightened and her jaw muscles clenched. "Ah, Nysa," he said. "If my dear sister spent more time spinning and less time reading history books, I'd have a husband for her by now."

He sought to embarrass her, so I paid her a compliment. "She's a charming lady," I said. "She's been gracious and witty, and I've quite enjoyed our talk today."

"You want to marry her?" said Kratisto. "She's all yours. I'm serious. Just say the word."

"Learchos!" said Nysa. She was the only one who called him by his real name. "The man is our guest! Don't put him on the spot like that. Besides, you know nothing about him."

"If your offer is real, Kratisto, I must decline," I said. "I am not yet nineteen years old. I promised my father I would not marry before I was twenty-five." Then I winked at him and said, "In six years, let's talk." The funny thing, Ephander, is that I could picture Nysa as my wife. She was a sensible, intelligent woman who would run a household well—I could already see how well she ran this one—and she wasn't too old to give me sensible, intelligent sons and daughters.

Kratisto reared his head back and cackled loudly. "I like you, Markos!" he said. "You're tactful and quick witted."

There was my cue if ever there was one. "Sir, with Mastropos laid up, you're a man short," I said. "Hire me to fill in for him. I'm pretty good with a sword."

The smile never left his face, though his eyes momentarily widened in surprise. "You're too young," he said. "Young men always think they're better swordsmen than they actually are."

"Let me demonstrate my skill," I said. "Let me spar with you or one of your men."

Kratisto agreed. The demonstration would take place in

the walled courtyard behind the house. As we left the dining room, Nysa came up behind me and grabbed my hand. "If you have any sense," she said quietly, "you will turn around and leave this house right now. You do *not* want to work for my brother."

She was dead serious, and I didn't doubt her, but I had to suffer through whatever awaited me. If I left this house now, I might never get Kandra out of here. How bad could Kratisto be to the men who worked for him? Mastropos certainly didn't have any complaints.

In the courtyard, all of his guards except the injured Mastropos were there. There were five of them and Kratisto had a special name for each. He introduced Choiros, 'pig,' whose name derived from his flat, turned-up nose. Briareus, the red-bearded one I'd met earlier, was named for the monstrous, many-armed son of Zeus. His arms were too long for his body and looked like furry sticks attached to his bloated torso. Another guard was Skatocephalos, 'shit for brains.' I didn't want to know how he got that name. Orestes was the only one that Kratisto called by his real name. This was because, I would learn later, he was the only guard who'd also worked for Kratisto's father, and attempts to saddle him with a demeaning nickname had never succeeded. The last man was called Mikropeos, 'tiny penis.' All of these guards accepted their humiliating names and grinned when they saw me. The next humiliation would be mine, they figured, and they looked forward to it.

Mikropeos handed me a sword, a real one. "Good luck, asshole," he sneered. "Orestes'll cut you good. Haw!"

I looked at Kratisto. "Real swords, sir?" I said. "Wouldn't

wooden ones be more practical?"

"Well, I can get you a wooden one," said Kratisto, the smile never leaving his face. "But you'll want a real one here today. This fight is to the death. Did I not mention that?"

The guards laughed, except for Orestes. I immediately spotted the flaw in the logic of this: if I killed Orestes and won Mastropos' job, or if Orestes killed me, Kratisto would still be a man short. In fact, if this was his hiring method, he would always be a man short, at least until Mastropos recovered. I was about to ask Kratisto if he was serious about this, but then Orestes took a swipe at me with his sword. I saw it at the last second and ducked away from it, but not before the tip cut my left bicep. A warm trickle ran down my arm.

I faced my opponent and sized him up quickly, as Xenocrates had taught me. Orestes wore armour. I did not. He had a defensive advantage, but without armour I could move more quickly. He was almost forty, but I was young. Though not as fat as the others, he was still a little pudgy. My conditioning was better than his—I ran every day—but I had to assume that he had more sword-fighting experience than me. The cut on my arm bled freely and could be a factor if it caused me to lose too much blood. There was no fear in Orestes' eyes, which meant one of two things. He was either a very good swordsman or he simply didn't take me seriously as an opponent. I suspected the latter but had to be ready for the former.

In addition to his sword, Orestes had a dagger in his left hand. It didn't worry me. He could not attack with the dagger. It was too short against by my sword, so as long as I didn't let him get in close and tie up my sword arm, the dagger was strictly for show. He feinted with his sword, then with his dagger, and then he took a real cut at my head with the sword. It was predictable. I ducked away from it. The miss made him over-commit on his follow-through, which gave me the chance to stomp on his right foot and drive the pommel of my sword into his shoulder bone. He cried out and backed away limping.

"Ho HO!" laughed Kratisto. "Looks like the kid can fight! You want new odds, Choiros? Too fucking bad!"

I already despised Kratisto. I fought for my life but it was a game to him. Everything was. Orestes came back at me with an overhand sword-chop—an effective move when your opponent has no shield—but I blocked it with my sword. With my left hand, I grabbed his right wrist—his sword arm—which I knew would make him try to stab me with his dagger. But he wasn't fast enough. I head-butted him in the face before the dagger was anywhere near me. Blood ran from his smashed nose. I'll give Orestes credit for courage. He did not back down. When I came at him again, he stood his ground. I feinted with my sword, then with my left hand. My left hand was empty, yet he reacted like it too held a weapon. His eyes were cloudy from the head-butt and he survived now on his reflexes. I faked a short stab at his ribs with my sword, then drove the point hard into his right wrist. It cut him enough to make him drop his sword. Then I kicked him in the instep. He dropped his dagger and fell flat on his ass.

Suddenly, I felt a sharp pain in the back of my left shoulder. I swung around to see Mikropeos holding a blood-tipped sword, a big dumb grin on his face.

"I poked you good," he said. "Haw!"

I used the Scythian sweep-kick—I call it that because my

Scythian friend Madyes taught it to me—to take Mikropeos' legs out from under him, then while he was down I kicked him in the head. I needed him dazed, temporarily incapacitated, before Orestes could recover.

"Good show, Mikropeos," said Kratisto, who was delighted by this bloody little side-spectacle to the main event. "But do that again and I'll cut your tiny balls off."

Orestes was back on his feet, but now he limped. He'd picked up his sword again, but he needed both hands to hold it. He moved sluggishly. He made a clumsy cut at me. I blocked it with my sword, then used my left hand to punch him in the stomach. I caught his sword-hilt with my own and wrenched the weapon away from him. It clattered across the paving stones.

He was done. He dropped to his knees and did not resist when I moved behind him and held my sword to his throat.

"Wonderful!" said Kratisto as he clapped his hands. The others clapped too. "Now kill him."

Orestes fought bravely. He did not deserve to die. I would learn that he'd been loyal to Kratisto and his father for over twenty years. Is this how Kratisto repaid loyalty?

Years earlier, when I was a child on Skiathos, my instructor Xenocrates ordered me to kill a smaller child he'd tied to a fencepost. The little boy was helpless, no threat to anyone, but Xenocrates still ordered me to do it. I refused. Xenocrates screamed at me—and believe me, Ephander, he was the most intimidating man I ever knew—but still I refused. It turned out that my refusal was the correct response. It was a test of my judgment. Xenocrates wanted to see how readily I would kill the helpless. If I had no concern for the lives I took, he would not train me to kill.

I thought of this as Kratisto ordered me again to kill Orestes. "I will not, sir," I said. "I have proven my skill with the sword, and Orestes has proven his courage."

"Kill him," Kratisto repeated.

"No, sir. If I do, you'll still be a man short."

He shrugged. "Suit yourself. I'll take that sword back."

I handed it back to him. He should have been impressed with my good judgment. Men who employ bodyguards usually prefer them to have some discretion, some restraint.

How little I knew Kratisto.

He nodded to the other guards. Before I knew what was happening, Briareus and Choiros held my left arm, and Mikropeos and Skatocephalos held my right. They turned me around so that I faced the wall.

Kratisto punched me in the kidneys. "When I give an order," he said, still smiling, "I expect you to follow it *without question.*"

Then he pressed my left hand up against the wall and used the sword to cut off my little finger. The smile never once left his face.

"Next time—if there is a next time—it's your whole fucking hand, New Guy."

The other guards laughed and released my arms. Kratisto examined my severed finger, held it up close to his eyes like he'd never seen one before. "Guess I'll just add it to the collection," he said. "I'm thirsty, boys, let's hit the wine shop. You coming, New Guy?"

Before I could answer, I passed out.

16–NYSA

I wasn't out for more than a few seconds. I was conscious by the time Nysa ordered two of the house slaves to carry me to a bedchamber. I insisted I was okay. "I can walk," I said. I took a wobbly step but would have fallen flat on my face if the slaves hadn't caught me.

"You're in shock," Nysa said. "You've lost a lot of blood." She was disturbingly calm. In the house of Kratisto, she had seen this many times. One of the slaves had a gaping hole where his nose should have been. The other was missing both ears.

She'd wrapped the stub of my finger in linen. It had already stopped bleeding. "Doesn't look too bad," I mumbled.

"It's not," she said. "It's your other injury that has weakened you."

That was when I felt blood run down my back. The slaves got me into the bedchamber. I didn't want to lie on the bed and get the blankets bloody. So Nysa just put her hands on my shoulders and gently pushed me onto the bed. I was too weak to resist.

"Are you thirsty?" she asked me.

I nodded.

"Here, drink this," she said. She handed me a cup. I drank it. Within seconds I felt myself nodding off. I wondered if I'd just made another mistake.

I awoke a few hours later. My wounds were cleaned and dressed. I got out of bed, stood up, took a few steps. I was weak, still a little woozy, but I didn't fall over. Then the slave without a nose ran into the room.

"Apologies, young master," he said. "I had to step out for a second. I'm at that age where nature doesn't call, it *commands*. You should rest. Both the master and the lady want to talk to you."

He took my arm and guided me back to the bed. "My name is Kallum, sir," he said. "If you want anything–food, drink, poppy juice–I will get it for you, but the lady says you're not to have wine until you're stronger."

"That's okay, Kallum," I said. "I don't much like wine. I'd like some water, though."

"Right away, sir," he said. He left the room and returned a minute later with a jug of water and a cup. He was in his fifties, round faced and bright-eyed, and he was probably pleasant looking at one time. His missing nose was an old injury.

"When did Kratisto do that to you?" I asked.

"This, sir?" he said, pointing at his face. "The master didn't do this. I'm originally from the far north, where the winter nights freeze. One night I drank myself stupid at a tavern. On my way home, I passed out in a snowbank. When I woke up, my nose was frostbitten. Over the next few days it turned black, got infected, and I had to have it cut off. Nobody's fault but mine, sir."

I couldn't tell if it was true or if it was what Kratisto told him to tell people. He spoke with a Keltic accent, so at least part of his story was true.

Nysa came into the bedchamber. "Ah, good, you're awake," she said.

"Thanks for looking after me, Nysa," I said.

"When a man is injured in my house," she said, "he should be healed in my house, at least as much as he can be healed. The sleeping potion, by the way, came from the despoina. She's taught me a great deal about medicines."

"The lady in the litter," I said. "Is she your brother's wife?" I knew she wasn't but had to pretend I knew less than I did.

"Kallum, leave us," she said. Kallum nodded and scurried away.

"She is *not* his wife," Nysa said, "and never will be, at least willingly. She was married to Father when he died. My brother wants to marry her, but she knows him too well. Unfortunately, we can't send her back to her own father, Simonides, because we don't know where he is. I've sent men out to find him, but none have returned yet. The despoina came from some piddle-twit island near Euboea, so I've sent a man to see if he's there."

I knew, but couldn't say without revealing too much about myself, that Simonides was not on piddle-twit Skiathos. He once had a house there but had given it to his former slaves. I needed to give Nysa a better hint.

"There is a poet named Simonides of Keos," I said. "It's not the same man, is it?"

"Yes, I believe it is," said Nysa. "You know his poetry?"

"A little," I said. "He has a following in Athens and visits there frequently. Have you sent someone to look for him there?"

"No," she said, "but I will now."

Simonides may not have known yet that Kyrios was dead. He would not want his daughter married to a maniac like Kratisto, so if Nysa's man found him in Athens, Simonides would get her out of this house. It would take him some time, so I would continue to try to do it myself. If I failed here—or got killed, a stark possibility with Kratisto—then at least Kandra would still have a chance of rescue.

"You should stay for a few days," Nysa said, "so I can make sure nothing gets infected."

"I plan to stay longer than a few days, dear lady," I said. "It cost me a finger to earn the bodyguard job. I plan to keep it."

Then Nysa's eyes bore into me like a charging bull. "What are you thinking, Markos?" she said. "My brother is not human. People around him lose body parts and get killed by his whims. When you're well enough, you should leave this house and never come back."

"I'm well aware of his inclinations," I said, holding up the stump of my finger. "Still, I will stay. I will take up my duties as soon as I can. Tomorrow, possibly."

"What you've seen so far," she said, "is only a sample of what he does. He places no value on life. When he was a boy, he tortured dogs, then moved up to horses. Then one of our slaves disappeared, then another. Father—may the gods let him rest in peace—refused to see what was happening. He figured the slaves ran away, so he sent out trackers. Of course they came back empty handed. Father insisted that Learchos was just curious, but I've got a dozen burn scars on my body. Mere curiosity would have been sated by the first one or two. When our father was alive, Learchos always had to rein in his darkest urges, but now he has no limits. Why would you possibly want to stay here?"

"I have my reasons," I said.

"He toys with you," she said. "You do know that, right? He will continue to toy with you until he gets bored. Then he'll have you killed. So unless you plan to kill him before he kills you, your time here will not end well."

"I appreciate the warning," I said, "and I thank you for it. I will stay."

"Can I count on you," she said, "not to tell him that I've sent men to find Simonides? Sister or not, he would kill me if it suited him. He'd probably give me to his guards first, though."

"You can count on my discretion, Nysa," I said.

"You won't fit in with the other guards," she said. "You're a trained swordsman with some education. The men he hires are all illiterate lowlifes whose only qualification is that they share his taste for cruelty."

"Orestes doesn't seem like that," I said.

"Learchos didn't hire him," she said. "He's the last of the guards who served Father. The others all became disgusted with my brother's excesses and left us. Orestes stays on because he swore an oath to Father that he would look after Learchos and me. Orestes is the only voice of reason in my brother's retinue. When he leaves—and he will eventually, oath or no oath—Learchos will become even worse."

"Your brother chose Orestes to fight me to the death," I said, "because there was a chance he would get killed."

"Exactly," she said. "When you defeated Orestes, my brother was thrilled. He thought you'd just solved a problem for him, but when you refused to kill him, he was furious. He will continue to put Orestes at risk. He will insult known killers, then get Orestes to protect him. Orestes is a man of honour, so he will not refuse. Can I ask you a favour?"

"Yes, lady," I said. "I owe you one."

"When Orestes is in those dangerous situations, can you help him out? That is, if you can do it without endangering yourself."

She knew little of a bodyguard's duties. If Orestes was in a dangerous situation and I was present, I would be in the same danger. But I still agreed.

"Mikropeos," she said, "is a piece of work. He hates people who are more intelligent than him. That's pretty much everyone. You're already his enemy. The others are local scum, but Mikropeos came from Ephesus. He was about to be publicly beheaded, but my brother bribed the local officials to spare him, which they did only on the condition that he take Mikropeos away from Ephesus and never return."

"Why was he being executed?" I asked. I didn't really want to know, but if he was my enemy, I probably needed to.

"Mikropeos rapes and murders," Nysa said, "and not necessarily in that order. Men, women, children, old ladies, he doesn't care. He's impulsive. He's not capable of forethought. He's the only man I've ever met who has fewer moral restraints than my brother. When he looks at me, I get a chill, because it's obvious what's on his mind. I shudder to think how much more of a menace he'd be if he had a shred of intelligence. Whatever you do, Markos, do not turn your back on Mikropeos. If your duties cause you to fight, make sure you know where Mikropeos is at all times. You would not be the first of my brother's guards that Mikropeos stabbed in the back. My brother keeps him because he finds him amusing."

She was slightly pale. Talking about Mikropeos upset her. I could understand why. Kratisto retained the services of a man that every other right-thinking person in the world wanted dead.

"When Learchos asked you if you wanted to marry me," Nysa said, "he was actually serious. He wanted to embarrass us both."

"I did not lie, Nysa," I said, "when I said I promised my father that I'd wait until I was twenty-five."

"He says he can't find me a husband," she said, "because I have no interest in spinning and weaving and other traditional women's tasks. It's true, I don't care much for those things. But the reason he can't find me a husband is because of him. I've got a good mind and a huge dowry. I know my wifely duties and can manage a household. There are good men who want me as a wife, but there are no good men who want Learchos as a brother-in-law."

I believed it. Nysa did not have a beautiful face, but she was not unattractive. She was heavy-breasted with curvaceous hips. Men notice a body like that, even when they don't want to. She was pretty when she laughed, although with Kratisto for a brother that did not happen often.

Nysa told me she'd been married once. The man, named Doron, was the son of one of her Father's friends. "He was always nice to me," she said, "always kind, always bringing me gifts. But every night he drank and gambled. He didn't chase women. How can I be so sure? He didn't *like* women. He liked boys. He bedded our male slaves but left the girls alone. I didn't hate him. I was frustrated because we'd never have children, but I was mostly indifferent to him. Learchos hated him ferociously. I'm still not sure why. Learchos has no moral objections to drinking and gambling and chasing boys. It might have been because Father liked Doron so much. When it came to Father, Learchos was as territorial as a mad bull. Doron was a charmer, knew how to say what Father wanted to hear, and Father was as blind about Doron as he was about Learchos. He thought Doron would get tired of his boys sooner or later and would get down to the business of starting a family with me. But I knew he would not. He was the type of man who loved men exclusively. He would not grow out of it.

"One night, Doron didn't come home. This happened occasionally, so I didn't think anything of it. The next morning, he was found dead in a back street. His neck had been snapped. All his money was gone, his gold rings too. It looked like a night-time street robbery. I knew it wasn't, though. Doron was a dandy fool, but he wasn't stupid enough to walk home alone through a rough part of the city at night. He was found nowhere near his usual dicing haunts. There were skinned areas on the backs of his heels, a sign that his body had been killed somewhere else and then dragged to the place where it was found.

"We had a funeral for Doron. I did not weep. Father did. He was genuinely fond of Doron. Learchos pretended he was sad too. During the funeral procession, he winked at me and showed me that he had one of Doron's gold rings on his finger. So Learchos killed him, or had someone else do it.

"That's when I learned just how dangerous Learchos had become. Doron wasn't a threat to him, or me, or anyone else. Learchos killed Doron simply because he didn't like him."

I was drowsy again. It came on suddenly. “You look ready to sleep again,” Nysa said.

“I am, dear lady,” I said. “I swear it’s not because I’m bored. I’m not quite myself yet.”

“Fatigue is a symptom of blood loss,” she said. “I will let you rest.”

17–NEW GUY

I see Kandra, face twisted in pain, white with shock, fired with dread, blood on her forehead, blood in her mouth, terror in her eyes. Her bloodied hands feebly try to cover her nakedness, she screams but no sound comes, pleads but no one hears, prays to every god but no god cares. I must help her, but I can't move. My head throbs. Something crushes my chest. I can't breathe. Kandra cries out again. Sound comes out this time, but it's not her voice. It's a man's voice. He says one word. I can't make it out. The voice speaks again. This time I hear. "Agrios!" Agrios? It means *the savage*. Is she being tormented by a savage? I try to speak her name, but no sound comes out of me.

I'm shaken awake. The first thing I see is Kratisto's face. I suspect that his presence causes nightmares. As usual, he laughs.

"Wake up, old New Guy," he says. The weight on my chest is a sword in a scabbard, with a helmet and breastplate. Kratisto thinks it hilarious to put these things on top of a sleeping man.

It takes me a few seconds to remember where I am, in the house of Kratisto. I know it was a dream, but I really want to see Kandra, to make sure she's all right, even though it is not possible to see her right now. In the dream, when I tried to call her name, I was lucky that no sound came. If Kratisto heard that, he'd kill me today.

"Agrios is the perfect name for you, old New Guy," he says. "You're half donkey or half wildcat or something."

Old New Guy? This makes no sense. Then I see the smirking man who stands behind Kratisto. I've never seen him before. He has a sword, helmet and breastplate, like Kratisto's other guards, like me now. I get it now. I am the old New Guy because he is the new New Guy. When Kratisto hires a new guard, he calls him New Guy until he can think of a degrading nickname for him. I was New Guy for less than a day.

Agrios. Unbelievable. He cuts parts off of people, and I'm the one he calls savage.

"Agrios, meet New Guy," he says. I nod to the new man. He nods back. I notice he's missing two fingers on his left hand, old wounds. Will Kratisto find it necessary to cut something off if New Guy already has something missing? I have already learned not to expect a particularly logical thought process from Kratisto.

In one way, however, he is very predictable: imagine the worst thing a man can do, and Kratisto will do it.

"The new New Guy," Kratisto goes on, "takes the place of Skatocephalos, who has met with an accident. Or, more accurately, Skatocephalos' liver accidentally met with the new New Guy's dagger in the whorehouse last night." I did not need to ask where Skatocephalos' body was. Kratisto probably just left it where it fell.

"He insulted my whore's honour," says New Guy. "That was *my* job."

Kratisto brays with laughter. Then he becomes serious,

even though the smile remains.

"Naptime's over, Agrios," he says. "I've got a job for you. Put on the armour and meet me in the courtyard in two minutes."

I'm still weak, not completely recovered yet, but Kratisto doesn't care. I don't expect him to. I put on the armour.

*   *   *   *   *   *

"Please, math-ter," the boy begged between sobs. "I'll be more careful." He laid on the paving stones in the courtyard, his face already a red-pulped mess. He lisped because some of his teeth had been knocked out and were on the ground beside his head. There was wine on the stones and the remains of a broken cup. The boy must have dropped it.

"Oh, I don't care a mosquito-fart about the cup," Kratisto said as he kicked the boy in the ribs. The boy groaned. "I just feel like kicking someone to death today, and you're the lucky lad I've chosen." The other guards were all there. They all laughed, although Orestes' laugh was forced. He didn't like this, but knew that if he spoke out, Kratisto would make him regret it.

Kratisto kicked the boy a few more times, in the ribs, in the head, in the testicles. The boy whimpered and groaned. One eye was now swollen shut.

"Agrios," Kratisto said. "I tire of this. Finish him for me."

I drew my sword. This boy suffered and would continue to suffer as long as he lived in the house of Kratisto. If I didn't kill him, one of the others would. I consoled myself that at least I'd give him the mercy of a quick death.

"Not with your sword," said Kratisto. "I'm kicking him to death. That's the job I want you to finish."

I re-sheathed my sword. I went to the boy, looked down at his destroyed face, saw the despairing resignation in his eyes, and kicked him hard, once, in the temple. It killed him instantly. Xenocrates taught me this. Xenocrates was heartless at times, but he thought it wrong to prolong agony. When you need to kill a man, he always said, you just do it, if for no other reason than to not give him a chance to strike back.

Orestes reached down and pressed his fingers to the boy's neck to feel for a pulse, then shook his head. The other guards hooted and hollered. They were impressed that I could kill someone so quickly.

Kratisto was not impressed. The smile remained on his lips, but his eyes turned snowstorm cold. "When I told you to finish what I was doing," he said, "I meant for you to make the boy suffer for as long as possible. Have you already forgotten what happens when you fail to follow my orders?"

"Sir," I said. "I did exactly as you told me. You said kick the boy to death, and so I did." I was ready to fight. I was up on the balls of my feet and I'd gone into a slight crouch. I couldn't help myself. If Kratisto tried to cut something else off of me, I would kill him. If that happened, I would never get Kandra out of here. The other guards would overpower me and turn me over to the authorities of Halicarnassus to be tried for the murder of one of the city's citizens—if I was lucky. Except for Orestes, the guards would hate me for killing the man who sponsored their depravity. They'd have their own notions of justice for me.

Kratisto looked me in the eye for a good long time. Then his eyes smiled again. "You are right, Agrios," he said. "You're new here, so I can't blame you for taking my words literally, but know this, boy: in the future, when I order you to kill someone, you will make him suffer for as long as possible, unless I tell you otherwise."

*   *   *   *   *   *

Kratisto provided me with a sleeping cubicle and paid me a monthly wage of half a pittance. The other guards didn't care about the low wage. Kratisto was their hero because they got wine and whores almost every night.

Kratisto had a routine. He slept late, usually to midday. Sometimes he went to the chariot races in the afternoon, but usually he just lounged around his courtyard and amused himself by tormenting his slaves and his sister. This was also the time of day that he'd attend to business matters. There weren't many. He did not inherit his father's metallurgical gift and his only ambition was debauchery. He did, however, go to the slave market in Halicarnassus several times a month because he always needed to replace his slaves. The day after he made me kick the slave boy to death, he ordered two of the house girls to strip naked in the courtyard. Then he gave them swords and helmets, and ordered them to fight to the death.

The girls, a tall slender blonde and a short dark-haired girl, were both pretty and about fifteen years old. Neither one of them looked like she'd ever even held a sword before, let alone used one. When Kratisto told them to fight, they looked at each other in disbelief.

"You want me make killing on her, master?" said the tall girl in a thick Northern accent.

"That's what I said, sweetheart," said Kratisto. "I'll free whichever one of you wins. Now get to it."

The blonde was tall and strong, a kitchen slave, which required her to do some lifting, but the dark-haired girl was one of Nysa's hairdressers. She was delicate, with soft hands and a pale complexion. She didn't lift anything heavier than a hairbrush and looked like she hadn't even been outdoors in years. She used both hands just to hold her weapon. The blonde swung her sword overhand and it clanged as it hit the sword of the other girl, who countered by swinging her own sword against the blonde girl's weapon.

Both blows were aimed at the opponent's sword, not the opponent's body. They were not trying to hurt each other, quite possibly because they didn't know how. Kratisto was not amused.

"You two cunts fight properly," he said, "or I'll just let my men fuck you to death. That might take days."

The dark-haired girl looked at the leering guards, and a wave of horror passed through her eyes. She charged at the tall girl, swung the sword overhand at her, which the tall girl blocked. The dark-haired girl then lunged forward and stabbed the blonde in the stomach. The blonde cried out, as blood seeped from the wound, then swung her own sword clumsily, but effectively enough, into the dark-haired girl's shoulder. The dark-haired girl screamed, dropped her sword, and fell to her knees. The tall girl may never have used a sword before, but must have seen at least one swordfight in her life. She would not have otherwise known to grab her defenseless opponent's dark hair, pull her head back and slit her throat.

Then the blonde touched her own wound. I knew it was fatal before she did. She was dizzy from blood loss and dropped to her knees. She looked pleadingly at Kratisto, probably in the hope that he'd get her a doctor, but she was beyond medicine now.

"Look at the bright side, sweetheart," Kratisto said. "I wasn't actually going to free you." Then he pulled out his dagger and plunged it into her heart.

Mikropeos was excited. He wanted to have his way with the girl's bodies. "Not today, Mikropeos," said Kratisto. "Save it for the whorehouse later."

Nysa came into the courtyard and saw the dead slaves. Her eyes widened a little, but otherwise she barely reacted. She'd learned, over the years, to contain her emotions.

"Brother," she said, "what did these two girls do?

"It's not obvious?" Kratisto said. "They killed each other in a splendid display that I wish had lasted longer."

"No, before that. Why did you punish them?"

"Punish them?" Kratisto snorted. "I gave these two barbarian sluts the opportunity to die in glory. The blonde was from the savage north, where such deaths are highly desirable. The other slaves envy these two."

I silently agreed. The other slaves envied the dead, but not for the reason Kratisto suggested.

Nysa fought back tears. She'd been fond of the girls. "Myra was the best hairdresser I ever had," she said. "She'll need to be replaced. The other one, Hannah, I also need replaced, as well as Nikos from yesterday."

Nysa said no more. If she criticized Kratisto in front of his men, she would regret it. She was helpless in this house, alone, with only slaves for company, and if she befriended any of them, there was the real possibility that Kratisto would kill them for one flimsy reason or another. Kratisto probably chose these two girls to fight *because* Nysa was fond of them. On top of this, Nysa had to train new slaves constantly. Kratisto actually thought this was a good thing because it gave her something constructive to do with her time—as if he used his own time constructively. I pitied Nysa so much at that moment. She ordered two of the other house slaves to bring the bodies inside, where she would clean them herself and anoint them and give them proper funeral rites. If it had been Kratisto's task to dispose of the bodies, he'd just have his men toss them in a rubbish heap for the dogs and kites and crows to feast on.

"Well, boys," said Kratisto, "looks like we're taking a trip to the slave-market."

The other guards hooted with glee. At first, I didn't know why, but it wasn't exactly a Pythagorean tetractys to figure out. Whoever accompanied him to the slave market would get a chance to try out the goods. When Kratisto bought new slaves, he and his men would fuck them a few times before they brought them home. "It's only common sense," Kratisto reasoned. "Would you buy a horse without riding it first?" If Kratisto found the experience unsatisfactory—if the slaves became too hysterical, or just bled too much afterwards—he would take them back to the market and either get his money back or exchange the slaves for different ones—whom his men would also fuck a few times before they brought them home.

When Kratisto went out, he usually left two men to guard the house. I learned later that his main concern was not just to protect Nysa and Kandra but also to prevent the women from escaping. On this day, he designated Orestes and me to remain behind.

Orestes didn't object to this, and neither did I. Orestes was past forty, by far the oldest of us, so I figured sexual urges did not dominate his thoughts as much as they would a younger man. Myself, I had several reasons for not wanting to screw slave prostitutes. For one thing, I worried that they'd be diseased. Some of those diseases were incurable. I also hated the idea of bedding the unwilling. Even though it was legal to do anything you wanted to a slave, in my mind it was still a form of rape. My few sexual experiences had been great precisely because the women involved were highly enthusiastic. I doubted that a slave who tolerated me, rather than enjoyed me, would be equal to the task. My main reason for restraint, though, was Kandra. If I screwed slaves, she would hear about it. As absurd as this sounds, Ephander, I wanted Kandra to know that I was here because I loved her, and my love was somehow nobler because I saved myself for her alone. This would not be easy. Kratisto took all of his men to the whorehouse, and they would wonder why I didn't screw everything in sight like they did. It would be suspicious, but on this day, I was to guard the house so it wasn't an immediate concern.

Or so I thought.

Kratisto and the other four guards left. Orestes and I split up. He patrolled the outside of the house while I remained in the courtyard. Every hour, we would switch places. Kratisto and the others hadn't been gone ten minutes when I heard pounding on the front door and some shouts. I drew my sword and ran to the door. I was barely out of the courtyard before a large man barreled past me so quickly that he knocked me over. I almost plunged my sword into his guts before I recognized Mikropeos. I was not his target. He was terrified. In the courtyard, he cowered behind a statue of Artemis.

"What's going on, Mikropeos?" I asked. He did not answer. Some sounds came out of him, but they were not words. His eyes were wide with naked fear, like a spooked child.

Briareus came into the courtyard. "Fuck," he said when he saw Mikropeos cowering in the corner. "He's useless when he's like this."

"What happened?" I asked.

"He saw a crow," said Briareus. "Actually, three crows, on a rooftop. You don't see a lot of them here in the city. What's worse, the moment he looked at them, they flew away." So Mikropeos was deeply superstitious. I could use that against him.

Briareus walked over to the shaking Mikropeos. "Mikro," he said. "Mikro, can you hear me?"

Mikropeos gave no sign that he did. "Mikro, you stay here today, okay? You understand?"

Mikropeos muttered something. Briareus just shook his head. "We'll leave him here. Agrios, you come with us to the slave market."

"Don't you need two of us here, sir?" I said. "In his

current state, Mikropeos doesn't count."

"It's okay, Orestes can handle it on his own for a couple of hours."

The slave market was close to the port. It was a small wooden building with a platform on the street side. Slaves, each one naked and chained, stood in a line across the back of the stage. The slave auctioneer, a small man in a tattered purple robe, motioned for the slaves to step forward one at a time. The first slave, a tall muscular dark-skinned man, was pretty scary, even with his ankles manacled and his hands chained behind him. He scowled at the small crowd, then shouted what was probably a curse in his own language. The auctioneer struck the man across the shoulders with a stick. The big slave turned towards him, so the auctioneer kicked him in the nuts. The big slave cringed a little but didn't go down. He was still ready to fight. There's tough for you, Ephander: a kick in the balls and he barely flinched. If his hands had been free, the auctioneer would already be dead.

"Who wants to bid on Ktinos?" the auctioneer called out. "Big and tough and stronger than two plough-horses. Ktinos can tear a man's head right off his shoulders. He once killed a lion with his bare hands. What a magnificent bodyguard he'd make! Who will give me a thousand drachmas?"

I didn't expect anyone to bid on Ktinos, whose name meant 'the brute.' The auctioneer's claims were far-fetched nonsense, but even if they'd been true, the big man had not accepted his fate as a slave. Some slaves never do. He would be dangerous and near impossible to train. Any man who bought him would risk his own life just getting him home.

"Five hundred!" a man shouted. He stood next to a litter

that six slaves carried. He was bidding for the litter's occupant. The litter looked so much like the one Kandra used that I momentarily thought she was inside it. Then, the lady inside pulled the curtain back so she could admire the man-flesh on the platform. She was past forty and had red hair. She wore no veil, a sign that she was no man's wife.

"That's Medea," said Briareus with a grin. "We'll be seeing her later."

"Seven hundred!" shouted another man.

The lady nodded to the man beside the litter. "Eight!" he called out. Several other bidders jumped in—I'm certain that at least two of them were not buyers and were only there to jack up the price—but in the end, the lady bought the big slave for twenty-two hundred drachmae.

Kratisto approached the platform and said something quietly to the auctioneer, who nodded and smiled and said, "Yes, that'll work for me." The auctioneer then called to his own slave, who then led three of the naked female slaves—the three prettiest ones—away from the platform. Kratisto had just bought them at a price that the auctioneer knew no one else would match, even at auction. Kratisto was too rich to care that he'd paid too much, and too lazy to go through the bidding process.

The three women actually looked relieved. The auctioneer must have treated them horribly. I pitied them if they thought Kratisto would treat them any better. Kratisto's plan was to take the three women to the tavern next door. He would rent an upstairs room so he and his men could try out the goods.

As we were leaving, the women, still naked, realized the intentions of Kratisto and his men and now looked worried.

One wept. One of the others resembled her, probably her sister, and tried to comfort her with soft words and a hug. The third woman, the tallest of the three, concealed her fear. When I looked at her face, she looked back at me defiantly.

"You ladies are in for a treat," said Kratisto. "You're about to get fucked senseless by the greatest band of degenerates in all Hellas."

The guards hooted. The tall woman suddenly began to cry. At the front door of the tavern, we were still close enough to the auction to see and hear it. I stopped and listened. At the front of the platform, the auctioneer had a woman who was so small that I initially thought she was a child. She had bruises on her legs and a swollen eye. She was pretty, but what struck me most was that despite her fear, she looked wary, assessing the situation and trying to figure out if there was a way out of it. I recognized this because it's what I do in tough situations. And I swear she looked right at me. She nodded slightly.

"Who will bid on Kalliope?" called the auctioneer. "Not much to look at, not very strong, but she can suck your cock till you cry out to the heavens! Who'll start me off at a hundred? A hundred here! Who'll give me one-fifty? One-fifty here! Who'll give me two?"

"Hey Agrios," said Kratisto snapping me out of it. "What the fuck you doing? Forget that titless wonder. The action's over here."

I dreaded this. When we got to the room in the tavern, Kratisto grabbed the tall woman, twisted her arm behind her back—completely unnecessary, she didn't resist, he just liked to cause pain—and began to screw her standing up. Briareus whooped and came up behind one of the others and squeezed her breasts hard enough to make her cry out. He did not penetrate her, though. The other guards, New Guy and Choiros, pinched the other girl and mauled her breasts, but neither did anything more. First fuck always went to Kratisto. He finished with the tall woman, then sat down on the rough bed. Briareus pushed the woman he was holding closer to Kratisto, who now sat on the room's ratty bed, and forced her to her knees. Kratisto pulled the woman's face into his groin.

"Suck it up, girl," he said. "No biting, though. Try anything like that and I'll fuck you to death with a fencepost." The others guffawed. New Guy and Choiros now grabbed the tall woman and both fucked her at the same time.

I left. I waited for the others down on the street.

Two hours later, Kratisto led his smiling guards and the unsmiling women down to the street. The women now wore sack-cloth tunics. All three of them just stared at the ground. Their eyes were dead, their faces sad, their movements labored as if every step was painful. One of the blonde women had blood on her thighs and legs.

"You missed some primo pussy, Agrios," Kratisto said to me.

"I wasn't interested, sir," I said.

"Next time I need to buy a boy," he said, "I'll bring you along."

"No sir, it's not that," I said. "I like girls. It's just that I've never developed a liking for rape."

"What are you talking about?" he said. The smile never left his face but his eyes looked confused. "They're slaves. Their consent is not an issue."

"Still seems like rape to me, sir," I said.

"You're a strange young man, Agrios of Athens. Well, I guess that means more pussy for the rest of us." Right on cue, Briareus, New Guy and Choiros hooted with laughter like a chorus of monkeys.

* * * * * *

I spotted the young man immediately, in this dockside shit-hole tavern, not for what he was but for what he was not. As soon as he appeared in the doorway, it was clear he did not belong here. He was young, maybe seventeen, healthy, and he had all his teeth. He also lacked the ingrained desperation of the usual customers. This was a place for hard men, scarred faces, noses broken in brawls, eyes glazed with too much wine even though the sun had not yet set this day. The smell of men's sweaty bodies filled the room. The young man was not here to drink, which became obvious the moment he locked his eyes on Kratisto and could not look away.

The wine here was a notch more palatable than horse-piss, I heard, but Kratisto liked the rough company here sometimes. Kratisto liked me with him when he came to places like this because I always stayed sober and could spot dangerous situations before they started. This was an adventure for him, to drink with lowlifes who tolerated him mostly because he was buying. They laughed at his stories so he'd keep the wine flowing. Danger always lurked here for Kratisto, which thrilled him.

If he'd been aware of the young man who'd come here to kill him, it would have thrilled him more. I was tempted to let the young man go through with it. If he killed Kratisto, it might become easier for me to get Kandra out of Halicarnassus, but the more likely possibility was that the young man would fail—I spotted his intentions quickly, so there was a good chance Kratisto would too—which would mean I'd have to explain why I didn't stop him.

Kratisto sat at a table with several sodden half-wits and boasted about the time he had three girls at once.

"Turn around right now," I said to the young man. He jumped when I spoke. I'd sidled up to him and surprised him. Big as I am, I've always been good at that.

"What?" said the young man.

"I know what you've come here to do," I said. I saw the bulge of a weapon inside his tunic. "I have a sword. You have only a dagger. You won't even get near him. Turn around and go back home right now."

"He killed my sister," the young man said.

He was brave, I'll give him that, but impulsive. Even with me standing beside him—he barely reached my shoulder—he still wanted to go through with it. He reached for his dagger, but I was faster. I pulled out my sword and jammed the pommel into his face. It knocked him over backwards out the door of the tavern. He laid stunned on the ground and put his hand to his bloodied lip. His dagger laid on the ground beside him.

"That's a warning, buddy," I said, "and the only one you'll get. Listen: Kratisto will get his. He has too many enemies *not* to, but if you try it tonight, you'll only get yourself killed. Go back home."

The boy nodded. He finally saw sense. He picked up his dagger, tucked it back into his tunic, and was about to turn to leave when a sword-point suddenly protruded through his midsection. Diastrefo, the New Guy, had thrust it through the boy's back. The boy sputtered, looked at me in shock, then fell over backwards as Diastrefo pulled his sword out of him.

"Well played, Agrios!" laughed Diastrefo. His name meant 'pervert,' and I shuddered to think of what unspeakable perversion he had to indulge in to get Kratisto to think him a deviant. "You actually had the silly fucker believing you."

"I saw you back there," I lied. "Glad you picked up on it." He'd heard me tell the boy that Kratisto would get his, and this worried me. I was serious when I said it, but I had to hope Diastrefo thought I was not. Of all the guards, Diastrefo worried me the most. He was intelligent, cunning, and the best swordsman. Mikropeos was my enemy but so simple-minded that he was predictable. I would have to watch Diastrefo. He was not my friend—none of these men were, not even Orestes—but so far he was not my enemy either. Diastrefo went back into the tavern to keep an eye on Kratisto while I dragged the boy's body to the alley to leave it there for the dogs and the kites and the crows.

18–KALLIOPE

The huge bastard wore loose yellow silk trousers, like a Persian flute boy, but was shirtless to showcase his dark biceps, thick as Dorian columns. He wore a turban and had a finely-crafted scimitar, which had a gold-plated hilt and an ivory handle, a nobleman's weapon, tucked into his belt. He stood inside the door of the House of Medea, Kratisto's favourite whorehouse, and glared at us. Mikropeos, Choiros, and Briareus looked afraid, so the big man focused on me. I wasn't afraid because none of us was here to fight with him. He was a brothel doorman. He glared at us because that was his job.

"You making trouble," he said to me, "and I fuck it kill you."

It was Ktinos, the same brute we saw at the slave auction a few days before. I would have sworn then that he would be an untrainable slave, but here he was, working for Medea and taking his duties very seriously.

Kratisto whooped a laugh. "Medea, he's magnificent!" he said. "How'd you tame the beast?"

"I may be old," Medea said, with a wink, "but I have my ways." She and Kratisto hugged like old friends. Kratisto kissed her on the cheek. I saw her up close for the first time. She was much older than I originally thought, closer to sixty than forty, and her red hair was actually a wig. Powder concealed her wrinkles from afar, but not from up close.

"I wouldn't have thought," said Kratisto, "that Ktinos would be a very good slave."

"Me neither," said Medea. "So the first thing I did was free him."

"Really?" said Kratisto. "And he doesn't run away?"

"Well, he's a free man," said Medea, "so he wouldn't technically be running away. Ktinos: do you understand that you're a free man, and you can leave anytime you want to?"

"I stay," said Ktinos. "I making promise to master lady Medea. Ktinos keeping it promise."

The House of Medea was not the largest brothel in Halicarnassus, or the finest, and the girls and boys here, though attractive enough, were not the best-looking. The large house was also on the east side of the harbour district, the only rich house in a troubled neighbourhood. It was dangerous to walk here at night, even with bodyguards, but Medea's clientele included some of the city's wealthiest citizens, men who were accustomed to taking guards everywhere they went. They liked the ambiance here—inside, it looked like what most Hellenes imagined the Great King's harem looked like—and Medea was known for her discretion. The main attraction here, though, was that she offered variety like no other brothel-keeper. She fulfilled special requests, no matter how cruel or bizarre. If your tastes were for men, women, boys, girls, or animals—and Ephander, I'm not kidding about the animals, one high-born Hallicarnassan lady supposedly came here from time to time to indulge her fantasy to be fucked by a horse—Medea would accommodate you, as long as you paid her price.

In Medea's lounge, we sat on couches draped in silks of many colours. The walls were painted with scenes of gods and satyrs who frolicked with jiggly maidens, and shepherds who were visited by randy goddesses. There was a clear area against one wall where a dozen girls and several pretty boys were displayed for us. The boys were completely naked, while the girls wore thin red veils. The veils covered them from head to toe and concealed almost nothing but helped define the curves of hip and breast, a much more arousing effect than if they'd just been naked. The women tried to look cheerful, but the cruelty of Kratisto and his men was well-known, so the women's fear showed through their forced smiles. These men liked to beat whores, and had even killed a few, for no reason other than they felt like doing it. When this happened, Kratisto would pay triple the replacement value of the dead whore. One of the women began to sob. Medea glared at her, so the girl made an extra effort to control herself.

Another of the girls, the smallest of them, did not show fear. She was the only one who looked wary rather than afraid. It was Kalliope, the girl from the auction. I didn't know Medea had bought her. Again, she looked right at me and nodded slightly. Then she continued to look the other men over, like she was sizing them up, looking for advantage.

This was a survivor. I already liked her.

"Agrios," said Kratisto. "My other men don't normally choose boys when they come here, but I had Medea put a few out for you. Take your pick."

"As I told you before, sir," I said, "I like girls."

"So you say," laughed Kratisto.

"I do say, sir," I said. I pointed to Kalliope. "If it's okay with you, I'll take this one."

"As you wish," said Kratisto. "Can't help but notice, though, that you've chosen the girl with the smallest tits, the one here who looks most like a boy." He laughed again, but said no more to me. He grabbed a busty blonde slave and dragged her ungently by the hair to one of the bedrooms. Kalliope came forward, took my hand and led me to another.

I sat on the bed. Kalliope stood in front of me. "What would you have me do, my lord?" she asked.

"Nothing," I said. "I will rest. You can too."

"Sir, you must let me do something," she said. "If I fail to please you, Medea will have Ktinos beat me."

Her hair was black, but her skin was chalk white, much lighter than it looked at the slave market. The room was dimly lit by a single oil lamp, but I could still see that the flesh around one of her eyes was slightly swollen. Heavy powder concealed a black eye.

"If it will help, I'll tell Medea that I am unwell," I said. "The truth is, that I do not rut with the unwilling."

"But my lord, I *am* willing."

"No you're not. You're a slave. If I choose to fuck you, you don't have the option of refusing."

"If you don't find me attractive, then why did you choose me?"

"You mistake me. You're very cute. In fact, you remind me of the first woman I ever slept with. I just don't like to fuck slaves. I also believe you've got a sharp mind behind those sweet dark eyes. What's your real name?"

"My real name doesn't matter," she said sadly. "I'm Kalliope now. I saw you at the slave market with Kratisto and his men."

"I noticed you too. You looked more wary than afraid."

"Survival instinct. I wondered what you were doing with those guys," she said. She sat on the bed beside me. As she became more relaxed with me, her language got rougher. "Those sick fucks really hate women. A couple nights ago, three of them fucked me at the same time. The asshole with the tiny dick kept punching me in the back while he fucked me in the ass. I still have the bruises. Like it's somehow my fault his dick is so small."

"Where are you from originally?" I asked. I wanted to change the subject. Her suffering depressed me.

"I'm from Halicarnassus, my lord. I'm an orphan. I've lived on the streets my whole life. A month ago, I broke into a rich man's house and stole his wife's gold bracelet. I got caught, so I was sold to that sack of pigshit slave trader, bought by Medea, and now I'm here in the fucking bowels of Hades. Take me with you."

"Take you with me? What makes you think I'm going somewhere?" She caught me off guard. Was it really so obvious that I didn't plan to stay in Halicarnassus? If she spotted it in two minutes, would others?

"Just a hunch," she said. "You're not like Kratisto or his men." There was a sudden yowl of pain, a woman's voice, from one of the other rooms. For the others, getting laid was never enough.

"You're far too intelligent," Kalliope continued, "and civilized to spend time with those sick fucks if you're not up to something. When you leave Halicarnassus, take me with you. I know the streets. The alleys, too. I can help you get out of town if you need to leave in a hurry."

What she said made sense. I'd been in Halicarnassus long enough to know the main streets but not long enough to know the back alleys. To take Kandra away from here, I might need local assistance. That didn't mean I was ready to trust an orphan, whore and thief I'd just met.

"I'll think about it," I said. "Whatever you suspect about me, you are not to speak of it with anyone. If you do, I'll kill you."

"No you won't," she said.

Damn. She'd read me correctly. I wouldn't kill her. It wasn't my nature. Besides, if Kratisto found out what I was up to, I wouldn't get the chance. So I had Kalliope give me a back rub while she told me what she knew about the city.

"I have another specialty, my lord," she said softly, "that you will like very, very, very much."

She was absolutely right about that, Ephander. Smart, too, because now I had a reason to request her every time I came back here.

* * * * * *

The other guards laughed at me. They thought I was some kind of lunatic. I did not care. I wasn't like them and could not even pretend to be. I didn't rut with every slave and whore I encountered. When I accompanied Kratisto around the city, I did my duty and defended him when necessary, but I didn't harass people who were merely going about their business, as all the others except Orestes did, as Mastropos had done when he was injured. There was no sign that the others had learned from Mastropos' mistake. Their unprovoked violence had one practical benefit: when most Halicarnassans saw Kratisto's entourage coming, they got off the street. So the times that I had to actually defend Kratisto were few.

The others teased me about my civilized ways. It was behaviour they could not understand. Sometimes they called me *Agios*, 'the saint.' It was not intended as a compliment. Mikropeos thought 'Agios Agrios,' Saint Savage, was the funniest thing he'd ever heard and laughed every time someone said it.

My dislike of wine mystified them utterly. Even Orestes, the most restrained of them, wondered about this. "I don't believe in getting slobber-faced every night, lad," he said, "but never taking a few drinks? That's a life unthinkable."

The others drank and ate until they passed out every night. They slept much more than I did—very few people did not—but their sleeping cubicles, ironically, were used less than mine was, mostly because they usually slept wherever they happened to pass out. On warm nights, they slept in the courtyard, snorting and grunting and farting the night away under the stars.

I slept my usual two or three hours a night. I liked the solitude of the wee hours of the morning. I would run through the streets, which initially confused the city watchmen, who stopped me at swordpoint the first few times—they figured a man running at night was fleeing a crime he'd just committed—but once they got to know me, they would just nod and greet me by name.

I also drilled with weighted swords. I tied rocks to two wooden swords Kratisto had given me. My drills were mostly repetitions of sword moves, thrusts and parries, feints and cuts, but also included stamina exercises like holding the weighted swords over my head for a full hour. I did most of these in the courtyard. Occasionally, when the others were passed out there, one or another of them would wake up and look at me like I was an apparition, a hallucination, but they rarely said anything and usually just went back to sleep.

Some nights Kratisto would rise from his stupor long enough to spar with me. Even half-soused, he was a pretty good swordsman who could have been great if he applied himself. He was naturally deceptive—an asset for a swordsman—and naturally athletic. Unfortunately, he was also naturally lazy. We used the wooden swords, so I always let him win. I foresaw the possibility that we might fight for real, and I wanted him to think he was a better swordsman than me. As with most egomaniacs, it was not difficult to trick him into thinking he was better than he actually was.

Most nights I went to sleep long after the others did and rose long before them. But one day I did not. I don't know why I slept longer on that particular morning. I woke up slowly with a weight on my chest. It wasn't particularly heavy, and my first instinct was to reach for it, but I resisted at the last second because whatever it was, it moved.

This hesitation saved my life. A horned viper sat on my chest. Its merciless green eyes looked right into mine. I froze.

The horned viper does not like cities. It is a countryside snake, and it didn't crawl on me by itself. Its venom was fatal. I'd heard that you longed for death for many hours before it came. I knew who was responsible. I couldn't see him—if I turned my head, I might startle the viper—but I heard the donkey chortle of Mikropeos.

I didn't panic. If I stayed calm, the snake would too.

Lucky for me, Grandfather had taught me about snakes. We'd see them sometimes when we camped out. The first time I saw a poisonous one, a horned viper even bigger than the one on my chest, it was on a forest trail ahead of Grandfather and me. I was nine years old. My first instinct was to run as fast as I could in the opposite direction.

Grandfather clamped his hand on my shoulder and held me back. "While running away is not the worst thing you can do when you see a snake, lad," he said quietly, "it is rarely necessary. Stop and look. What is the snake doing? Is he attacking us?"

"No, sir," I said. "He looks afraid that we'll attack *him*."

"Correct. Always respect snakes–this big bugger has enough venom to kill ten men–but there is no need to fear them. They do not go around looking for people to bite. They see us as predators and stay away. They bite only in self-defense."

As he spoke, the big viper slithered away into the undergrowth as fast as it possibly could. I learned the lesson. And here in the House of Kratisto, as death stared me in the face, I remembered it.

Mikropeos laughed and poked the viper with a stick. He apparently thought this would make the snake bite me, and was genuinely surprised when it coiled up and tried to bite the stick. After its second strike in his direction, the snake slid off of my chest and onto the floor. It remained coiled, but Mikropeos gasped like a frightened child, dropped his stick and ran away.

My sword leaned against my pallet, so I grabbed the weapon and used the flat side to pin the snake's head to the ground. I used my other hand to grab the snake behind its head, so that it could not coil back and bite me. Grandfather had taught me this. Then I went looking for Mikropeos.

He'd returned to his own cubicle. The simpleton was actually hiding, like he thought the snake would look in every room until it found him.

I hid the snake behind my back. It coiled angrily around my left arm, but I was safe as long as I kept a firm grip behind its head. "Mikropeos, or whatever the fuck your name is," I said. "Do you think you're smart enough to contend with me?"

He peeked out of his cubicle. "Snake bite you?" he asked hopefully.

"No," I said. "And it's no coincidence. My father was a sorcerer who taught me how to talk to serpents. This one's name is Pistos, and he's really pissed at the guy who brought him here. He asked me where your room was."

I pulled the snake from behind my back and held it out towards Mikropeos. His jaw dropped so quickly that it must've bruised his chest. I don't know what scared him more, the snake itself or the idea that I could communicate with it. I dropped the snake a couple of feet in front of Mikropeos and said, "Pistos—attack!"

The snake for some reason moved towards Mikropeos instead of me. I have no idea why, probably a coincidence, but who knows, maybe it really *was* pissed at the man who'd brought it here. Mikropeos pissed himself, literally, and wailed like a baby, then dove back into his bed and pulled the blanket over his head. The snake, probably alarmed at the sound

Mikropeos made, coiled up and hissed but didn't actually strike at him. Orestes suddenly ran up from behind me and hacked its head off with his sword.

"Are you guys *nuts*?" he said. "Bringing a killer snake in here?" Then he thought for a second, looked at me and said, "That's not your style, Agrios. Only a moron of Mikro's stature would do something like this."

Orestes looked into Mikro's cubicle and saw him cowering under his blanket, where he wept like a three-year-old. "You fucking idiot," Orestes said. "You got a beef with Agrios, that's one thing, but you bring a viper in here, other people might get killed too, including yourself. Aww, he's not listening to me. Agrios, let's get the snake out of here before the women see it."

Two good things resulted from this incident with the snake. The first was that from this point onward, Mikropeos was spooked by me. He believed that I really was the son of a wizard and could bring all sorts of evil juju down on him if he tried to torment me. At times I would turn and find him looking at me with a distinctly worried expression, and he'd look away as soon as I noticed him. When I walked by him for any reason, he now stepped back and looked at the ground until I passed, like I was lightning he hoped would strike somebody else.

The second good thing was that it opened a form of communication between Kandra and me.

I'd been in the house of Kratisto for more than a month now, but I had not communicated in any way with Kandra, not a word or a gesture. One late night, as Kratisto and the others had drank themselves into their usual stupor and dozed in the courtyard, I did my weighted sword exercises. I held one upright in each hand out to my sides for ten seconds, then held them over my head for ten seconds. I repeated this for twenty minutes without resting either arm. Much harder than it sounds, Ephander, try it some time. It was a cool late summer night, perfect for training. I looked at the endless stars in the clear sky. Then I noticed a silhouetted figure in one of the upper windows of the house. A tall woman watched me from the gynaikon. I did not see enough detail to know for certain it was Kandra, but no other woman in the household—Hades, no other woman in Halicarnassus—was as tall as her. Whether or not it was her, she did the right thing when she quickly pulled the curtain back over the window. I looked over at Kratisto, and was relieved to see him snoring away. It did not have to be him who saw anything. In a house full of slaves, secrets were rare. There were simply too many eyes here. If a slave-girl saw Kandra watching me, she might run and report it immediately to Kratisto, not because she hated Kandra, but because she knew Kratisto flogged slaves that he suspected of holding back information.

The daily trips to accompany Kandra's litter to the shrine of Artemis were pure torture.

As I walked alongside the litter, we could have conversed easily but both knew it was too dangerous to try. The litter-slaves would hear. She chatted sometimes with Orestes when he was present, but did not speak to any of the others except to issue sharp commands. If she spoke to me, even in whispers, it would get noticed. When she spoke to Orestes, I heard an edge to her voice, a bite that wasn't there when I knew her on Skiathos. I wanted to jump into the litter with her, hold her, kiss her, smell her hair, nuzzle the soft skin on the back of her neck, and make her laugh that magical laugh of hers. I also knew I must drive such thoughts from my head.

The worst task was when we got to the shrine and had to help her out of the litter. Kandra was a proper lady now, and a proper lady did not clamour out of a litter like a serving wench. A wooden box was kept on the back of the litter, and when she alighted, the box was placed as a step for her. Whichever one of us was on that side of the litter took one of her hands as she stepped primly down. The first time I did this, I almost blew everything. The warmth of her hand on mine radiated through me from head to toe like I'd been hit by lightning. I needed every ounce of concentration I had to not put my arms around her. I kept my eyes fixed on the ground, and released her before she had completely stepped down. She stumbled, but caught herself. If she'd tripped, and I'd had to catch her, it would all be over.

"Oaf," she muttered. "Pay attention."

"Apologies, despoina," I said quickly.

"Don't mind him," Orestes said to Kandra. "He's new."

Kandra's eyes bore into me. I looked down, at her feet, but I realized that if I did that for long enough, I'd start to think about the rest of her body, and this was no time for distraction, so I shifted my gaze to my own feet.

"I heard we have a new guard who doesn't drink wine," she said to Orestes. "Is this him?"

"It is," said Orestes. "So far, despoina, he's been all right."

"How long do you think a sober man will last with Kratisto?" she said.

"Not very," said Orestes. He and Kandra chuckled. She proceeded into the temple. We'd wait outside. I noticed she limped a little.

So Kandra and I had no way to communicate until after Mikropeos put the snake in my bed. When anyone in the household had a health problem, Kandra helped them. From her father Simonides, she'd learned herblore. She knew which plants healed and which ones killed. When Nysa treated those many household injuries, she could count on Kandra to supply the right medicinal plant. When Orestes was banged up, after we sparred on my first day here, he found a small vial of leopard's bane, calendula and milk of opium on his bed that night. The attached note said, 'To ease your pain.' As I walked past his sleeping cubicle that night, I happened to see the handwriting on the parchment, and it startled me. It was exactly like my own. Back on Skiathos, Kandra learned to write by copying my handwriting, and soon did it so well that I couldn't tell hers from mine. When Mikropeos was spooked by the crows, he found a vial of ashwaganda and chamomile waiting for him. The note said, 'To comfort you at night,' although Mikropeos had to get Orestes to read it for him.

After my little snake incident, I found a small vial on my bed that night. The note said, 'To bring sleep.'

It confused me at first. Kandra knew that I did not sleep much, and she knew I wouldn't be spooked by a snake. Yet she sent me this medicine, and this note, for a reason. I stared at the words as if that would somehow shake loose their true meaning. Didn't work.

So that night, after the others dozed in the courtyard, I went for a run. When I returned, I drilled with my weighted swords. That's when it hit me like gods-sent inspiration. It was not the words in the note but the *missing* word that was the key to its meaning. Orestes' note had said 'To ease *your* pain.' Mikropeos' note said, 'To comfort *you* at night.' My note said 'To bring sleep.' Kandra did not specify that it was I who might need sleep. It was brilliant. If the note was read by someone who would report it to Kratisto, and it almost certainly was, no one would see anything other than the actual words and their literal meaning.

I was to use this vial to put someone to sleep. Kratisto? Maybe. Now I needed to figure out the rest of this puzzle.

19–BETROTHAL

Early one afternoon, Nysa summoned me to her sun room, which was on the second floor of the house. This was not unusual. I'd been there many times. She was lonely, I knew, and liked my company. Apart from Orestes, none of the other guards could provide her with anything close to an intelligent conversation. She wanted to know all about Athens and my time there as an *ephebe*, a military trainee. She was keenly interested in military matters, and her knowledge of battle strategies and generals was exceptional. She'd questioned me closely about why I left Athens before my training was finished. I told her it was because my father died bankrupt, not because my slave birth had been discovered. Since I'd been in Halicarnassus, I'd maintained the pretense that I was a native Athenian. I don't know if Nysa believed me–Themistocles himself once told me I was a conspicuously inept liar–but she at least had the decency to pretend she did. There was no need to conceal our conversations. Kratisto knew that his sister liked to talk to me, but told me in no uncertain terms–in fact, he said he'd force-feed me my own testicles–if I ever touched her. The threat was unnecessary. I did not lust for Nysa, although under different circumstances I might have. She was a dozen years older than me but not unattractive and would make a good wife.

On this day, she did not want to talk about Athens or warfare. First, she just stared at me, with no expression. This was unlike her, she usually smiled when I came to chat with her. She wore a yellow chiton and a dark-green shawl that matched her eyes almost perfectly.

"Is something wrong, Nysa?" I said. "You didn't even answer when I said hello."

"I can't figure you out, Markos," she finally said. "You've hoarded enough of the sleeping potion to kill three elephants."

It was true. Every night for the last month, since my encounter with the horned viper, Kandra had sent me a potion made of valerian, lemon balm, and one or two other sleep-inducing ingredients. I saved them all. They were a key component of my plan to get Kandra away from here. Then I did something really stupid: I hid the vials under the straw mattress in my sleeping cubicle. Even Mikropeos could have come up with a better hiding place.

"The despoina sends me a vial every night," I said. "She heard that I don't sleep much."

"So why don't you take the potion?" Nysa asked. "It's perfectly safe. I take it myself sometimes. You sleep calmly, and the next day you feel no ill effects."

"I don't need much sleep," I said. "Never have. My father was the same. A couple of hours is usually enough."

"Then why didn't you tell Kandra to stop sending you the vials?"

"She went to the trouble to try and help me. I didn't want to insult her by refusing these gifts."

Nysa smiled. "What exactly are you up to, Markos of

Athens?" she said. "Or should I say, Markos of *Skiathos.*"

I don't know if my face changed colour at that particular moment, but it sure felt like it did. I also knew that this was my hardest test. How I handled the next few seconds would determine the success or failure of my entire plan.

So I did not confirm or deny. I kept my face as neutral as possible. I shrugged, like it was no big deal. "What makes you say that?" I asked.

"I'm not a complete idiot," she said.

"I never thought so," I said. "I've always thought the opposite."

"You say too many words exactly the way Kandra says them," she said. "I noticed it after you'd been here a couple of days. You've spent time in Athens, but like her, you're from Skiathos. It's no fluke that you're here. So what are you up to?"

Nysa could have reported her suspicions about me to Kratisto, but she hadn't yet, so I had to hope I could trust her further.

There were no slaves with us. One had brought us water and wine and honeycakes but did not stay. I went to the door, looked out to see if any slaves were within earshot. When I was satisfied no one could overhear us, I returned to my chair and spoke in a low voice.

"It's true," I said. "I've known Kandra since we were children. She is the love of my life. I've come to take her away from here. I knew that I could not just barge into Halicarnassus and steal her, so I've infiltrated your household to give myself time to come up with a plan. Will you keep my secret?"

At that moment, I realized something unpleasant about myself: I was prepared to kill Nysa, an innocent bystander and someone I genuinely liked, if she interfered with my plan.

"Of course," she said. "As long as you give me your word that your plan does not involve killing us all with your hoard of sleeping potion."

"I swear to sacred Athena," I said. "No one in this household will be harmed, with the possible exception of Mikropeos, and only because that worthless asshole tried to kill me. Keep my secret, Nysa, and I'll keep yours."

"My secret?" she said with a smile. "What secret do you think I have?"

"Your brother doesn't know about you and Orestes," I said.

Now it was Nysa's turn to squirm. The colour drained from her face like wine from a tipped cup. She stammered helplessly. Her lips blubbered like she'd forgotten how to form words. Even when Kratisto had killed two of her favourite slaves, she did not lose her composure the way she did now.

"P-please," she said, as she grabbed my hand in both of hers and squeezed it desperately. "We were secretly married last spring. If you tell my brother, he'll kill Orestes, then he'll torture every slave in the house for not telling him."

Married? This was news to me. In fact, I'd suspected—and I emphasize, Ephander, only *suspected*—that she and Orestes were lovers. I always went to bed very late at night and had to walk past Orestes' sleeping cubicle to reach my own. Most nights, it was empty. I initially thought he'd been warming the bed of one of the slaves, but then I noticed how Nysa's eyes shone in Orestes' presence, and in no one else's, and a barely noticeable pink tinge came to her cheeks. It meant she liked him, perhaps even loved him. I had no inkling that they were man and wife.

"I'll give you anything you want," she pleaded. She got down on her knees in front of me and tried to lift my tunic. "Take me right now if you want to. I'll suck your dick. I'll let you—"

"Please stop, Nysa," I said. "Keep your voice down. I've already promised to keep your secret if you'll keep mine. Now I know why you refuse the husbands Kratisto brings you."

"Yes," she said, as the panic slowly faded from her eyes, "but it's not the only reason. He once tried to get me to marry a filthy seventy-five-year-old beggar. He thought it would have been a grand joke. He's also tried to fix me up with degenerates, eunuchs, condemned criminals, and men who were clearly insane. In fact, it will now be harder to refuse if he ever does make a suitable match for me. It hasn't happened yet, so I'll deal with it if and when it does."

"If you were on to me from the start," I said, "why didn't you tell your brother?"

"Well, you're a man of character," she said, "unlike the other lowlifes my brother collects. If you came to take Kandra away from here, as I've always suspected, that's a good thing. In some ways, though, I share my brother's motivations."

"You're nothing like your brother."

"In most ways, true. But he does many terrible things because, at the heart of it all, he's bored. I too am bored. I rarely leave the house. I've never been out of Halicarnassus. This is why I dream of visiting Athens—and Susa and Sardis and Aegyptos and practically everywhere else. I've never been to the chariot races—my brother has decreed that the racetrack is no place for a lady—and I've never seen the port, the slave market, or much else in this city. Halicarnassus has a reputation for great beauty, but based on how little of it I've seen, I wouldn't know, even though I've lived here my whole life.

"So to relieve my boredom, I let this drama unfold, and I must admit that it's been magnificent. I do like you, and I sincerely hope my brother's men do not kill you. So I will let this stage-play finish. Choerilus himself could not have written a better one. I'm dying to see how it ends."

* * * * * *

"Silk fight!"

Kandra's handmaidens and the other slave girls in the house of Kratisto suddenly rolled swathes of silk, precious silk, into balls and threw them at each other. There were fifteen girls and women, and they laughed like children, even though only one or two of them actually were. They were unusually boisterous because tomorrow was the start of the Lenaia. It was a minor winter festival in Athens, but in Halicarnassus it was the high point in the life of a slave. On the morning of the first day, there was a procession from the city centre to the shrine of Dionysus, where twelve white calves were sacrificed. It featured two days of comic plays. Tragedies were for other festivals. On the second day, the slaves were allowed to drink their fill of their masters' best wine. In most households, one person was designated to abstain, to handle any emergencies that might arise. The guards considered it a punishment to be sober in a house full of drunken slave girls, so none of the others objected—and none was surprised—when I volunteered.

The slave girls laughed and joked as they decorated the house, inside and out, with ribbons and swathes of coloured silk. They also sang randy songs that would have been deemed unladylike at any other time. They were having the time of their lives, so Nysa was genuinely unhappy to break it up. "Girls, finish the decorating later," she said, not unkindly. "We have guests."

The slaves were so caught up in their merriment that they hadn't initially notice the three stern-faced men Kallum led through the house and out to the courtyard. The men had an appointment with Kratisto. Their business was serious, they said, and they refused Nysa's offer of wine and honeycakes. In the courtyard, they sat in stony silence. They were unarmed, and their own bodyguards had been forced to wait outside. Mikropeos, Diastréfo and I had been ordered to be present when they arrived. Kratisto wanted us here, especially Mikropeos, to unnerve and distract the visitors. They were here to negotiate, and no man could concentrate well with a deranged idiot like Mikropeos staring at him.

The three men were aristocrats from an ancient Hallicarnassan family. Two of them were pot-bellied, bald, and about fifty years old, clearly brothers. The third man was maybe thirty, much fitter than the others, and while he had a full head of hair, he resembled the other two, so I figured he was the son of one of them. They all wore belted knee-length tunics of finely woven linen, a sign of their wealth.

One of the older men held a scented cloth to his nose. The younger man, who did not have a scented cloth, took on a greenish hue. The previous night, one or more of the guards had vomited here. The slaves had cleaned it up but the smell lingered. This was also tactical. Men who were nauseated—and intimidated—would give in more easily, simply to get the Hades out of here. I wasn't ill myself because vomiting happened here so often that I'd simply gotten used to the smell.

Kratisto made them wait for an hour. Several times we heard Kratisto laugh loudly, even though we could not see him from the courtyard. One of the older men said to me, "Well? Is he coming or not?"

Kratisto was just being an asshole—he couldn't *not* be an asshole—but there was nothing I could do. "Sir, I do not speak for the despotis," I said.

"Then go get him, damn you!"

"I cannot, sir. My orders come from him, not you, and he ordered me to stay here."

His face reddened and he began to sweat, even though it wasn't a particularly hot day. He wanted to send one of the others to fetch Kratisto, but took one look at drooling Mikropeos and thought better of it.

Finally, Kratisto appeared. "So, who the hell are you guys?" he said. Kratisto knew who they were. He just wanted to insult them further.

The oldest man sighed. "You know damned well who we are!" he said. "I made this appointment with you personally three days ago!"

"Sorry, fella," said Kratisto, whose smile never faded once. "Not ringing any bells. You sure it was me?"

The oldest man jumped to his feet. "You fucking well know it was!" I was closest to him so I pulled my sword partway out of its scabbard, put a hand on his shoulder and directed him back to his chair. He sat but became no calmer. Kratisto's tactics had worked very well so far.

"I'll remind you," said the other older man. "This is my brother Abantes and his son Vettias. I am Iachkos. We're here to discuss an incident a few days ago involving you and Abantes' daughter."

"Was she the blonde with the big tits?" Kratisto said innocently. "I tell you, pal, she was terrible. Just laid there like a corpse. Are you here to give me my money back?"

"My daughter is not a whore!" growled Abantes. "You and your men raped her!"

"I'm sorry," said Kratisto, "but you'll need to be more specific. What did she look like?" Diastrefo and Mikropeos laughed, but I couldn't even pretend that I found this amusing.

Abantes looked like he wanted to wring Kratisto's neck.

"Dark-haired, pretty girl, about twenty," Iachkos said. The men knew that Kratisto toyed with them, but also knew that they'd get nowhere if they didn't play this game.

"Short, big round ass?" said Kratisto.

"No sir," said Iachkos. "Tall. Slender."

"Oh, *her*!" said Kratisto, as he clapped his hands in delight. "She was terrific! Very lively from start to finish. I tell you, Abantes, if she ever does become a whore, she'll be a great one. Let me know if that happens."

"My daughter," said Abantes, fists clenched, face tightened with rage, "is not a whore and never will be."

"She's a natural," said Kratisto. "You'd really make a lot of money from her. I'd pay double to fuck her again."

Abantes was too enraged to speak, so his brother stepped in. "Learchos," said Iachkos. "Enough of this game you're playing. You and your men raped my niece and her slave-girl. This is a courtesy call before we bring in the legal authorities. The issue here is not whether you enjoyed it, but how you plan to compensate us. This sort of thing gets around, so we won't be able to find her a good husband. Right now, she's terrified to leave the house."

Kratisto's smile never diminished. The threat of legal action was laughable because he was rich enough to bribe his way out of criminal charges. He'd done it twice in the short time I'd been with him.

"Sir," said Abantes, "do you have children of your own?"

"Probably, somewhere," said Kratisto. Mikropeos and Diastrefo laughed.

"She is my child," said Abantes. "My special little flower. Now she has been defiled by you and the thugs you employ. She'll never be the same. You think it is a joke. This would never happen if your father was still with us."

Kratisto bristled slightly at the mention of his father. "Hey buddy," he said. "We're stuck with the world the gods give us, not the one we want, and definitely not the one that no longer exists. So unless you know how to raise my father's rotting corpse from the dead, don't mention him again."

Abantes face turned purple. He was angry but knew he was helpless. He wanted to kill Kratisto here and now but knew he'd be dead in a second if he tried.

"Okay, all kidding aside," said Kratisto. "A serious offer. Your daughter can marry Mikropeos here."

Mikropeos laughed his donkey laugh. Iachkos looked ill at the prospect. Abantes just shook his head. "Are you fucking kidding me?" he said. "You rescued this degenerate from the noose in Ephesus. My daughter would kill herself if I betrothed her to this animal."

"Okay," said Kratisto, "then *I'll* marry her." Believe it or not, Ephander, he was serious. He would go through with the wedding, torment the girl until he got tired of it, then she would disappear.

"Absolutely not!" said Abantes. "Completely unacceptable. She breaks into tears at the mention of your name. We're leaving. You haven't heard the last of this, Learchos. You will pay, one way or another."

"One last offer," said Kratisto. "Take it or fucking leave it."

"Do I even want to ask?" said Abantes. "You've insulted us from the moment we arrived here, and you haven't taken this matter seriously for a second. Why would I believe that you suddenly will?"

"Your son," said Kratisto, nodding towards Vettias, who hadn't said a word since he'd arrived. "He is unmarried, yes? How'd you like my sister for a wife?"

Abantes' eyes widened. "You're serious?"

Iachkos did not like where this was going. "Abantes, don't even—"

"She's my daughter, brother, not yours," said Abantes. To Kratisto, he said, "We'll want this in writing."

"Draw up the contract," said Kratisto. "Meet me here the day after the Lenaia and I'll sign it."

Kratisto held out his hand. Abantes clasped it gladly. At this moment, I was more disgusted with Abantes than with

Kratisto. Nysa's dowry would be huge, but Abantes was already wealthy. Vettias looked terrified.

Who could blame him? Kratisto would be the brother-in-law from Hades.

20–LENAIA

Kratisto was the soul of sober propriety in the grand open-air theatre of Dionysus. He sat proudly in a front row seat reserved for the *choregoi*, the wealthy citizens who sponsored the Lenaia comedies. His hair was neatly brushed, his long barbarian moustache oiled and trimmed, and he wore a fine cedar-green tunic. He was a striking man when he chose to be, a man who commanded attention even when he did nothing. He chatted quietly with the sixty-year-old matron and her husband in the seats next to his. I stood ready at the edge of the seating area. I was not close enough to hear what he just said, but whatever it was made the lady and her husband laugh. Then the old man said something and Kratisto laughed.

I'd been in his employ for almost three months now, and until a few days earlier, I'd had no idea that Kratisto was a choregos. He'd always given the impression of complete indifference to civic duty. I only found out about it because he stopped at a small warehouse on his way to the brothel. As we approached the building, we heard singing. Inside, in a large empty room, a chorus of twenty-four boys stood off to one side, with several actors in various places near them. It was a rehearsal, so none wore a costume or mask. A small thin balding man in his forties, with the determinedly unkempt beard of a playwright, stood in front of the actors. He shouted at the chorus, "Better, but you're still coming in too early! Tobias, I can barely hear you. When we perform, you'll need to be twice as loud as you are now. Ah, Kratisto." He held out his hand and Kratisto clasped it and smiled warmly. Until that moment, I didn't know Kratisto was *capable* of smiling warmly.

"How goes it, Epicharmos?" Kratisto said. "Will we be ready?"

The little man was Epicharmos of Kos, a comic playwright famous throughout Hellas. Kratisto had brought him to Halicarnassus and hired him to write, rehearse, and stage a play for the Lenaia. It cost a small fortune. He'd rented a large house for Epicharmos, and stocked it with the fourteen-year-old slave-boys the playwright was reputed to love so much. It was all very shrewd. Hiring Epicharmos was exactly the sort of public-minded action that would make people doubt the horrible rumours about Kratisto, or perhaps dismiss them altogether as the exaggerations of the envious.

"I think we'll be okay," said Epicharmos. "We're still rough in places, but we're much better than we were a few days ago. The boys are working hard."

"Good work, my friend," said Kratisto as he patted Epicharmos on the back. "I'll check back with you later."

As we resumed our trip to the whorehouse, Kratisto caught my eye and said, "Why are you looking at me like that, Agrios?"

I wasn't aware I'd been doing it. "I have to say I'm impressed, sir," I said. "Every choregos in all Hellas would give his left nut to get Epicharmos for the Lenaia, but you, testicles intact, did it. How did you manage it?"

"I have friends in low places," he said with a wink, "but friends in high places too. Epicharmos was one of my father's friends. I've known him for years."

Then Kratisto just stared at me. So I said, "Why are *you* looking at *me* like that, sir?"

He laughed. "I'm impressed with you too, lad," he said. "You're the only one of my men who realizes how much prestige Epicharmos brings to this city."

At the Lenaia a few days later, Epicharmos' play was about to begin. I noticed how much attention people paid to Kratisto, even though he just sat and chatted amiably with the people around him. All the women present, young or old, snuck glances at him. Married women glanced flirtatiously at him, even with their husbands present. The unmarried ones wanted to meet him. He was the most sought-after bachelor in Halicarnassus, wealthy, god-handsome, witty, charming. Many of the men looked at him, too, a few because they desired him, but most because they had sisters or daughters to betroth. It was hard to believe that this was the same monster who would kick a slave to death simply because he felt like it.

Diastrefo and I were assigned to guard Kratisto today. We were not in a whorehouse, or on a street at night, so Kratisto had us dress down: clean blue tunics, no armour, no swords, no helmets. The Lenaia was a religious festival, so we were technically not allowed to bring weapons in, but the city watchmen overlooked our daggers because, well, we worked for Kratisto.

I did not like this situation. I stood off to one side of the theatre, Diastrefo on the opposite side. If anyone attacked Kratisto, we'd be too far away to help him. There were dozens of people between us and him. I needed Kratisto alive. I would escape with Kandra that evening, but my plan would not work unless Kratisto's slaves and bodyguards drank wine freely. If someone killed him, his entire household would go into mourning and refrain from wine. Plus, I confess, I wanted to kill Kratisto myself.

When we arrived at the theatre, Kratisto told Diastrefo and me where we would be stationed.

"We should be by your side, sir," I protested.

Kratisto merely laughed. "Agrios, no one would dare lift a finger against me here," he said. I did not understand his lack of concern. During the Lenaia, this theatre was a sacred place, and the play itself was performed in honour of the god Dionysus, but anyone who wanted to kill Kratisto wouldn't care about gods or rites or festivals. As the play began, I worried.

The play was called *The Three Wives of Paliatsos.* I wasn't the only one to worry here. Epicharmos paced and fidgeted helplessly. Everything was out of his hands now. The performance belonged to his actors and chorus. He could not coach the actors anymore, but he also understood that if he fidgeted too much, he might communicate panic to the men and boys on stage, so he did his fidgeting out of the actors' sight.

Epicharmos was known for complex domestic farces. He didn't disappoint here. In the first few minutes of the play, the main character, Paliatsos, had gotten himself engaged to two women at the same time. Then, as he romped with a married woman, her husband came home. Paliatsos talked his way out of it by putting on the wife's clothes and pretending to be a woman. The husband believed the ruse, flirted with Paliatsos himself, and then arranged for Paliatsos to marry his son.

I had to be alert here, so I was not able to focus too much on the play—I only caught bits of pieces of it—but what I saw was performed masterfully. The chorus was a little shaky at the beginning, probably nerves, but settled down nicely for the rest of the performance, and the actor Tobias was much funnier onstage—and much louder, even through his mask—than he was in rehearsal. Laughter thundered from the audience time and again. At the end of the play, Paliatsos' ruse is revealed when, dressed as a woman, he tries to convince the cuckolded husband that he's not worthy of the man's son, but he forgets he's supposed to be a woman and speaks to the man in his normal deep voice. Right at that moment, one of the women he was supposed to marry shows up and recognizes him. I would not see the other plays, and don't know much about theatre in the first place, so I could not say if *The Three Wives of Paliatsos* was worthy of the grand prize, but there could be no doubt about its popularity with this audience.

When the play ended, the people around Kratisto congratulated him for sponsoring it, and the crowd applauded long and hard. That's when I caught a glimpse of Iachkos. He had with him two rough-looking bruisers who I recognized as the bodyguards who'd accompanied him and his brother and nephew to the house of Kratisto a few days earlier. Iachkos pointed in Kratisto's direction. The two men nodded grimly and ran forward.

I screamed a warning, but in the crowd, no one heard me. I pushed in the direction of Kratisto. I stepped over seats and shoved people ungently out of my way. It was no time for good manners. A woman shrieked. Another voice, a man's, groaned loudly in pain. There were still a dozen people between Kratisto and me. This was the one thing I worried about. As I grabbed a man by the arm and pulled him out of my way, he took a swing at me and cut me on the chin as he went down. A woman, probably that man's wife, grabbed my arm and scratched it with her long fingernails. "Asshole!" she screeched at me.

"Get the fuck out of my way!" I yelled as I shoved her aside. Another man crossed in front of me. Our feet tangled together and we collapsed in a heap.

I leaped to my feet and pushed two more people out of the way to get to the man in the cedar-green tunic lying on the ground ahead. He was dead, his throat cut, and the blood that pooled around him had already slowed to a trickle. The cedar-green tunic was blood-soaked.

The man wearing it wasn't Kratisto.

He startled me when he came up behind me and clamped his hand on my shoulder. "Did you imagine for a second," he whispered in my ear, "that I was the only man in Halicarnassus with enemies?"

"Any idea what this was all about, sir?" I said, nodding towards the body.

"You'll love this," he said. "Before I offered him my sister, Abantes' son was going to marry this man's daughter. When Abantes backed out, this man promised payback."

Kratisto was delighted by this, and while everyone else looked at the body in revulsion or avoided looking altogether, Kratisto smiled even more broadly than usual.

I'd gotten to Kratisto as quickly as I could, and even

though I wouldn't have been able to protect him from an attack, he was nonetheless pleased with the effort I'd made. Diastrefo was just getting here now. "Gotta love a man, Agrios," he said, "who's willing to knock down man or woman, friend or foe, to protect his master. Looks like you took a couple of wounds, too."

The cut on my chin, where the man had punched me, still bled a little, as did the scratch on my arm. Kratisto wanted to reward me for my attempted valour. He knew I did not drink, so he asked me if I wanted a woman.

"Can I have Kalliope come and sleep with me tonight?" I said.

"Done," he said.

Another key piece of my plan had just fallen, serendipitously, unexpectedly, god-directedly, into place.

*   *   *   *   *   *   *

"Wine for everyone! Yes, even you, Ina," called the lady, the tall despoina who hadn't exchanged more than two words with me in all the time I'd lived in her house. This was not the frowning young matron that we took to the temple every day, the one who scowled at us guards like we were something she'd just scraped off her sandals. She was the heartbeat of this party. Some of the new slave girls were shy about drinking in the presence of their mistress, but Kandra's ready smile soon convinced them. It was the first time I'd seen Kandra smile here. Nysa was not here, so it was Kandra who mixed the wine with water. "We're not barbarians—or Thebans—so the wine is watered, but everyone *will* have fun tonight. I command it. Who's next? Why isn't anyone singing?"

Right on cue, four slave-girl musicians—two flautists, a kithara player and one who tapped rhythm on woodblocks and little bells—began to play. Pretty much everyone sang the song, a randy ballad of an old tanner with a pretty young wife who wore him out nightly, then looked for someone younger and stronger.

Kandra was always thinking. She got everyone to sing so she and I could talk with less chance of being overheard. I knew not to look at her—if I did, my desire for her would be obvious to a blind man—but I stood beside her, at a polite distance, eyes respectfully forward.

She handed me a cup of wine. She knew I didn't like it, but she couldn't let anyone know she already knew me. "Thank you, despoina," I said, "but I cannot. I'm the dry-mouth tonight."

"The what?" she said.

"The dry-mouth. Kratisto's idea. One guard remains sober today in case anything happens."

"Why you? You're not the New Guy anymore. Are you being punished?"

"I volunteered, despoina. I don't like wine."

"Now I remember," she looked. "Until this moment, I didn't completely believe it."

"It's true, dear lady," I said. "I've never liked wine. Gives me a headache."

"That's just more for the rest of us," she said with a smile "Kallum! Why is your cup empty? Get over here!"

Kandra drank wine too—it would have been suspicious if

she did not—but hers was ninety percent water. Everyone else's wine was initially two-thirds water, but by the time they were on their third cup, it was about fifty-fifty. Later, the mix would be twenty percent water. She did it so gradually that no one would notice. Or care.

"Despoina," I said. "I must thank you for the sleeping-draughts you send me, but I don't need them anymore. I should return them to you. I can go get them for you now, if you'd like."

She winked at me, very risky if anyone spotted it. "I don't need them back," she said quietly. "I've got some with me now. You're holding my backup supply."

I looked at her in confusion. "Sometimes," she said, "Kratisto tosses out my herbs and medicines. So I sent you a regular supply in case that happened."

This, Ephander, was the keen mind I'd recognized when we were still children, and one of the things that made her the love of my life. We had the same plan for this evening, *even though we'd not spoken a word about it to each other*. We *thought* alike, and while my understanding of the plan's finer details differed from hers, we had the same thought process. When she sent me the sleeping potion, I figured out that it wasn't for me and that she wanted me to hoard it. When I heard that everyone in the house would get drunk for the Lenaia, I figured the sleeping potion would end up in the wine. Kandra made sure that she had a backup stash, which was, pardon my Phoenician, fucking brilliant.

She put two small bundles of dried leaves on the table. "Put them in your pocket," she said quietly. "If you start to get sleepy, eat half of one bundle. A few hours later, eat the other half. It'll keep you awake all night without loss of alertness."

I recognized the bundles as *khat,* a plant from Asia and Africa. It was fresh, so Kandra must've grown her own somehow. I stuffed the little bundles in my tunic pocket.

"The second bundle," Kandra added, "is for your whore. I assume that you want to bring her with us."

There was ice in her voice when she said that. She referred, of course, to Kalliope. "We'll need her," I said. "She knows the city well. We don't."

"Really? Have you slept with her?"

"Yes," I said, "but only because I had to."

"Really?" she said. "You *had* to? Did you feel it was your solemn duty?" She looked at me like I'd just said something uproariously funny.

"If I didn't, it would have been suspicious," I said. "We can discuss this later."

"She'll be an escaped slave," Kandra said. "Her presence will increase our danger."

"Maybe," I said, "but she's lived in Halicarnassus all her life. She knows the streets, alleys and port district far better than you or I do. She's worth the risk."

Kalliope had arrived here a couple of hours earlier, in the late afternoon. I immediately sent her to my sleeping cubicle to wait for me. I had to make it look like I would screw her once I was off duty tonight. I'd also given her a dagger, in case any of the other guards tried to take advantage of her.

The party continued. The slaves got drunker. Voices got louder. Songs got randier. Everyone danced, except for a couple of the slaves, the matronly Bella and the very young Ina, who had both nodded off already, even though Kandra had not drugged the wine yet. Bella was old. Ina was young and unused to the effects of wine. Kandra would not drug the wine until Kratisto arrived. If he was late and everyone was already passed out, he would be suspicions. He was many things, but stupid wasn't one of them.

Orestes was not here because he and Nysa went to the temple for a separate sacrifice. Their absence could be a problem. Our plan was to escape unopposed by getting everyone in the household to drink the sleep-inducing wine. The absence of Nysa and Orestes was a loose end, especially if they showed up at the wrong time. I could probably trust Nysa enough to allow her to remain undrugged. The other guards would all drink our sleep-wine, so I wasn't worried about them. Orestes would be trouble. He did not approve of the way Kratisto kept Kandra as a prisoner, but he'd sworn an oath to serve Kratisto. He was a man of honour and would oppose me if I tried to take Kandra away without Kratisto's permission.

How's that for screwy, eh, Ephander? The only man in the house with any sense of honour was my biggest potential problem.

Kratisto wasn't here either, but we knew where he was. The other guards, except for Orestes, were all with him. The play he sponsored had taken the grand prize. I don't know if the contest was rigged—with Kratisto, you always had to consider that possibility. *The Three Wives of Paliatsos* was a fine comedy, however, well received by its audience, so it could have won without a bribed jury. Kratisto would join us later, but for now there were ceremonies he had to attend at the great Temple of Dionysus, words of praise he had to hear, libations he had to drink, speeches he had to endure.

An hour later, we heard shouts and laughter outside. I instinctively drew my sword and ran outside to look. A group of about fifty people approached. It was no angry mob, though. They carried Kratisto on their shoulders. He wore a laurel crown—I wondered why it was awarded to him and not to Epicharmos, although that may just have been how they did things in Halicarnassus—and he drank unwatered wine from a small jug.

"Look at this fucking guy!" he said as he pointed me out. "He hears a mob approach, so he comes out to investigate with his sword drawn. I swear, if he thought we were a threat, he'd fight the lot of us. He'd lose, but he'd probably kill ten or twelve of us first. Best fucking bodyguard a man could ever have. To Agrios!" He held up the jug of wine towards me, a sort of drunken salute, then drank deeply. Others cheered and drank from their own jugs. Kratisto spilled as much wine onto his tunic as into his mouth.

I re-sheathed my sword and went back into the house.

"Good news and bad news," I said to Kandra. "The good: Kratisto's well-besotted already. The bad: he's brought fifty people with him."

Kandra just laughed. "Looks like I'm going to need that second stash after all," she said. I went to my cubicle and fetched it for her.

More people arrived, Kratisto's friends and near-friends, so there were about eighty people here now, all getting drunker and louder. The singing became rowdier and more off-key. The room smelled of wine and sweaty bodies. If I was not on duty, I would not be here. As people get drunker, especially those unaccustomed to wine, they get stupider. They think that drink makes them more charming–it does, but only for the first half hour. After that, their sodden attempts at wit degenerate into inanity, their charm into obnoxiousness.

The wine emboldened the household slave girls. A few looked at me and liked what they saw. I was not here to take advantage, so I did not speak to or even look at any of them. A pretty dark-haired girl, who I think was Nysa's new hairstylist, smiled at me. I looked away, hoping one of the other men here would catch her eye, but when I looked up again she stood in front of me and smiled in a way that left little doubt. It's a situation that most men dream of, Ephander, and I know you do: a very pretty slave-girl gets a few drinks in her and then lets you know she wants you. Then she suddenly looked very frightened and turned away. She crossed the room and stood with several other girls. She did not look back. I didn't know what had just happened. As she drew nearer, did she get a better look at me and suddenly decide I was repulsive? I doubted it. While I wasn't as handsome as Kratisto–by the gods, no man was–I was tall and lean and athletic. My dark Scythian features intimidated some women but made me exotic to others. Nysa had told me that some of her girls were quite taken with me, not least because I was the most civilized of the guards. So the pretty slave-girl's sudden turnabout made no sense.

Then it happened again. A blonde slave girl, a shortish large-breasted kitchen girl that I'd noticed a few times before, sidled up to me. On another day, her smile would have melted me.

"Hello there," I said. "Enjoying yourself?"

She nodded, still smiling. Then the smile instantly vanished, and she walked away, almost ran, without another word.

I was about to ask Kandra if I was scaring the girls away because I'd suddenly gotten leprosy, but the stony look in her eye answered my question. The girls kept away because Kandra had glared at them. In some circumstances, Kandra scared *me*, so it's no wonder the slave girls did not want to cross her. Word got around the room, and no more pretty girls came my way that night.

A young man, one of Kratisto's friends, came up to me and began to spout off about all the damned foreigners in Halicarnassus. A rich man's son, he wore a long silk tunic with a jewel-studded horsehide belt. I'm not sure what he intended, but he was emboldened because he'd mistaken me for a slave who could not react to his taunts. "I don't even like having you ornamental shit-licks here as slaves," he slurred at me. He said *ornamental* but I think he meant *oriental.* "If you were my slave, I'd have you whipped, just out of principle." He thought this was high wit and laughed. No one else did.

"I'm on duty here, sir," I said. "You should just enjoy the master's hospitality and not give me another thought."

"Who the fuck are you to tell me what to enjoy?!?" he slobbered at me. "Hey, Krato, your barbarian slave-boy is giving me some lip over here."

The young man grinned at me like he thought I was in big trouble. I gave him a quick short shot to the jaw that he didn't even see. He was flat on his ass with no clear idea how he'd gotten there.

"I'm a free man," I said calmly. "You ever call me a slave

again, you little pussy, and I'll *really* hit you."

The man, stunned, looked like he'd just been struck by lightning. He scampered away like a frightened vole. I was a little concerned that I'd overstepped, that Kratisto might take exception to me striking one of his friends, but he laughed so hard that he couldn't speak for a full minute. When he finally recovered, he shouted, "Know you, every man here! Don't fuck with my Scythian."

Cheers erupted, cups were refilled, and one of Kratisto's other friends came up and shook my hand. "I'm glad somebody finally popped Keno," he said. "And I'm especially happy that I got to see it. The little bastard is always spouting off about foreigners, yet his own father is from Thrace."

The party ran on. "A toast to your host," shouted Kratisto. Then he grabbed his crotch and said, "Later, I plan to give the most-est to our hostess!" Some of the partyers had already nodded off, but the ones who were still awake laughed and cheered. It was approaching midnight. Kandra had drugged the wine a couple of hours earlier.

Food was brought in. Bread sweetened with raisins and figs, olives, dried apricots, nuts, and a thick lentil soup were served to the guests as appetizers. The main course was a huge roasted boar, wheeled out on a cart fitted with a brazier to keep it warm. It was greeted with cheers. Several guests stood up and patted Kratisto on the back even harder than they did at the end of *The Three Wives of Paliatsos.* Mutton and goose were also on the menu.

As soon as the food had been brought out, Kandra went to the kitchen to toast with the serving slaves and the cooks. They were half asleep before she returned to the dining room. The remaining guests who were awake would not be for long.

Men and women paired off. A few men paired with other men, and a few of the women paired off with women. Some had sex with each other right here in the dining room. Such indiscreetness would have alarmed most Hellenes, who tend towards prudishness about public displays, but Kandra did not object to it because it was acceptable behaviour in the house of Kratisto. It was hard not to laugh at the man who nodded off as he screwed a slave girl from behind. She was asleep too, and when they collapsed to the floor, they remained in position.

Not everyone stayed. Others led their paramours to more private locations. Before they left the dining room, Kandra was on these people like lightning. She wanted to get more wine into them. "A drink with your hostess," she would say with a big smile, "to celebrate the act of love." Who could refuse? None of these couples suspected that the wine she gave them had a knockout dosage of the sleeping drug.

Another man was eating a mutton-leg when he nodded off. He sat on a couch shouting something that he thought was truly profound at his friend, and gestured with the mutton-leg, which looked like a meat club in his hand. The mutton-leg fell from his hand, his eyes closed, and he rolled backwards and passed out on the couch.

"Can't argue with that," said his friend, who promptly passed out beside him.

An hour past midnight, Kratisto was the only reveler awake in the dining room. When he finally dropped off, Kandra slipped away. She would change from her silk chiton to a loose linen tunic that would give her more freedom of movement—we would need to walk quickly, possibly even run, later that night—and she also wanted to confirm that everyone else in the household was asleep.

I wanted to kill Kratisto right there and then. Nysa could be openly married to Orestes and every slave in the household would be better off. The only ones who would miss him would be the lowlifes he hired as guards. Delay conflicted with every instinct I had. Xenocrates had always taught me to do what you need to do the moment you recognize you need to do it. But I held off because Kandra wanted to kill Kratisto herself. He'd cut off my little finger, and I wanted to kill him for that alone. I did not know the details of what he'd done to her, but I believed her when she said he'd done infinitely more than a pinky's worth of wrong to her. So I waited.

I looked closely at Kratisto. The evil fuck had that smile stuck on his face even as he slept. What a waste of a life. He had the intelligence, charisma, and opportunity to be a great man in this city, yet he chose a life that was no better than a beggar's dream. I walked around the dining room, just to make sure everyone here was completely out. They all were. A bellowing elephant wouldn't have woken them.

I thought about how well our plan had gone so far. In an hour, we'd be out of Halicarnassus, on a ship I'd hired two days earlier. I returned to the table where Kandra had mixed the wine. I drank a cup of sweet clean water, then another.

Then I felt the cold steel of a sword blade against the back of my neck.

21–LUCK

"Put your sword to my stomach," Xenocrates ordered. "Point first. Come on, lad, jam it in there. Don't be shy."

We were in the training area he'd set up beside the goat pen behind his shack, back on Skiathos. I was eleven years old and had no idea why he wanted me to do this. He sometimes made me do pointless things just to distract me. Then he would kick or punch me. He did it to develop my reflexes and to always remind me that my opponent would be as devious as possible and would try to get me to lower my guard. Much as I hated getting kicked and punched, literally thousands of times over the years, there was no denying that his methods worked. At the end of my eight years of training with Xenocrates, I had the reflexes of an Anatolian wildcat.

I put the point of my sword to his stomach. I never once took my eyes off him, watching for any movement of his hands and feet. He towered over me. I was tall for my age, almost as tall as my father already, but I barely reached Xenocrates' shoulder. He stared down at me, grinning. With his long grey-streaked hair and wild beard, I thought of him as a demented god.

"Okay, shithead," he said. "Stick your sword into me. I'm unarmed." He dropped his own sword to the ground, but I'd learned long ago that you could *never* consider Xenocrates unarmed. He could easily kill you with his bare hands, and if he wanted your weapon, he knew a dozen ways to get it from you. He wore no armour, but against me he didn't need it yet.

It seemed too easy, which meant it was one of Xenocrates' tricks. I thrust my sword into his torso, even though I knew this would probably end with him unharmed and me flat on my ass with a new bruise or two.

He sidestepped my lunge easily and laughed as I stumbled past him.

"Again," he ordered.

I tried it again and he sidestepped it just as easily the second time, except this time he cuffed me in the back of the head as I passed him and knocked me down on my hands and knees. Then he kicked me in the arse while I was down. And he laughed, of course.

"You see your mistake?" he said.

"It is always a mistake to challenge you with a sword, despotis," I said, a picked myself up off the ground.

"True. Even so, when you held your sword to my gut, your arm was fully extended. That would be a mistake against anybody. The only way you could put your sword into me was to take a couple of steps forward. That made your next move predictable."

He then told me to put my sword to his stomach again but to come in closer so I could thrust forward with a single arm motion that did not require extra forward steps. Getting in close to Xenocrates still had its own plethora of hazards. Before I'd completely settled into position, he punched me in the jaw. I saw it coming and ducked away. The blow barely touched me. I rolled backwards, in less time than it takes me to tell it, and came up on my feet, facing him, sword ready. It was a move he made me practice for hours. He did not smile or tell me I had done well—that was not his way—but I knew by the look in his eye, by the slight diminishment of his permanent expression of disdain for me, that he was pleased with my reaction.

This incident so many years ago flashed through my head as I felt Kratisto's sword on the back of my neck.

"I've been on to you for weeks, asshole," he said. "I know you plan to steal my woman tonight, and I know the two of you drugged the wine. I let it happen because it's been so highly amusing to watch."

He was behind me, so I couldn't see his face. I couldn't understand was how he was still standing. He'd downed at least five cups of the drugged wine, enough to knock out a plough-horse, yet his voice betrayed no sign of slurring or sleepiness.

"I will miss you, Agrios," he said. "You are easily the most entertaining of my men, with your fanatical need to train and your screwy notions of honour. I'll still enjoy killing you, though. I'll do it slowly. I'll let you live if you get down on your knees right now and suck my cock. You know you've always wanted to."

If he'd been trained by Xenocrates, I'd be dead already. Kratisto had already made three key mistakes. The first was delay, which was to my advantage, not his. He'd caught me by surprise. If he'd just plunged his sword into me, Ephander, I wouldn't be here to tell you this story.

"I want to live, sir," I said. "I'll do it."

I wouldn't, of course. His word couldn't be trusted. I'd already seen him kill slaves whose lives he'd promised to spare.

His second mistake was that he talked too much. I was able to gauge, from the sound of his voice, that he was at least four feet behind me. That meant his sword arm was fully extended. He would not be able to put his sword into my neck without taking two steps forward. As often as I cursed Xenocrates for being such a heartless asshole, I just as often thanked the gods for all he taught me.

I dove forward, over the table, too quickly for Kratisto to react. I knocked the wine and water bowls and pitchers off the table. They smashed, and when I slid over the table and landed on the floor, I cut my shoulder on a broken shard. I came up facing Kratisto, sword in hand.

His third mistake: he didn't take my sword from me when he had the chance. Now I faced him and could see why he was still awake. His eyes were wide, pupils so dilated that they looked like black coins. He'd eaten khat, a heavy dosage, which he'd probably gotten from the same source Kandra did. It would keep him alert. It would make him faster and more confident. It would not, however, magically correct his flaws as a swordsman.

"After I kill you," he said, "I'm going to fuck Kandra in the ass and piss in her face afterwards. You'd be amazed how much she loves that."

No student of Xenocrates would ever fall for this. A swordsman must not react to taunts, because an angry swordsman is a predictable one. He will go on the offensive, often with an amateurish forward charge. His first anger-driven blows will be formidable, but he'll tense up his arms and shoulders, which makes it impossible to sustain the effort for very long. A calm swordsman who assesses your weaknesses is much more likely to kill you.

Kratisto couldn't rile me. But I might rile him.

"Kandra can't possibly like it," I said, "as much as Nysa likes giving me blowjobs. She's a real suck artist, you know. The very best. After I cut your fucking head off, I think I'll take her with me and make her my personal cock monkey."

It was untrue, of course, but my words did their damage. Kratisto was an amateur. He lost his temper and charged. This was no small problem. Even enraged, numbed by wine and high on khat, he moved with the silken fluidity of a natural athlete. What a swordsmen he could have been if he hadn't been too lazy to train properly. He and I had sparred many times, but there was no regularity to it. Sometimes we'd do it three or four days in a row, then we wouldn't do it again for another month. He was too egotistical to recognize that he always beat me only because I let him. He never did the drills and exercises that I did daily to build strength and stamina in the arms and shoulders.

He swung his sword in a vicious overhand cut at my head. I knew it was coming before he did. I jumped aside easily. His momentum carried him past me and he stumbled. If he'd fallen, the fight would have been over right there and then, but he managed to stay on his feet.

"You fucking shit-bag slave-ass fucking lunatic *fuck*!" he screamed. "I'll cut you up and fucking feed you to the mangiest fucking dogs I can find!" His smile disappeared, the first time I'd ever seen that. He charged at me again with the same overhand cut. It didn't work the first time, but he didn't learn from it, another mistake an angry swordsman makes. This time

I blocked it. No easy feat: he'd put all his weight into it, so when his blade slid down mine and our hilts caught, pain radiated down my right arm. With all the wine in him, he didn't feel pain like I did. While our swords were locked together, I drove my left fist into his ribs, a solid shot. It would have put most men down, but Kratisto barely flinched. He pulled his sword back and hacked at me again and again and again.

I blocked every cut. When we'd sparred, I'd noticed that he revealed his attack in advance. He would feint three or four times, but he would always crinkle his left eye before the actual blow. It was just short of a wink. I didn't notice it at first, and when I finally did, I thought it was a trick, but I soon learned that he wasn't aware that he did it. Many swordsmen do something like that. I did it myself at one time—I would always open my mouth before a real thrust—but Xenocrates made me thrust a thousand times with a metal clamp holding my lips shut. Painful as Hades, but it cured me.

Kratisto fought in a frenzy, his face contorted with purple rage, but he would lose this battle. He expended far more energy than I did. It was so obvious that a child would have seen it. The khat overrode his fatigue, but that wouldn't last forever. He would feint five or six times, but I always blocked the real blow easily because I knew it was coming. I didn't count the number of times he hacked at me, but it was at least twenty. He was so worked up that he actually foamed at the mouth a little, and cursed me every time my sword blocked his.

His blows gradually began to lose force. He was tiring to the point that not even khat could sustain him. I let one of his cuts come through. Instead of blocking it, I sidestepped it with little trouble—I was still fresh—and as he lurched past me I punched him in the face with my left hand. It broke his nose. Then I slammed the pommel of my sword into the side of his head. He was already going down, but I kicked him in the leg to make sure. He fell on his face and dropped his sword. I kicked it away from him, then kicked him in the head. He was still conscious but too dazed to move.

I hesitated—contrary to my own instincts—only because I knew Kandra wanted to kill him herself, or at the very least witness his death. I was too much a disciple of Xenocrates, so I did not think about it for long. I'd hesitated earlier, and if Kratisto had been a smarter swordsman, he would have killed me. I would not make the same mistake again.

I would kill him. Now. For all the unnecessary suffering he'd caused, he did not deserve a quick death, but I needed it done because, for Kandra and me, this night had barely begun.

I raised my sword to plunge it into his neck when I heard movement to my right. I ducked away just in time as a sword whizzed past my head. I felt the wind of it. It missed my neck by less than an inch.

It was Mikropeos. He hadn't been in the dining room with the other revelers. I don't know where he came from, but I don't think he drank any of the drugged wine. He'd eaten khat, too, and it had made him brave, but he was a bully, not swordsman. I'd only ever seen him use a weapon on unarmed men, or men too drunk to fight back properly, or with the other guards there to back him up. To defeat me, his success rode entirely on surprising me from behind, which he'd now failed to do. The khat had given him confidence, but he practiced with the sword even less than Kratisto did. I had to finish him quickly, before Kratisto recovered.

Mikropeos smiled and said, "I'm gonna cut you good, Agrios Agios." I saw fear behind the smile. He charged and drove his sword straight at my midsection. He was clumsy and slow, even with the khat. I stepped to my left and brought my sword down on his sword hand, and cut him so badly that he let go of his sword, clutched his bleeding hand, and fell to his knees. He wailed like a child. He disgusted me. Whatever else happened here tonight, this household, this city, this world would be better off without him. He was so preoccupied with his wounded hand that he didn't even try to get out of the way when I drove my sword into his throat. He gurgled and sputtered and collapsed, then bled out on the floor.

I turned back to Kratisto.

He was gone.

I wasn't surprised. It was true to his character. He could have helped Mikropeos but chose instead to sacrifice him.

I was about to go after Kratisto when the door opened and Orestes burst into the dining room, his sword drawn. He moved cautiously towards me.

He was here to fight me. It took me a few seconds to realize that.

"Orestes," I said. "I spared your life once before, but I'll kill you if you try to stop me now."

"I swore an oath to Kyrios," said Orestes, "a better man than you'll ever be. I swore on his deathbed that I'd defend his children—*both* of them—to the death if necessary."

Orestes was a passable swordsman, but he was forty-six years old. I also guessed that in all his years with Kyrios, who unlike Kratisto was not an abrasive jackass who offended people everywhere he went, Orestes did not have cause to fight often. So he was out of practice and past his prime. I didn't want to kill Orestes, a decent man whom I actually liked, but I was committed to a course of action. I could not, would not, turn back now. I would spare him if I could, but I would kill him if I had to. I would find a way to live with it afterwards.

I also knew that delay now worked to Kratisto's advantage, not mine. The longer I tarried here, the greater chance he'd have to either gather help or get away. As with Mikropeos, I had to defeat Orestes quickly.

I feinted high, then low, then high again, then I stomped hard on the arch of his foot. I swear I could actually *see* the pain run like lightning up his leg and up the entire length of his body. Then I faked a cut at his head, and as he moved to block it, I grabbed the wrist of his sword arm with my free left hand, then drove the pommel of my own sword into his jaw. It stunned him. I hit him in the jaw again. He reeled, stumbled backwards, and dropped his sword, which I caught by the hilt before it hit the ground. He fell flat on his ass and sat there silent and cloudy-eyed.

I had a few seconds to look behind me, just in case Kratisto or someone else had snuck up on me. There was no one there, so I turned back to Orestes, but what I saw next was not him but Nysa's tear-soaked face. She stood only a few feet away, between me and Orestes, who still sat dazed on the floor.

By the gods, what a brave woman she was, Ephander. I don't know if she'd actually seen how quickly I'd put Orestes down, but she certainly knew that I'd done it. Yet she still stood between him and me. I wouldn't have done that on the bravest day of my life.

"Please," she said, her eyes brimmed with tears. "I beg you. Don't kill him. He's—he's all I have now."

It was no time for delicacy or delay. I shoved her aside, none too gently. I stood over Orestes. "This is no longer your fight, Orestes," I said. "I will take Kandra away from here tonight. I will not kill you if you promise not to hinder me. I know you are a man of honour, so if you give me your word, I will accept it. Swear it!"

"I—I swear it," he said, "on sacred Athena." His face was twisted in agony. His ankle was already swelling. I might have broken it.

"And I won't kill you either, Nysa," I said, "*if you drop that fucking dagger right now.*" She didn't think I'd seen it, but a woman in a silk chiton has only so many places to hide a weapon, and all of them show. When I'd looked away from her to speak to Orestes, she'd taken it in her hand and now held it behind her back.

The dagger clanked on the floor as she dropped it. I left the dining room and went after Kratisto. I followed the trail of blood he'd left on the stairs to the second floor. Then the trail stopped. I counted seven rooms and he could have been in any of them. He may also have gone up to the third floor. So I had to check each room, one by one. I found no one in the first room, two sleeping slave girls in the second, and nose-less Kallum passed out on the bed in the third. I was just about to go into the fourth room when I heard screaming from one of the other rooms. It was a woman's voice. At first I thought it was a ruse by Kratisto, he was certainly capable of it, but then I realized it was Kandra. Kratisto was torturing her!

The screams came from the room at the end of the hallway. The door was open a crack. If it hadn't been, I would've run right through it. As I got closer, I was able to make out words. "You *motherfucker*! You worthless *asshole*! You piss-poor *excuse* for a *man*!"

I charged into the room. It was a disturbing sight.

Kratisto laid on his back on a large bed as Kandra plunged a dagger into his chest again and again and again. There was blood on her hands and on her tunic. But it wasn't hers.

Kratisto was quite dead. When Kandra saw me, she dropped her dagger and fell into my arms, crying. "I didn't kill him," she said between sobs. "I wanted to—I *needed* to—but someone beat me to it. He was dead when I found him here."

I reached down and put my fingers to Kratisto's neck. No pulse, definitely dead. A dagger, not the one Kandra had used, was still hilt-deep in his chest.

And that smile, eerie now, demonic, was frozen on Kratisto's dead face.

NAMES & TERMINOLOGY

*indicates real historical character

Abantes, citizen of Halicarnassus.
Acharnian Gate, northern gate of Athens.
Adina, a Lydian slave, Belkos' housekeeper.
Agapios, 'beloved,' slave boy of Xenocrates. Aka Krites, "the Cretan."
Agrios, 'savage,' Kratisto's nickname for Elektros
Aki, Scythian archer in Athens.
Alexandros, Athenian ephebe.
Anakletos, slave tracker.
***Anacreon**, poet.
Antiochis, Athenian tribe, led by Aristides.
Apollo, god of music, medicine.
Archidamos, Eretrian partygoer.
archon, one of nine elected chief magistrates in Athens.
archon basileus, literally "magistrate king," the archon designated to oversee religious rites and homicide trials.
***Archilochos**, poet.
Ares, god of war.
Argus, bodyguard in the house of Kratisto.
***Aristides**, nicknamed Aristides the Just, Athenian statesman.
Artemis, goddess of the hunt, twin sister of Apollo.
Athene, goddess of diplomacy and strategy.
Belkos, father of Phyloctetes and Elektros.
Bella, matronly slave in the house of Kratisto.
The 'black mist,' a form of battle frenzy in which

soldiers become uncontrollable and determinedly homicidal.

Boreas, prominent citizen of Halicarnassus.

Borysthenes, Scythian uncle of Elektros.

Briareus, bodyguard in the house of Kratisto.

Brontes, "the thunderer," Athenian strategos at Marathon.

Capros, Athenian ephebe.

Carneia, the religious festival observed by the Spartans that delayed their arrival at Marathon.

Castor, father of Xenocrates.

Ceramicus, section of Athens that was the potters' district.

***Choerilus**, playwright of tragedies.

Choiros, 'pig,' bodyguard in the house of Kratisto

choregos, pl. ***choregoi.*** Wealthy citizen appointed by the archon to sponsor one of the plays for a religious festival. It was considered an honour.

Cutter, tavern habitué.

Damon, Skiathian ironsmith, brother of Belkos, priest of Apollo.

Damoxenos, Athenian ephebe.

***Darius**, Great King of Persia

***Datis**, Persian general

Demetrios, son of Hermistocles.

diaulos, a footrace of about 400 metres.

Diochares Gate, eastern gate of Athens

Diocles, student of Xenocrates.

Diodoros, ephebe at Athens.

Dionysos, Athenian keeper of Dio's tavern.

dolichos, a footrace of about 2.5 miles.

Doron, 'gift,' late husband of Nysa.

Dromeos, Athenian soldier at Marathon.

Elektros, slave-born swordsman.

Ephander, Elektros' friend.

*__Epicharmos of Kos__, comic playwright.
Epictetos, wealthy Athenian.
Ergos, Skiathan slave, husband of Adina.
Eurymachos, Athenian officer.
Gennadios, elder of the tribe Leontis
Gia, Scythian aunt to Elektros.
Hannah, slave in the house of Kratisto.
hazarapatis, a rank of Persian officer, commander of a thousand.
Hera, queen of Olympos, wife of Zeus.
Herakles, semi-divine son of Zeus, more commonly known by his Romanized name Hercules.
Hermistocles, Elektros' "Grandfather," though technically not his blood relation. Father of Phyloctetes' mother.
*__Hipparchos__, brother of Hippias.
*__Hippias__, Hellene tyrant and advisor to the Persians.
Hieronymos, Grandfather's other grandson, son of Demetrios.
hoplite (1) an ancient Hellenic infantryman, fully armoured from head to toe and armed with a nine-foot spear and sword. **(2)** The style of warfare favoured by the ancient Hellenes. During the Classical period it revolved around the **hoplite phalanx**, a mass of hoplites in formation that presented a wall of spears and shields to the enemy and relied on the men fighting as a single unit rather than as individuals.
Hyperion, Athenian ephebe.
Iachkos, citizen of Halicarnassus.
Ina, young slave in the house of Kratisto.

***Kallimachos**, Athenian polemarch—war archon—at Marathon.
Kallum, slave in the house of Kratisto.
Kandra, a woman from Skiathos.
Kenites, elder son of Damon, half-cousin to Elektros.
Keno, friend of Kratisto.
Korinthos, Athenian soldier.
koumiss, a beverage made of spices and fermented mare's milk, favoured by the Scythians, who also believed it had medical uses.
Krios, "the ram," Athenian ephebe.
Kratisto, 'the strongest,' a wealthy Hallicarnassan.
Krites, "the Cretan," Agapios' nickname in Athens.
Kyrios, Kandra's late husband, father of Nysa & Learchos.
Lasthenes, Athenian wagon driver.
Learchos, Kyrios, Kandra's late husband.
Leontis, Athenian tribe of Themistocles.
Ling, Asiatic wife of Xenocrates.
Madyes, Scythian archer in Athens.
***Mardonius,** Persian general.
Marta, Athenian prostitute
Mattina, mother of Phyloctetes, daughter of Hermistocles.
Metion, Athenian ephebe.
Milo, Athenian officer.
***Miltiades**, Athenian general
***Neokles,** father of Themistocles.
Oeneis, Athenian tribe of Miltiades.
Oiorpata, "man slayer," Scythian nickname for Roxella.
Pamphilos, Athenian horse owner.
Pantionis, one of the ten tribes of Athens.

Persos, Themistocles' spy whom Elektros meets in Thrace.

***Phaenippus**, archon basileus of Athens during Battle of Marathon

Phaleron, port of Athens during the Persian wars.

***Pheidippides**, legendary Athenian runner.

Phocas, Athenian officer.

Philostratos, Athenian ephebe.

Phyloctetes, "Phylo," Elektros' half-brother.

***Pindar**, poet.

polemarch, elected war archon in Athens.

Pyrrhic dance, military exercise at the end of Athenian ephebe training.

Pyrrhos, crony of Kermites.

Proxenos, ephebe instructor at Athens.

Roxella, aka Oiorpata, Scythian mother of Elektros.

satapatis, low-ranking Persian officer who commands a *sataba*, one hundred infantry.

Scylurus, Scythian archer in Athens.

Simeon, friend of Elektros at Athens

***Simonides**, well-known lyric poet, father of Kandra.

Skunxa, Scythian king.

Tammuz, Persian officer at Marathon.

***Themistocles**, Athenian general & archon

Thoas, Scythian archer in Athens, cousin to Elektros.

Tyros, younger son of Damon, cousin to Elektros.

Xenocrates, teacher/trainer of Elektros.

Zeus, king of the gods.

Zhongguo, ancient name for China.

Marcellus Durrell has been a freelance writer, musician, hot tar roofer, chicken catcher, fruit picker, auto assembly line worker, cab driver, movie theatre janitor, cardboard box factory worker, museum security guard, shipper/receiver, steelworker, and library clerk. He is currently a librarian in Hamilton, Ontario, Canada, where he lives with his wife Josie and two unspeakably spoiled cats. *The Owl and the Wolf* is his third novel.

67350187R00225

Made in the USA
Charleston, SC
11 February 2017